Rival

BY A.J. MACEY

BLURB:

Hey b*tches, my name's Kiera. You might know me as The Cat, famous cat burglar/thief.
No? Well, let me give you a little insight into my life as of late.

I was going about, minding my own damn business, when the mob boss who runs most of the Reno underground sent an assassin after me. Crazy, yeah? Anyway, six months later the previously mentioned assassin is now my partner in crime when we get a job from the local motorcycle club, The Aces. All good and dandy, right? Wrong. They're 1%ers, all three officers unbelievably attractive. Oh, yeah, the vice president of the MC? That's my asshole stepbrother and let's not even get started on the club's suspicious Enforcer or the President who's dripping in sexual swagger.

With four sexy as f*ck men at my back, can I get the job done or will our explosive personalities cause us to be at each other's throats? Oh, damn! Almost forgot in the thought of all the ruggedly attractive men, muscles, and tattoos that the rival MC, The Alloy Kings are moving in and seem intent to take me down with the Aces. F*cking bastards.

But I'm not the thief who became famous at 15 years old and survived the mob's hell in my past just to lie down and take that, they won't know what hit them.

I'm The Cat, and soon enough, they'll learn that I've got claws.

WARNING:

The Aces Series is a WhyChoose/Reverse Harem trilogy featuring MFMMM meaning the female main character doesn't have to choose between her love interests. Please note, future books will contain M/M contact.

This book contains references involving PTSD, sexual assault recollections, abuse, and other themes that some readers may find triggering.

Cover: Jodielocks Designs
Editing: Ms. Correct-All's Editing and Proofing Services
Formatting: Inked Inspiration Author Services

CONTENTS

PROLOGUE

AUGUST 2006
KIERA

I stared at my mother's photograph that I had pulled from the hidden spot within my room. I'd found the space a couple of years ago. One of the wooden wall panels in the very corner of my sitting room held a decent sized alcove on the other side. When I finally pried off the wood square in front of it, without damaging it, I started to hide the trinkets and treasures that actually meant something to me inside and out of the reach of anyone's grabby hands or prying eyes. That familiar pang of heartache squeezed my chest in a vise-like grip, anger quickly bubbling up behind it. It had been two years. Two years since my mom died, and it hadn't gotten any easier. But tonight was going to be the start of a new era. Tonight, I was going to *take* from the cruel hand that ruled our lives—my life—for too long.

Glancing at the clock, I realized I needed to be ready to be escorted to the party shortly, so I quickly set my mother's photo back in its home within a storybook she used to read to me when I was younger, and replaced the wooden cover on the wall. I took several deep breaths, centering myself as I brushed out any wrinkles in the uncomfortable dress my father's stylist had picked out for me.

The dress was a red sequin gown, and the halter top and cinched in waist gave me a fake hourglass shape despite my body being as skinny and lean as a stick with no curves to speak of. I mean, I was nine for crying out loud, I didn't need any more attention, but I knew one reason for this party was for my father to show me off to his snobby rich friends who invested in his *business*. I shoved back the tears that burned my eyes and swallowed the acid that attempted to escape my stomach, and focused. Lifting the flared mermaid-style hem of the dress, I made sure there were no spots or scuffs on my black shiny shoes since my father would freak if there were.

"Kiera," my bodyguard barked from the door. I stood tall and followed him out of my rooms and down into the party.

Let the show begin.

♠ ♠ ♠

"It was a pleasure to meet you, Kiera," the older gentleman sneered down at me, his jowls wobbling as he talked. I gave him a polite smile instead of throwing something at his face like I wanted to do, and walked away. I spent several minutes wandering through the crowd discreetly checking where people's attentions were focused. My father's action of clinking a knife against his champagne glass made sure everyone was focused on him, not his nine-year-old daughter who was forced to go to these stupid parties.

When there was no one looking toward me, I moved quickly and silently until I stood near the back of the room as I always did. This time I positioned myself near the case holding a shiny jeweled necklace. The rubies were a deep red contrast to the diamonds and light gold of the metal. The cameras were angled toward the crowd, not the display cases in this gaudy ballroom slash museum, allowing me to make quick work of the lock and pressure sensor before swapping the expensive piece with my freshly made calling card. I couldn't help the smugness that flooded me as I glanced down at the black paw print in the middle of the plain white of the cardstock business card.

After stashing the necklace in my previously designated hiding spot, I listened to my father's dragging speech about how thankful he was for all his friends. *Yeah, right*, I scoffed, but kept my face flat. The party and chitchat resumed quickly afterward, though it only took ten minutes before the first murmur of discontent whispered through the crowd. I couldn't stop the tiny curl of my lip or the flare of power that filled my chest.

I'm The Cat and this is just the beginning.

CHAPTER 1

Fuck!" With quick movements, I rolled out of bed and stepped into the god-awful jeans I'd picked for my cover. My hair was swiftly thrown into what my best bitch coined as my 'rat's nest' bun. I was running late. Again. After pulling a black turtleneck over my head, I swigged some mouthwash while I situated the itchy fabric around my neck.

I would have been out the door in less than five minutes if the damn door hadn't been so slow to open. *Need to get that fixed*. I made a mental note about the door in the fourth bay of the garage as I hopped into the used piece of junk I utilized as my job car. Shooting a text to Abby, I let her know I was on my way. With the windows rolled down, the quickly warming weather of the Nevada desert brushed against my face as I made my way to downtown Reno. The coffee shop's parking lot was partially filled with others who needed their fix before going on with the monotony of their daily life. I spotted Abby's dusty truck off to the side of the large lot. Hustling, I ordered a black coffee and went out to the side patio where my best bitch was seated.

"Hey," I greeted breathlessly, flopping ungracefully into the warm metal chair. I angled the chair slightly so I could keep an eye on Abby as well as discreetly watch the whole reason for being here, Harbold Law Office. The building was a tan, smooth stone with a grey shingled roof. The large windows and front door glimmered in the quickly rising sun. The tint of the glass was nearly black, hiding everything that happened within the building.

"You're late," she chastised, her rough voice low to not catch the attention of those around us. Her blue eyes situated on my face and a dark brown brow lifted in her usual judgmental facial expression. If I didn't give a shit about her, I'd have smacked that look off her face long ago. "Honestly, I don't know how you're able to do your jobs with your shitty time management skills."

"Your guess is as good as mine." I shrugged and took a small sip of my drink pushing past the bitter taste.

"You do know they make coffee that actually tastes good, right? You don't have to power through straight black." Abby nodded her head toward the cup in my hand, her own cup marked with different symbols signifying she had some girly frou-frou drink.

"I wouldn't drink it if I didn't have to," I muttered, taking another sip. "Besides, I can't handle all that shit you have loaded up in there. Is it even still coffee or is it just a giant cup of sugar?"

"Oh, shut up, bitch. If you weren't so damn stubborn..." she mumbled the rest of her statement incoherently into her coffee cup.

I chuckled, my gaze following the large man who had just stepped out of his fire red Lamborghini. He even had the balls to park perpendicular to the lines on the asphalt taking up over three slots of his own parking lot.

"How the fuck does he even fit in that?" I whispered to Abby, who choked on some of her sugar concoction when she tried to laugh at me. "I mean seriously, look at him. He's bigger than the Stay Puft Marshmallow Man." Cory Harbold's custom Italian suit strained against his large belly, the man's meat mitts clutching his briefcase close to his side. Waddling across the pavement of his firm's parking lot, he finally reached the front door that had been unlocked ten minutes earlier by his front desk secretary.

"How much longer until your job's done?" Her rough voice finally evened out after the bout of coughing.

"Tomorrow night." I leaned forward on my forearms. "There's some snazzy party over at the Solace." My voice wavered at the mere mention of that wretched casino and resort, and I ground my teeth to keep my mouth shut while I centered myself. "How's Nate?" *When in doubt, reroute the conversation.*

"He's good, they're coming back from their ride this morning. Going to meet him at the compound." Her face changed into a dreamy expression at the thought of her husband.

Gross. I contained the grimace that tried to break through, but barely. A ding from my phone saved me from having to continue talking about the fiasco that was the concept of marriage.

Dipshit: *Got it.*

I tucked my phone back into my pocket, focusing on leisurely drinking the last of my coffee. I made sure to give it five minutes before I would head out with Abby.

"Ready to go?" My tone remained at a normal volume, my husky voice abnormally cheerful. *Nothing to see here folks, just two normal friends getting coffee like normal people.* She nodded and rose from her seat. In the twenty minutes we were at the shop, the parking lot had mostly emptied. "You still need to hit up the store?" I asked as I climbed into Rocky, Abby's red Chevy Colorado truck.

"Yeah, just need to pick up a few things for the guys." She started the vehicle and we made our way to the grocery store near the edge of town.

Neutral colored businesses slowly transitioned into the residential neighborhoods and homes. The store's exterior matched the continual pattern of greys, beiges, and tans that littered the rest of the streets. We walked the empty aisles grabbing items for Abby's signature pasta dish before checking out. It was an oddly normal trip compared to what I was used to when I went out.

The grocery store parking lot was nearly barren in the mid-morning sun. The weather had transitioned from warm to hot, making the stupid outfit I was wearing even more uncomfortable. A tug at the neck of my sweater wasn't nearly enough to cool me down, so I abandoned that idea and helped load the last of the groceries into the open space of the cab. Taking the cart, I walked over to the return stall.

I mean, I am an asshole, but I'm not that much of an asshole to leave the cart in the middle of the lot. My name being shouted by a distraught Abby caught my attention. Whipping my head around, I noticed three men attempting to shove Abby into an unlabeled van.

Oh, hell no.

Game on, fuckers!

Sprinting, I tackled Bastard #1, a muscular guy holding on to Abby's boots. We made contact with the cement, the burning of the rough surface cutting through my shirt barely noticeable due to my pumping adrenaline. Abby had wiggled a thin arm free and had scratched up Bastard #2's face, blood welling up at the large, red welts. Arms clamped around my chest holding my elbows to my sides as Bastard #3 lifted me off his buddy's groaning, barely conscious body.

"We were only tasked with bringing the Aces' bitch, but a two-for-one deal I'm sure will be appreciated." Bastard #3's voice was harsh and taunting as he lifted me further off the ground and toward the van. Kicking back, my geriatric-style tennis shoe made solid contact with his knee. As he screamed I was able to maneuver myself slightly from his ironclad grip, noting the patch on his vest.

Prospect. Alloy Kings Motorcycle Club.

Fucking 1%ers. I growled, kicking my heel back and up, hitting him squarely where the sun doesn't shine. He lurched forward and released me so he could tend to his family jewels. *He won't be having kids for a while.* I mentally applauded my efforts at the sound of his cries. I stumbled forward a bit but regained my composure right in time to see Bastard #1 get up and scurry like the bitch he was back into the van. Abby, who was fighting for all she was worth in Bastard #2's arms, was being hauled over to the open van door. I threw myself at his back and latched on, distracting him enough to let go of Abby. She dropped and rolled out of his way like a pro and soon it was just me and Bastard #2. He attempted to grab me, but his large calloused hands missed as I jumped off. Several well-delivered punches later and Bastard #2 had retreated to their van with Bastard #3 hot on his heels, but before I could grab Abby and leave, Bastard #3 sucker punched me in the side of the head. Stars burst in front of my eyes as the van squealed its tires out of the parking lot.

"Kiera!" Abby's voice was the last thing I heard before slipping to the ground.

BROOKS

"What the fuck do you mean our shipment was taken?" I snapped. My Road Captain, Nate, stood before me, his face taut with irritation.

"Meaning exactly what I said, Boss." Nate's voice trembled harshly as he ground out the statement between clenched teeth. His anger radiating off him in waves as one of his hands curled and uncurled. "Our contact wasn't at the drop, only this." He held out the small piece of paper. Snatching it from him, I studied the crumpled page. A crown stared back at me.

"God fucking damn it!" I kicked out, putting a hole in the plaster of the office. "Fucking Alloy Kings. These fuckers are really starting to piss me off." Before Nate could respond, his phone rang loudly.

"Not a good time, babe…" His bearded face paled significantly. "You almost here?" More silence rang out as he waited for an answer. "Good, we'll meet you out front."

"What?" I scoffed. I had more important shit to take care of than whatever his Old Lady needed. *Like these fucking bastards who think they can take our damned shipments out from under our nose.*

"Abby and her friend were nearly kidnapped at the store this morning," he filled me in as we headed toward the front of the main compound building. The bar was empty and clean as Cheryl wiped down the lacquered surface erasing the last bit of evidence of the guys' party last night.

"And?" I knew there was more to it than what he had

revealed. His lip twitched, his large beard shifting with the movement, before continuing.

"She'll explain, they're almost here."

"They? We don't need outsiders here." Shooting a glare at Nate, I stepped outside into the hot spring weather, the desert dust glaringly bright in the overhead sun. I had to squint until my eyes adjusted from the stark change, the bar seemingly pitch black compared to the sunniness of Nevada's outdoors.

"Kiera's good, Boss. I've known her as long as I've known Abby."

Swallowing my retort I focused on the familiar red truck as Abby pulled up. Her thin face was set in a scowl as she climbed out and headed toward us, her dark brown hair starting to fall out of her ponytail. There was a darkening bruise on her arms and a swatch of blood dried on her fingers.

"What happened?" Nate immediately questioned his wife who stormed around the front of the truck, her boots pounding loudly against the pavement.

"Three guys tried to force us into their van." She pulled open the passenger side door to reveal a thin woman with wavy, dirty blonde hair. Her skin was tanned, but I couldn't get a good look at her face with the way she was slumped in the chair. "Punched Kiera on their way out." Nate lifted her out of the seat, his burly muscles able to hold her with ease.

"Take her to one of the back rooms." I sighed, rubbing my eyes. "How'd you get away?"

"Kiera took care of most of it. She's pretty scrappy when she wants to be." Abby followed us into the bar area, her husband continuing down the hall to one of the extra bedrooms. "There's something you need to know," she urged, her grave tone bringing my attention to her. "They were Alloy Kings' prospects; they knew I was an Aces' Old Lady." Building rage thrummed in my veins, my fists clenching at my sides. I ground my teeth thinking through what we should do before I spoke.

"Warn the other Ladies and any hang-arounds to keep an eye out." *Fuck.* Stone's thudding footsteps filled the quiet area as he entered the bar from the back office.

"What's wrong, Boss?" his deep voice asked quietly. Stone rarely raised his voice-- his near-permanent scowl, broad shoulders, and muscles conveyed more of a threat than his voice ever could.

"Alloy Kings are causing issues." Abby had pulled back from our huddle to go check on her friend at the first sight of Stone, figuring we would start talking club business. She had been around long enough to know when to give us privacy. When she was far enough away, I continued to explain what happened. "Jacked our latest shipment and tried to take Abby and her friend."

"She looked a bit scuffed up," Stone agreed. "What's the plan?"

I was about to answer when Abby and Nate filed back into the bar with their friend trailing behind them. I couldn't help myself, my gaze skimmed over her body and face trying to get a better look at her than when she was slumped in the seat of Abby's truck.

Her dirty blonde hair was knotted on the back of her head and stuck out at weird angles. Her outfit was drab and did nothing for her; I had to keep myself from grimacing at it. She sported a nice tan and her eyes, a dark green-brown, scanned her surroundings warily.

She might be pretty if she wasn't dressed like my grandmother...

KIERA

"Boss, this is Kiera." Nate's booming voice was restrained as we neared the two jacked guys standing near the bar. I recognized them from my file on the Aces Motorcycle Club—MC President Brooks 'Boss' Abbott and the MC's Enforcer Stone 'Grave' Ronin. Since I wasn't supposed to know anything about them, I kept a confused yet curious look on my face. *You know the one I'm talking about. The one when you've farted in a crowded room and you wonder if anyone is going to call you out on it, so you just look around with that 'who did it, it wasn't me' face.*

Thank fuck for my ugly ass outfit. I prayed it would be enough to keep them from looking too much into me. Glancing around, I made mental notes of everything I could see. I had blueprints of the building back home, but I didn't really *know* what it looked like.

The flooring was a dark cement, nearly as black as the ceiling tiles in the long rectangular room. The walls were a dark grey and covered in different motorcycle memorabilia. A lacquer topped bar ran almost the length of one of the short walls, only stopping by the open hallway that led to the rest of the building. There was a wall of liquor on glass shelving in front of a giant mirror, the reflective surface only broken up by a black unmarked door.

I tallied the exits: two main doors since I wasn't sure if the unmarked one was an exit, a large air conditioning system based on the vent grates, and a few windows that could be opened along the front of the room looking out over the parking lot. Several scuffed and chipped wooden tables and chairs were situated around the open space, broken up by leather lounge chairs. I had to keep my face devoid of emotion as to not gag at the amount of blood, spit, and other human fluids I was sure coated the surface of nearly everything in the building.

"You want a drink?" Brooks offered. His voice pulled my attention away from the dark, dingy bar. Waving toward the very boobilicious bartender with permed blonde hair, he took a sip of his drink while the woman shuffled around behind the counter. Her chest bounced with any minute movement as she picked up the half empty bottle and a clean, *well, hopefully clean*, glass.

A lowball of whiskey appeared in front of me, and I eyeballed the glass a few seconds before I lifted it to my lips. The drink pleasantly burned when I took a small sip, my eyes on the MC's president as I felt Abby and Nate shuffle a few steps away. Their soft words were muffled as I discreetly took in the sexy man in front of me. Brooks' golden blond hair, a bit on the long side, was brushed away from his too-pretty-for-his-own-good face. *Which is why he probably chose to cover his strong jaw with that rough looking beard*, I thought. He wore traditional rider's attire of jeans, plain t-shirt, and his cut, the skull in the Ace of Spades glaring at me from its position within the Aces' club name patches. I had to get ahold of the desire that slowly uncurled within my stomach at his muscled body clothed in his tight shirt.

"You got someone you can call?" Brooks' voice was as smooth as the whiskey I was drinking; the throaty quality warmed my body right along with the alcohol. I nodded softly, thankful Abby had been there when I came to so I could tell her to keep her mouth shut about me and my not-so-typical career choice.

Brooks nodded back at me, his grey-blue eyes darting

back toward the bar and his own glass. Stone's ebony eyes were locked on my face; the steely gaze seemed to take in every movement and nuance. Watching him, I caught the way his body shifted, as if he was readying for a fight. His dark skin stretched tightly over bulging muscles, and only a shadow of black hair dusted his scalp and jaw.

I busied myself with my phone knowing the one person who would, hopefully, put the suspicious man at ease. My top priority was to keep myself from being exposed to one of the few criminal enterprises of Nevada. Against my better judgment, I dialed Garrett's number.

"Yes?" his harsh voice gritted out. "What do you want?"

I held back my growl and used a 'normal' people voice to not draw attention to myself as I explained. My eyes were trained on my glass, refusing to make contact with anyone, even Abby. The amber liquid winked in the soft overhead lighting.

"I need you to grab my on-the-go bag," I murmured, not faking the embarrassment that flooded my cheeks. I *hated* being in a position to have to rely on him. *Of all the assholes in the world*, I mentally grumbled.

"Where are you? Damn it, Kiera." It was his turn to growl at me, the revving of his Harley loud in the background. "You better not be in the middle of fucking nowhere again."

"I'm at the bar. With Abby." His grumbling stopped as he processed what I said. He knew what I was attempting to say without giving myself away. *I mean, I am sitting here pretending I didn't know this was the home base for the main motorcycle gang in the area.*

"You're at the compound?" he stated very slowly, with a brief pause before screams erupted on the other end of the line. I had to yank the phone away from my ear in case he burst an eardrum. His obscenities cracked through the speaker at the volume at which he shouted them. Annoyed with the situation and his assholey behavior, I hung up on him. *Fucking bastard.* A small smile curled my lip when I imagined Garrett's face when he realized he was no longer screaming at me, but at a dead line. *Ha!*

"He'll be here shortly," I muttered, taking another sip of the delicious liquor. Brooks and Stone were both eying me with suspicion now, Garrett's tantrum having caught their attention. They didn't talk as we waited and, with Abby and Nate stepping over to the other side of the bar to let Nate check over her, I was left to fend for myself. The rumble of Garrett's bike filled the awkward silence fifteen minutes later, and his familiar grouchy face zoned in on me as he shoved the door open.

"Warden?" Stone finally spoke, choosing to use Garrett's road name. Surprise littered his single-worded question. Garrett briefly glanced at the other MC officers, a slight dip of his head in greeting before turning his full, seething attention on me.

"If you'll excuse us, gentlemen. I need to have a discussion with my stepsister," he bit out, his baritone voice laced with fury. I slipped off the worn wooden stool, looking toward the floor as if I was properly chastised by his words.

Yeah right, fuck this asshole, I thought privately.

I followed closely behind him as we made our way back to the same spare bedroom I had woken up in, taking note that it was the second door on the left-hand side of the dingy carpeted hall. When he shut the door with a slam behind me, Garrett took several steps to close the distance between us, our chests brushing together causing my nipples to peak. Fire burned my veins at the feeling of his taut, tattooed muscles rubbing against me. Pushing the heat down, I focused on what he was saying.

"What in the ever-loving fuck are you doing here?" Each word was enunciated with deadly precision. I snatched my bag away from his closed fist, his reflexes too slow to pull it away from me. Setting it on the bed, I unzipped the plain black duffle and pulled out another pair of mom jeans and another stupid turtleneck, this one a dark grey instead of black.

I am so ready to be done with this job so I can burn these fucking clothes.

"Abby and I got jumped and she brought me here. Don't worry though," I sneered, looking up at the asshole before me. His green eyes sharpened and sparked as I glared at him. "I'll be out of here after I change. I have to prep for a job tonight." I shucked the ruined sweater and blood splattered jeans, leaving me in a black bra and matching thong. Garrett's eyes zeroed in on my body as I dressed quickly, his intense perusal heating my blood. *There's no time for hate fucking,* I reminded myself, *unfortunately.*

Garrett Newlyn came into my life when I was sixteen. Having just turned eighteen years old himself when his mother married Frank, his tattooed, muscled body had caught my attention, but no amount of sexiness could take away the amount of assholey-ness that spewed from his damned, kissable mouth.

"What job?" he demanded. His eyes finally focused on my face as I adjusted the turtleneck, his anger unmollified by my nearly naked body minutes before.

"None of your damned business, *Warden,*" I mocked his nickname. "I'm going to leave with Abby, you're going to keep your nose in your own fucking shit, and you're not going to call attention to me or my jobs to your boy band buddies. Got it?" I jabbed him in the chest with a finger. His lip pulled back in a snarl.

"Fuck you, Kiera. I don't want you here in the first place, so you'll get no objections from me when you leave."

I flashed him a sardonic grin. *Good.* Weaving around him, I stepped back out into the hall, the weight of my duffle secured on my shoulder.

"What job?" he asked again, following me. I huffed at his annoying, overprotective persistence.

"Don't worry about it." I rolled my eyes before stepping back into the bar area. "I'm ready, Abby." I tried to make my voice sound polite, friendly, and overall like a normal person. All of which I wasn't. *At all.* Garrett's hand clamped down on my shoulder keeping me from stepping forward.

"Don't do this job, Kiera," he urged quietly, but not quietly enough for Brooks or Stone to be blissfully ignorant. *Damn him, this isn't keeping his nose to himself.*

"It's only some volunteer work at the law office." I glanced over my shoulder at him. My words filled with innocence hoping to direct any attention away from me. I kept my eyes away from the other MC members and glared at Garrett. "Don't worry, it's only for tomorrow." He gritted his teeth and let go of my shoulder. Taking the opening, I shuffled quickly to Abby and out into the hot desert sun.

CHAPTER 2

Abby's truck left a cloud of dirt floating above the road where her tires spun against the desert ground. Garrett was suspiciously quiet behind me, his body language closed off with crossed arms and hard-set jaw. Stone looked, well, like Stone, with a scowl, twitchy muscles with the urge to hit something, and suspicious eyes.

"Stone, go with Nate. Figure out what we can find out about our missing shipment," I commanded, the trouble with the Alloy Kings' coming to the forefront of my mind. "I want to know how they found out, if our contact snitched or if they found out some other way." Without further prompting, Stone strode back inside where Nate was still seated at the bar. Garrett remained unmoving, his eyes zoned out where the truck had just been.

"So," I started, turning to face him. "You never mentioned a sister." His eyes snapped to me.

"Stepsister," he emphasized. My brows raised at his defensive tone. "Don't worry about her, she won't be coming by the compound again." His steely inflection had me wondering why he was so intent to keep her away.

Clean up her outfit, maybe let down her hair, and she'd be absolutely fuckable. "Don't even fucking go there, Boss," he warned, taking half a step closer.

"Go where?" I scoffed, just because I thought so didn't mean I'd act on it.

"I know that face." He pointed toward my expression. "There's plenty of hang-arounds to fuck; you leave Kiera out of club business." I held my hands up in surrender.

"Damn, Warden. A little possessive, aren't we?" I taunted. In response, he turned and stormed off leaving me snickering in front of the clubhouse. Unfortunately, my semi-good mood faded as soon as Kevin, one of the club members, came storming up to me a few minutes later.

Fucking Alloy Kings...

APRIL 19TH
FRIDAY MORNING
STONE

Garrett, Nate, and I were seated in a half circle in front of Brooks. Church had been called between the four of us in an attempt to keep the rest of the guys at bay before moving against the Alloy Kings. My blood boiled at the thought of the rival club moving in on our merchandise and turf, the amount of anger only building after everything with Nate's Old Lady and her friend from earlier. I pushed the memory of the odd woman from my thoughts; club business was top priority right now.

"We have a major issue," Brooks started. "Not only did our shit get stolen and Abby was nearly kidnapped, but Maxine was taken only an hour after the attempt on Abby." All breath left my body. Maxine was Kevin's Old Lady, and I had been too caught up in dealing with our missing shipment when Kevin came in a few hours ago to hear what had happened.

"We have information from one of our contacts that she is being kept in a secure location for one of the Alloy Kings' sex trafficking auctions," Nate supplied, his bushy beard shaking as he talked. His eyes were dark, full of stormy clouds, no doubt remembering Abby and her close call earlier this morning. "What's the plan? Storm it?"

"We can't risk a blood bath," I added, my words filled with resolution, brooking no argument. We needed every man for the upcoming strikes on our rival's shipments and compound.

"Need something more subtle," Brooks agreed, nodding. "We could go in under the radar."

"I know someone," Garrett ground out reluctantly. "Kiera knows The Cat."

Kiera knows The Cat? I thought doubtfully. She looked more like someone who had ten cats and didn't leave the house rather than someone who would know an infamous criminal.

"The professional cat burglar slash thief?" Brooks' blond brows raised in surprise. Garrett nodded sharply before continuing. His eyes hardened as he clenched his jaw, obviously unhappy at having to offer up the information.

"If we give her some details and a price high enough, Kiera might be willing to pass on the information. The Cat will go for pretty much any job if the pay is up to their standards. Saves us from having to go in guns drawn." Garrett leaned forward, his tattooed arms resting on his knees. Kiera's mystery grew with each word he spoke. My gut told me that there was something else at play with her; suspicion made my stomach burn. I knew Garrett had some family, but he hadn't mentioned them in years and he definitely hadn't said anything about some crazy cat lady stepsister.

"How do we know she's reliable?" I questioned. Garrett's angry gaze focused on me.

"She's reliable," he huffed.

"How do we know she'll actually tell The Cat about the job?" I pushed further. Something with Kiera wasn't adding up and I wanted, no *needed*, to figure out what.

"I vouch for her," he ground out, his eyes burning even more as he stared at me.

"I thought you wanted her as far as possible from club business, *Warden*," Brooks prompted, placing heavy emphasis on his name. "Or did what you say earlier go out the window?" Brooks gave Garrett a sinful smile which seemed to fuel the fire.

"Boss," he bit out, his fists clenching.

"Kiera can handle herself," Nate chastised Garrett. "Hell, she can handle Abby with no problems and we all know how much of a handful she can be."

I nodded absently. He had a point, Abby was sharp as a tack and fast as a whip with her attitude. She only kept them tampered down when around other patch holders knowing the first rule of the club, Respect First. Abby was essentially the head Old Lady, coaching the other ladies and hang-arounds through different events or issues. Even I had reservations if it ever came to crossing her and I was the one everyone was afraid of in the club.

"I know she can handle herself, but that doesn't mean I want you thinking you can dip your dick like she's some hang-around," Garrett snapped at Brooks. He was loyal to a fault with the club, so seeing his allegiance to Kiera was peculiar. He'd been cold to any hang-around for the last six years, only fucking when he needed and tossing them aside when he was finished. Brooks didn't say anything, only smirked. Knowing him, he was going to do everything in his power to piss off Garrett.

Ten minutes of discussion later after we finally got back on topic, we had our plan settled.

APRIL 20TH
SATURDAY NIGHT
KIERA

Checking once more, I assured myself that we had everything we needed for the job. Chase's bag held binoculars, his extra ammo, rope, and some other miscellaneous items, while my thigh holster bag had my lock picks, an extra pair of gloves, one of my multiple fake IDs, and some cash. My night vision goggles were lying neatly on top, the band tightened to the proper amount so it wouldn't slide around over my hat which was situated next to my stuff. I mentally ran through the plan for the fifth time in the last few minutes looking for any potential issues or holes in our main scheme or backups options.

Chase was securing his holster straps to his chest and belt, his light brown hair messily combed to the side of his forehead. His jaw was covered in a dark blond layer of scruff, muscles flexing under his black shirt. His playful attitude sparkled inside his eyes despite his stoic expression. My mind flit back to when I first met Chase over half a year ago.

My beer bottle bit into my palm with how cold it was, the refrigerator set to near freezing temperatures. Kicking the stainless steel door shut, I made my way into the large living space flopping ungracefully onto the dark brown leather sofa. The TV volume was quiet, not really in the mood to fully pay attention to the cooking show I had thrown on. A sharp, staccato buzz accompanied a high-pitched squeal sending me into action. The alarm only tripped when someone broke in or was on the property without permission. I took my security very seriously.

You kind of have to when there's a list a mile long of people who want your head on a spike.

Yanking my Glock from the holster, I grabbed a spare magazine and tucked it in the waistband of my lounge shorts. I turned down the main hallway toward the security room and came face to face with one of the most handsome men I'd ever seen, his tall body standing still fifteen feet away from me. His face was uncovered revealing steel-grey eyes, a jaw full of scruff, and a head of either light brown or blond hair. The lighting in the hall was dimmed making it hard to identify his features. The one thing that didn't match his stoic body language was the small smile that curled his lips.

We stood staring at each other for a few silent moments, assessing, eyeing, and plotting our next moves. Out of the blue, I bolted to the right down the side hall next to me, and his hand raised at the same time. A loud crack sounded as he attempted to shoot me, his silencer dulling the ear-splitting sound of his gun only just; my ears still continued to ring ever so slightly as I ran. His near silent footsteps followed me down the hall.

"Oh, Kiera," *he sang out, taunting like a cat cornering a mouse. The irony of the comparison was not lost on me since I was The Cat.*

I snarled. I'm definitely not the fucking mouse. *The light, cheerful tone of his taunt gave me pause as I waited at the edge of the hall around the corner.* If he thinks I'm going to run away or lie down and give it up, he's got another thing coming. *I steeled my spine in anticipation of his attack, a small smirk tilting my lips. His black gloved hand curled around the edge of the wall, his silver gun glinting in the low light. Grabbing his hand, I delivered two swift punches, one to his stomach and one to his face. The butt of my gun added an extra oomph to the hits.*

Unfortunately, he wasn't as stunned as most people would have been and was able to wrestle his hand away from me, his gun swinging out wide. I ducked and elbowed him in the stomach before taking off again. Adrenaline coursed through my veins as we continued to play cat and mouse. A wave of excitement filled my body and I felt the pang of desire to really show this fucker exactly who he was dealing with. Serene calmness came over me as I waited for him once more. Crouching down, I nestled on the other side of the cabinet as to not give away my position. I saw him the moment he entered despite his quiet steps that were more cautious than before. This is my house, and I'll be damned if I let him get the upper hand, *I mentally growled.*

"Come out, come out, wherever you are!" he sing-songed. Light glinted off his black boots, as we had ended up in my fully lit kitchen. I sprung when he was within hitting range, finally knocking his gun loose from his grip. The metal skidded across the countertop before falling with a clunk on the other side of the large island. His body pressed against mine forcing me to lean back. His gloved hands resting flat on the quartz counter on either side of my torso. I noted the delicious feeling of his muscles flush with my hips and breasts, taking stock that he was also turned on by the chase between us.

"I suggest you watch your next move, assassin," I taunted back, my gun angled up his rib cage directly at his lung and heart. "I might slip and blow off the family jewels, and that would be a travesty."

"You're much more fun than my other marks." He rubbed his nose along my cheek and inhaled. "None of

those bastards fought back. They all whined and moaned like little bitches." I felt his lips widen into a broad smile against my flushed and heated skin. My heart pounded in my chest, the hard thuds pushing my breasts into his toned upper body in a harsh staccato rhythm. That pang within me moved from the desire to eliminate to the desire to dominate, need coursing through me at the shift.

"I won't ever beg for mercy," I responded, my statement breathy with desire. I felt my pussy throb as he pulled back and looked at me. His steel grey eyes were filled with excitement, his smiled crazed and manic. He was devastatingly handsome and clearly insane, but then again, so was I.

"I can make you beg," he whispered, moving closer until we were nose to nose. "But not for mercy. No, little kittycat, I'll make you beg to come and release as I relentlessly fuck you without leniency." I chuckled coldly, my chest heaving in time with my breathless pants.

"You think I would just let you fuck me?" I leaned even closer, brushing the edge of his lips with mine with each word spoken. "No, little assassin." Turning his words against him had his eyes blazing with the thrill of the upcoming challenge. "You've got to fight for the privilege to fuck me." On the last word, I moved, maneuvering myself out from between him and the counter.

A cruelly handsome smile appeared on his kissable lips, while he took his gloves off sensually slow, one finger at a time. I disengaged the hammer on my gun before sliding it into the holster at my hip, pulling the extra magazine out and laying it on the counter. My assassin's eyes tracked the movement before flashing me his manic smile once more.

"It would be my pleasure to fight for your pussy, my little kittycat." Every time he spoke, even when laced with desire

and need, it was abnormally cheerful and jolly, as if he was constantly happy despite the fact he was about to murder someone. In this case, murder me. Well, fuck me now, we'll get back to the attempted murdering later, after I get my fill. I took off again, this time heading for the living room and hallway. His footsteps were no longer silent but pounding as his long legs ate up the distance between us.

I almost rounded the corner into the front entryway when his body smashed into mine, his muscled arms pinning me chest first against the wall. His impressive erection pressed along my ass in a rough manner as he ground his hips against me. Gritting my teeth to keep a moan contained, I threw an elbow back into his ribs. He grunted, shifting back from me just enough allowing me to turn around. Before I could try and run, his rough fingers wrapped around my wrists and held me to the wall.

"Is that all you've got?" he whispered sinfully in my ear, his breath hot on my skin. My lips tilted up at his tone, my eyes half-lidded in my lustful haze.

"I'll kiss it all better later, promise." I nipped his ear lobe at the end of my statement. His curiosity burned in his eyes as he looked down at me before slamming closed as I kneed him right between the legs. His pained groan echoed in the silent hall behind me as I sprinted up the staircase two at a time, grabbing the leather belt hanging from my chair before hiding. I had made sure not to hit too hard, I mean, I did want him to be able to fuck me as he promised. Can't do that with a sore dick, now can you?

"My kittycat fights dirty," he purred when he reached the top of the stairs. His steps were purposeful as he stalked to my bedroom. The crazed look made his steel eyes glow in the near blackness of the room, the only light from the full moon outside the many windows of my master suite. He stepped farther into the room eyeing the large California King bed with blazing appreciation.

I struck when he was distracted, jumping and latching onto his back. My legs wrapped tightly around his muscled abdomen holding me to him as I wrapped the leather around his throat. Try as he might, he couldn't dislodge or stop me until the belt was fastened snugly, but not too tightly, around his pulsing neck. He stilled under me when he realized I wasn't attempting to strangle him to death, his fingers exploringly brushing the leather. Slipping down his body, I placed my feet on the plush carpet.

"Let's see here," I said as I slowly walked around him, the excess of the belt held tightly in my fist. "Looks like you're my pet now, little assassin." I looked up at him, my head coming to right below his broad shoulders. The maniacal smile that spread across his face had me breathing in sharply, his eyes burning me from the inside out.

"Then I'm yours, Kittycat." He dipped down sharply finally pressing his lips to mine. His hands immediately going to my loose tank and ripping it right down the front baring my breasts to him. "Fuck me," he groaned happily cupping my chest, the pads of his thumbs running over the point of each nipple bringing another throb to my already soaking pussy.

"That's what I plan on doing," I murmured, tearing his shirt from his body as he had done to me. Chiseled muscles met my fingers as I gripped his shoulders, and without hesitation, I dug my nails in and tore down his chest and abs until I was met with his waistband, blood welling up in the wounds. I wanted to see how far into pain my assassin liked to go, and based on his shudder and goosebump rising on his tanned skin, I'd say pretty damn far.

I barely got his jeans unbuttoned and shoved down his hips before he had me turned and pushed into the wall *as he had downstairs. Only this time, he had shoved my shorts down far enough to press against me. His large cock stretching me as he plunged into me in one slow, powerful stroke. Unable to hold back the curses on my tongue, I moaned obscenities as he thrust into my flooded pussy without leniency, just as he promised.*

My moans turned to unbridled screams as I neared my orgasm, the sharp pangs of release pressing down against me making me thrash between my assassin and the wall. Right as it neared, he pulled out, a large hand fisting around my throat holding me flush with his bleeding chest.

"You know what you have to do to get your release, my little thief," he threw my sentiment in my face with a heated, yet gleeful, intonation. He nibbled my neck as he held me steadfast against him. My anger bubbled to the surface which only fueled the lust-filled haze I was drowning in.

"Fuck you," I bit out, breaking his hold to grip the leather wrapped around his neck. Pulling sharply on the strap, I led him back to the bed. "I'll beg you when you've earned it, and the five minutes of pounding my greedy pussy you just did is nowhere near enough," I growled, yanking on the makeshift collar, his muscular body spread against my dark bedding. His crazed smile turned salacious as he looked at me standing at the foot of the bed.

"If you want it Kittycat, then you work for it," he taunted. Raising a single brow after shucking my ruined clothing, I climbed on top of him sinking immediately on his bobbing erection. Our throaty moans filled the air as I rode him hard, digging my nails into his already tortured chest. The minutes turned to long stretches, and as I neared that edge I bent over his blood smeared chest, the warmth of the liquid rubbing over my pert nipples and heavy breasts.

"Please, my assassin," I begged, my voice shaking with

the fire that burned my nerves, ready for release. As if I had spoken the magic words, he snatched me around my waist and flipped us over. The sound of his balls slapping against me was drowned out by our combined screams, my hands clawing once more at his chest and after a few more thrusts, I blacked out momentarily from the intensity of my orgasm. My assassin followed suit as I milked him of his own release.

"Kittycat?" Chase's elated voice pulled me from my memories, his steel eyes bright as he stood in front of me. "You all right?" I nodded, a small smile curling my lips.

"Yeah, just thinking," I responded softly. Despite the fact I hated pretty much everyone, this crazy, happy-go-lucky ex-assassin somehow earned my loyalty in a night of an adrenaline-pumping, unbridled, sex-filled game of cat and mouse.

"What about?" He curled me in his arms, his nose nuzzling into my hair as he liked to do.

"When we first met, my little assassin," I teased. "Unfortunately, we can't have a repeat right now since we need to head out."

"Aw..." He pouted his luscious bottom lip out. "Later?" He gave me a cheeky grin as he bounced lightly on his toes in excitement. I nodded, a small laugh bubbling out of me at his enthusiasm. Pushing him away, I handed him his gear before strapping mine to the various parts of my body.

"Ready?" I questioned as I secured my goggles on my forehead over my beanie. He nodded, the thrill of tonight's challenge making his eyes glow in two pools of molten metal. "Good, let's go steal us some files."

CHAPTER 3

M eow," Chase's cheery voice purred in my ear piece. "You look pretty yummy in those tight black pants." I rolled my eyes at his heated compliment, my lock picks clicking quietly in the deserted parking lot. After a few more adjustments of my metal instruments, the lock gave way. The faint scent of paper greeted me as I slipped into the empty law office. I knelt down behind Cory Harbold's desk where the heavy oak door on the left side of the hideously gaudy piece of furniture opened silently, revealing a safe.

"Passcode?" I prompted, my fingers poised over the keypad.

"22410893," my partner rattled off the eight-digit code. The light shifted green, and the sound of the lock opening was like music to my ears. *Bingo, this is too easy.* I had to bite back a satisfied smiled at how seamlessly the job was moving along. Despite all the dirty little secrets Cory held in his office, his safe and security were mediocre at best, thinking the threat of his boss would be deterrent enough for criminals and thieves.

Like me.

But he was clearly wrong.

"What the…" I reached into the safe, and instead of finding a stack of papers, my gloved fingers brushed cool metal. *Nothing, the safe was empty.* "You've got to be fucking kidding me," I growled.

"What's that, Kittycat?" Chase's voice filled my ear, not at all concerned at the turn of events. *Of course*, I grumbled.

"The safe's fucking emptied out." I shut the safe and desk door, turning to his other drawers. "Everything else in his office is the same as it has been for the last week when we were casing the place. He knew we were coming," I realized with a start. At that same moment, a door opening at the front of the building caught my attention.

"I'd get out of there, Kittycat," he happily urged. "Harbold is here." I sighed in irritation. *Fucking shit.* Slipping out the office window that I had oiled last night for emergencies, I disappeared into the night and headed straight for my bike.

APRIL 21ST
SUNDAY EARLY MORNING
GARRETT

The squeaky stool was hard under me as I sank onto the wooden surface. Groaning, I rubbed my face in irritation at how early it was. *Who fucking gets up at seven in the morning?* I pushed the whiny thought away in an attempt to focus on the matter at hand, the Alloy Kings. A whoosh of air from outside whirling into the bar caught my attention. Chase's teasing smile and skip-like step filled the doorway before he started toward us.

"Who are you?" Brooks questioned, his brows furrowing.

"Kiera's friend, Chase," I informed him. I flashed Chase a look to relay he needed to keep his damned mouth shut about himself.

"Nice to meet you." He disregarded me with a brief wave of his hand before sticking it out for Boss to shake. Stone just stared, in a very Stone-like manner, at the former assassin as Chase slipped an arm over my shoulder. After a few moments of tense silence, Kiera's angry face appeared from the door as she made her way inside. Her fury added to the sexy fire that always burned within her. Her lean muscles were covered in tight black pants, and a loose black band t-shirt that had been cut off at the shoulder seams, the open sides revealing the band of her typical lacy bra. Completing the look, she wore riding boots and a leather jacket was clenched tightly in her fist. Her outfit offered a glimpse of the tattoos that swirled in both black and color, curling around her arms, chest, sides, and right half of her neck, but I knew from previous glimpses of her naked body that the artwork covered nearly every inch of her smooth skin.

"You might want to run," Chase whispered in my ear, his hot breath caressing my cheek. His overly puppy-like behavior was apparent on his face as he smiled toward me, his light grey eyes laughing at what was about to unfold. He thrived on chaos despite the meticulousness he employed during his previous career.

Glancing at Brooks and Stone, I noticed both wore looks of suspicion and arousal as they eyefucked Kiera. I couldn't blame them, she looked like a frump in her work clothes, but in this outfit... I mentally groaned at the sight. Even my jeans were growing snug. Stone's expression was a bit worrisome, the cold look of mistrust blatant in his deep scowl and narrowed eyes. She immediately walked behind the unmanned bar and poured a large glass of the closest alcohol she could grab.

"Kiera..." I started preparing to ask her for help when

suddenly, I was staring down the barrel of her Glock.

"Don't even fucking start with me," her husky voice snarled in rage. Her wrath made her chest heave as she made her way slowly around the bar. The sudden appearance of her weapon had Brooks and Stone reaching for their own, but Chase noticed their movements first, freeing his matching set of silver guns from their shoulder holsters. *Ugh*, I huffed, *just what we fucking need right now--a stand off in the bar*.

"Oh, no, boys. That won't do at all." Chase's manic smile appeared only moments before bobbing his weapons. "Hands down and I will consider not shooting both of you."

"No killing," Kiera commanded. She was the only person on the planet Chase would ever listen too, and the words pulled his eyes to her.

"No killing? Ah, man," he whined, pouting his bottom lip before looking back at my fellow club officers. "I guess I won't shoot you. Unless you go for your weapons again." Kiera's burning eyes centered on my face.

"You little fucking rat bastard," she ground out.

I knew she needed to hear what I had to say and what I had to offer before she ended up shooting me, or before she found out that her anger had me as hard as steel in my jeans.

"We need your help, Kiera. We can focus on what I did later," I urged, trying desperately to sound contrite when all I wanted to do was throw her sexy ass on the bar and fuck her until her anger was only a memory. "Another Old Lady was kidnapped, and we're willing to pay for her retrieval." Her eyes narrowed slightly as she pondered the offer for a moment, her shoulders finally relaxing before she spoke.

"How much? Location?" she asked as she dropped the weapon to her side, her attention focused on the prospect of a job instead of making a target out of my face.

"Five million. Half up front, half after it's complete," Brooks took over for me. His eyes narrowed as he watched her, the grey-blue depths dipping down to her perky tits quickly before returning to her face. "We need to get her back before they sell her to the highest bidder."

"Do you know The Cat?" Stone directed his question to Chase, who had finally lowered his weapons.

"Yeah, you could say I know that pussy real well. Don't I, Kiera?" Chase's grin turned from manic to wicked as he eyed her. Grinding my teeth, I pushed the thought of them together from my head. Stone's glare was disbelieving, not realizing that Chase very rarely, if ever, took anything seriously. He truly was an odd character.

"You want me to steal back a person?" Kiera's voice was incredulous, her brows dipping down as she tilted her head to look at the president. *Ugh, here we go.*

"You?" Stone interrupted, his next question full of doubt. "You're The Cat?"

"Uh, yes." She shook her head as if it was the stupidest question she'd ever heard. "I thought you knew that." Her darkened green eyes looked to me and narrowed. "You didn't tell them, did you?"

"I said you knew The Cat, not that you were the professional thief who's climbed their way up the ranks in the Nevada underground," I snarked, the anger that had been thrumming in my veins for the last few days flaring to life. "You know how I feel about your extracurricular activities. I mean, fuck, Kiera! You went after Cory Harbold, do you even realize he's Frankie Casterelli's personal lawyer?" She pointed her gun at me again, her vehemence bright in her eyes.

"Of course I fucking knew that! Why do you think I went after him in the first place? Frankie," she sneered the name, "is my ultimate target, and I'm not scared of that fat fuck either. Hell"—her hands flew up in the air in irritation, her anger about me overstepping into her job forgotten for the slight he had committed against her—"he already tried to have me killed."

"Wait, let me get this straight." Brooks' head shook back and forth quickly, his hands out to stop the conversation. "Frankie 'Smokes' Casterelli tried to have you killed? Who the hell did he send?" His voice filled with astonishment as he eyed the aggravating kitten next to me.

"Oh," Chase piped up, bending slightly in a small bow, his palm pressed into his chest. "That would be me." Silence followed his admission, his Cheshire Cat smile pasted on his smug face despite the tension that filled the room.

"You're an assassin?" Brooks' question dripped in skepticism. Chase nodded enthusiastically.

"Yes sir, I am." He was practically bouncing on his toes in excitement. I mean, he even clapped his hands in front of himself in a quick rhythm. *God, he's worse than a puppy.* "Skill Shot, at your service." *For fuck's sake.* I rolled my eyes at his imaginary hat tip. *Always with the fucking miming act.* Stone immediately stepped between the jittery assassin and his shocked boss.

"The highest paid assassin on the market? The one who went off the grid and retired?" Stone growled, seeing the happy-go-lucky Chase as nothing but a threat to the club.

"That's right, I found something better than killing. Didn't I, Kittycat?" Chase poked Kiera softly in the side a few times, his eyes filled with adoration as he stared at her. Kiera's eyes rolled, but she couldn't hide the ever so slight curl of her lips.

"He latched onto me," she explained, laughing as he continued to prod her ribs. "Like a leech or a barnacle."

"Now, I'm her partner in crime!" he squealed, scooping her up in his muscled arms. "Ain't that right?" His question was muffled as he buried his face into her dirty blonde-brown hair that was braided over her left shoulder. He continued to nuzzle her as she turned to face the rest of us. I bit back the urge to shoot him as his hands worked their way around her lean stomach.

"Why would Frankie 'Smokes' want to kill you?" Brooks continued his questioning, blatantly ignoring the grab happy assassin.

"Seriously?" she snarked looking to me. "Did you not tell them anything?" I shook my head, anger fusing my tongue to the roof of my mouth. "Well then, it's nice to meet you, Brooks." Her hand shot out to shake his. "My name's Kiera Casterelli." Neither of the officers moved, stunned into shock at her admission.

"Ex-hit man turned mob boss, Frank 'Smokes' Casterelli," Stone emphasized slowly, "is your father?" She nodded, no joy or smile evident on her face. She *hated* Frankie more than probably anyone on the planet. What he had done to her when she was younger was unforgivable and his death was marked in big, bold letters on my to-do list.

"When do you need me to get her by?" Kiera redirected the conversation choosing to focus on business, despite Chase's grabby paws kneading her stomach. I bit back my growl at his nuzzling and let Brooks take over when he came to from his stupor.

"As soon as possible." He tried to hide it, but it was blatantly apparent in his jeans how he felt about *my kitten*. Chase's hands crept up Kiera's sides almost brushing her delectable tits and I finally snapped.

"Keep your hands to yourself." I shoved his shoulder back, his stumbling steps moved him a foot away from her. Her eyes zeroed in on my face. The hatred burned, and I had to hold myself back from taking her right here in the middle of the room.

"I can do whatever the fuck I want with whoever I want, Garrett," she bit out taking half a step toward me, her gun twitching in her hand as if she wanted to point it at me again.

"Aw, somebody's a bit possessive of our kittycat," Chase teased good-heartedly, his arm sliding around me once more. A hand squeezed my bicep lightly. *Is he feeling me up?* "Don't worry, Gar, I share. Hey, that rhymed." He chuckled at himself, his suede jacket soft against the back of my neck.

"I thought she was your sister?" Stone's voice was full of accusation at Chase's not-so-subtle innuendo.

"Stepsister," Kiera and I responded in unison glancing at Stone before our attention fell back on each other.

"Frankie married his tramp of a mother when I was sixteen," Kiera explained not holding back on the disgust in her voice at the mention of Frankie and Barbara. Both of which were a match made in shitty heaven. *They deserve each other*, I internally growled.

"I was eighteen, about to go through patching in," I explained glancing at Brooks and Stone, both of who nodded in understanding. They knew what it had been like at that time. It had been a rough few years trying to survive with Barbara's drug addiction. Her pissing the money for rent and food down the drain on her heroine left both of us shit out of luck until I started hanging around the club doing odd jobs. After a few months, I started through my prospect shit, patched in, and never looked back at Frankie or my shit mom. The only part of my past I couldn't seem to let go of was standing right in front of me: tattoos, sexy ass, and more, all wrapped in one snarky package.

CHASE

My eyes darted between my kittycat and her stepbrother, the stand-off between them nearly suffocating me in sexual tension. *If I throw them at each other enough, maybe they'll finally just fuck and get it over with.* I knew that night when Kiera taunted about blowing off my family jewels that she was one of a kind, but when she leashed me? Hot damn. She owned me from that moment onward; no one else had *ever* caught my eye or made my blood pump, especially not like her. Her blazing inferno scorched me from the inside out and I couldn't get enough, but I knew that Kiera would never solely be mine, she was too much of a loaded gun. *Not that I would keep her from others.* I was giddy at the thought. My kittycat's power held me captive and when she eventually used it on others, it ensnared me even more. *Now, to push them a little more.*

"So, Gar," I paused, my eyes glittering with what I was about to do, "want to explain why you tipped off our mark?" Having lit the powder keg that was Kiera's rage, she blew, her gun trained again on his forehead.

"Thanks, Chase," he bit out glaring at me. He was only an inch shorter than my 6'4", but his muscles were slightly bulkier than mine, but still considered lean compared to Brooks or Stone.

"Well, no need to thank me," I teased. "I just like

watching my little kittycat point that large piece in your face. Her anger really is something, isn't it?" Kiera's dark eyes had flared with fury, only now the desire I knew pumped within her for Garrett and me unfolded in the mossy depths. *Hmm.* I let my imagination run wild. *Wouldn't that be fun*? I felt Garrett stiffen under me, his jaw ticking giving him away. *He thought so too.* Smug at the revelation, I pushed on. "No need to be ashamed of it, Gar. I love it when she's all fiery too." I threw him a saucy wink, a tiny smirk on my face at his angry scowl.

"Fuck off, assassin," he snapped. Shoving my arm off his shoulders he crossed his arms over his chest. His tanned cheeks were ever so slightly pink in anger, but he couldn't hide the boner he was sporting in his jeans. It didn't escape my notice that Brooks, and even Stone, had one as well. *My, my...* I smiled widely. *Lots of not-so-little toys for my kittycat to play with...*

"Start talking, *Warden*," our girl sneered, her eyes narrowing.

"Who gave you permission to address us by our road names?" Stone interrupted Garrett, his words harsh and short as he glared down at Kiera. Her attitude and sass ratcheted up another ten levels as she swung her eyes to the suspicious enforcer.

"Fuck you very much," she snapped. "I get you're all about ties that bind and respect and all that other useless bullshit, but I, my dear Stone, am not. I don't give two fucks about your leather-clad boy band here. I'm here for a job that you want to hire me for, nothing more. I don't owe shit to the club, and you sure as hell don't have my respect because of the patches you wear. Got it?" She huffed the end of her rant.

Stone was seething. Her lack of respect for their

hierarchy had his blood boiling based on his hardened ebony eyes and the harsh frown slashed across his tense jaw. While I knew she could handle herself, if she didn't shut that pretty little mouth of hers, she was going to find out first hand why he's the enforcer to a motorcycle gang. *Not that he'd be successful since I was standing right here. I might be willing to share her, but no one hurts my kittycat and gets away with it... or with all of their fingers.*

"If I think you're a threat to the Aces, I have absolutely no qualms putting a bullet between your eyes and burying you out back. Got it?"

She scoffed, rolling her eyes.

"Did you literally not hear what I just said? I'm here for a job, I'm here for the money," she enunciated slowly as if explaining things to a toddler. "I don't give a shit what you little boys do in the meantime whether it's fuck leather lovers, deal in arms, or snort cocaine, as long as you pay me for my work." Brooks finally stepped in, his arm bracing against Stone's chest when he opened his mouth with a retort.

"We got it," Brooks ground out eyeing Stone before focusing on Kiera. "Take a walk with me, will you?" He tilted his head toward the front door, his arm falling back to his side. Kiera's lips thinned and she nodded. Before heading to the door with Brooks, she poked Garrett in the chest sharply.

"Don't think because your babysitter distracted me that this conversation is over, Garrett. You owe me an explanation and you definitely fucking owe me some work for the amount of shit I'm going to have to go through to get those damned files now because of *your* fuck up," she growled, then stormed away from him, her gun going back into its holster.

As Kiera walked out with Brooks, the three of us stood in an awkward silence. *Well, I wasn't feeling awkward, but knowing Gar I'm sure he was.* While they stood there stoic and tense, I glanced around. The bar was dingy, but certainly not the worst place I had ever been. During my perusal, my eyes locked with the one person who seemed upset about my presence, Stone. His stony gaze hadn't left me since I admitted who I was, glared at my inspection of their clubhouse. Chuckling slightly, I raised my hand from Garrett's bulging bicep and tossed him a little finger wave. I couldn't help the smug smile that curled my lips when Stone's glower flashed into a snarl before smoothing over into his permanent frown.

If he thinks I won't push his buttons just because of his position in the club, then he's a moron.

KIERA

The weather was warming quickly with the sun as I headed down the cemented trail with Brooks. Neither of us spoke as we walked toward what looked to be a picnic area. Several tall trees, desert bushes, and picnic tables littered the space. I saw a few other patch members roaming around the area walking from their garage to the clubhouse or to the other outer buildings. Lots of curious gazes filtered toward us making my skin itch. Brooks leaned back into one of the tables, his sexy ass propped against the top while his right boot planted on the bench. I continued to stand in front of him, my arms crossed under my breasts.

He stared at me shamelessly and I held his gaze unblinking. His grey-blue eyes were similar to Chase's but held the tiniest hint of icy blue within the steel-colored depths. The battle of wills that continued between us had my skin flushing and my blood surging. His rugged appeal was a lot like Garrett's, but instead of basking in anger and hatred, he was dripping in sexual swagger. The visible part of his arms held no tattoos, but the tanned skin was taut over large, sculpted muscles. His legs strained against his jeans, and the hardened bulge at the crest of his thighs was not disappointing in size. My mouth watered in hunger at the sight. *I'd certainly love to see if that portion of him was as tan as the rest of his body.*

"So," Brooks finally spoke, his smooth voice casual, but a thread of predatorial tone filled the word. "Professional cat burglar, huh?" I cocked a brow waiting for him to continue. *He seriously couldn't expect me to answer that.* "A mobster's daughter and the stepsister and friend to several MC members. You're full of surprises."

"I'd say I tried, but I really didn't." I shrugged nonchalantly. My statement was true. I merely did what I was good at, and what paid well; Abby, Nate, and Garrett just sort of happened along the way.

"How old were you when you started stealing?" His eyes narrowed slightly as he continued talking, as if he could look into my soul and learn everything about me. I shrugged a shoulder, silently refusing to answer his questions, and gave him a taunting smile. "How'd you become a thief anyway?"

"Maybe it was something I learned in the family." The lie left my lips easily, but Brooks leaned forward to look at me more intensely. The smoky sky irises of his eyes never left my face. A drip of my own arousal slicked my skin under my riding pants while I restrained the urge to shiver under the heated and determined stare.

"Now, Kiera, I know that's a lie," he refuted, his whiskey

voice lowering as his gaze drifted down my body.

"Oh, really?" I sassed, determined to show him that his sex god act wouldn't distract me. *Well, it was fucking distracting, but I'm not that kind of bitch to let a pretty man sidetrack me unless I say it's okay.* "How would you know that?"

"Cause there is a lot of shit that gets talked about when it comes to the Casterelli mob, and none of it included any kind of thief, let alone a famous one."

I hummed skeptically. *He doesn't get to pilfer into my past without me getting anything in return. Nothing ever comes free, remember that, people.*

"How'd you become a motorcycle club president?" I challenged. "Was it passed on from after your dad, the previous president, died, or did you have to have some kind of vote?" It was barely noticeable, but I wasn't just everyone so I saw the slight widening of his eyes at the tidbit of information I had thrown down on the table. Granted, I *had* heard that floating around the underground circles, the rumors being whispered about at my father's fancy parties, but I knew that as well as the answer from all of my research. Taking half a step forward, I laid a hand on his propped knee so I could lean into him. "You're not the only one who listens to whispers, Brooks Abbott."

We stared at each other for a long moment, the heat of his leg searing my hand, but I refused to back down first. Finally, he smiled and leaned back effectively breaking the stand off. *Ha, bitch.*

"You're definitely not what I expected," he complimented. *At least, I think it was a compliment... fuck it, that's how I'm taking it.*

"Good." I smiled, pulling my hand back to cross my arms once more. My movement shifted his attention back to my body.

"And I certainly didn't expect this underneath that hideous outfit you wore on Friday." His voice was thick with desire as he leisurely undressed me with his eyes once more. Seductively biting my lower lip, my greedy pussy throbbed at the sexual waves pouring off him, our banter only having fueled the fire.

"I've certainly got a lot more going on," I taunted, "if you think you're good enough to see it." His predatory smile zeroed in on my face after having stared at my breasts while I talked. *Clearly a boob guy,* I noted, *good to know.*

"Oh baby, I'm more than good," he uttered in a sinfully smooth tone, the sound melting me even further. "Want to take me for a test drive?" He cocked a brow, wrapping his hands around my waist so he could pull me toward him close enough that I could feel his breath on my face.

"Boss." Nate's booming voice cut through the little bubble of craving we had created, interrupting what I was about to say. *Which was a big resounding fuck yes with an extra cherry on top.* "We have news from our contact." Nate's eyes briefly flickered between us, curiosity brimming. Knowing him, he'd tell Abby later and I would get an earful of snark and sass about moving in on the MC president. Brooks didn't respond, but his jaw was clenched as he slipped off the bench, his eyes never leaving my face. I hadn't moved back when he shifted forward, so my breasts brushed against his t-shirt and leather cut only adding fuel to the intense desire that flared in his glacier eyes.

"I'll be right there," he muttered not taking his eyes off of me. Nate nodded before heading back to the clubhouse. "As for you, baby, go get the details from Garrett about the job." Leaning down, his beard tickled my cheek as he whispered in my ear. "Don't maim or kill Warden. Also, our conversation is far from over; keep that in mind next time I get you alone." Before I could respond he strode away confidently, his riding boots thudding rhythmically on the sidewalk.

Fuck me, I internally groaned. My pussy was dripping down my bare leg and soaking into the fabric of my dark pants. *I need to fuck someone, and soon. This lady boner makes it a tad bit difficult to walk.*

Taking a few deep breaths so I wouldn't jump Garrett when I got to him, I followed Brooks' path back toward the compound's main building. I kept my head high as I entered the bar and found Garrett and Chase alone. Both seated at the bar sipping the same alcohol I had pulled from the shelf earlier. My previous anger simmered in the background mixing with my lustful haze as I stared at my attractive stepbrother. *Damn him,* I growled, *why did he have to be such as ass?* Closing the distance between us, I snatched the lowball from his hand right before he could take another drink. Downing the whole thing in one gulp, I set the glass on the bar top and stared at Garrett, my left hand resting against the lacquered surface.

"What are the details of the retrieval?"

"The warehouse is off Coney Island Drive in Sparks, right by the Truckee River and Glendale Park," Garrett answered, barely keeping his irritation at bay as he poured another drink. "The next pick-up of their merchandise is supposed to be next Thursday, the second, so the auction can happen next Friday."

"So we have eleven days until the merch move," I muttered to myself, mentally tallying the to-do's I would need to get done beforehand including how I was going to fix the massive shitshow my theft from Harbold's office turned into. I couldn't move against Frankie until I had those files.

"Need to case the warehouse and surrounding area," Chase chimed in from behind me, his head bobbing in buoyant agreement as he created his own to-do list.

"List of security precautions, guard rotations, any restraints or drugs keeping the girls," I added, glancing over my shoulder at him. "Need blueprints of the warehouse first and foremost as well as information on the previous auctions. Who are the typical buyers, how much they go for, any outside associates that assist with the move or auction."

"Why would you need to know that?" Garrett asked. For once his question was genuine and not filled with snark.

"The higher the price, the more security precautions. The more outside people assisting, the more openings for infiltration," I explained, my mind still tallying things I had to get done. "We're going to need help," I murmured to Chase quietly. "It's too big of a risk to go it alone." He nodded, eyes flicking to Garrett before they lit up with an idea.

"Why don't we have Garrett, Stone, and Brooks help? They would know the Alloy Kings better than anyone." Chase was giddy at the idea; he loved seeing how others worked. He was like a preschooler making friends out on the playground. "How 'bout it, Gar? Want to make it up to our kittycat after your screw-up?" My attention flickered back to the man in question. His face was red in anger, but his eyes held the tiniest amount of guilt. *God damn, angry looked sexy on him.*

"Stop throwing that shit in my face," he grumbled, his tattooed hand running down his face as he spoke. "Yeah, I'll see what I can dig up for you. Stone will probably be able to figure out security and their rotations since he's got the background in that shit."

"Good"—I leaned into Garrett letting the full force of my anger with him fill me—"but don't think that will get you out of helping me with getting Harbold's files. You owe me." I stabbed him in the chest with a pointed finger. He glared at me, staying silent. Stepping back I tilted my head toward the door. "Come on, my little assassin, we have work to do." *Lucky for them, my middle name is work.*

♠ BROOKS

Passing a fuming Garrett and the assassin, Nate led me back to our main office toward the back of the building. Stone was standing with his arms crossed in front of his broad chest at the other end of the small room. His scowl was deeper than normal, but I wasn't sure if it was from the feisty thief outside or the information he had learned about our shipment.

"So, what's the news?" I questioned when nobody spoke. Nate stroked his beard lightly, a grimace passing over his face before he responded.

"We have a snitch," he said, his voice grave."Within the club." My blood turned from burning with desire about Kiera to ice, the severity of his statement washing over me.

"Who?" I barked out, my hands curling into tight fists. Nate shook his head signifying he didn't know.

"We don't think it's one of the patch holders. I'll be watching the prospects and the Old Ladies. They seem the most likely to have gotten ahold of club information," Stone bit out, his voice frosty matching the ice pumping through me.

"Good." I nodded rubbing my eyes. "Fucking Alloy Kings," I muttered to myself as the door opened. Garrett stepped into the room, his anger tucked away as he turned to us.

"Kiera will take the job," he offered quietly. "She needs our help."

Stone scoffed. "We have other shit to do than help the thief who's supposed to be the best," he sneered glaring at Garrett who now looked about ready to punch someone.

"Do you want Kevin's Old Lady back or not?" Garrett snapped. "Cause Kiera's the one who can make it happen, but I agree with her that it's too risky for her and Chase to take it on by themselves with the timeline they have to work with."

"I always knew she was into something shady, but I never would have put two and two together that she was The Cat," Nate added thoughtfully. "She and Abby are usually out for an hour or two every so often, wonder if she knew."

"Probably. Kiera and Abby have been inseparable since before any of us came into the picture," Garrett pointed out. "Kiera used to steal food and clothing for Abby when her dad gambled their money away, you know." I felt my eyebrows raise. I knew Abby had a shitty upbringing, as did most of us, but I didn't realize Kiera was her saving grace. Nate nodded.

"Yeah, Abby told me she helped a lot, but I didn't realize it was that way. I'll have to thank her next time I see her." Garrett chuckled, which was odd since he rarely ever laughed or even smiled. *He has it bad for Kiera.*

"She'll probably look at you like you grew a second head if you did that, so I advise against it," Garrett offered. "Her pride's bigger than this whole compound."

"Her attitude too," Stone said ruefully. He really didn't

seem to like Kiera, his surly attitude growing with each statement about the thief. "What does she need?"

Garrett outlined what Kiera had brought up about what we could work on in the meantime, making sure to tell us that when she had a better plan on what needs to be done, she'll come to us.

"All right." I rubbed my scruffy jaw. "Stone, go look into what security shit Kiera needs, and keep an eye on those potential snitches. Nate, get in contact with our guy and schedule another shipment pick-up, we need that to pass it on to our dealers. Garrett, you're with me on getting all the shit Kiera needs to get Kev's Lady back." We separated to work on our tasks, the threat of the Alloy Kings hanging over all of us.

CHAPTER 4

My fake work boots thudded on the drive as I wheeled the empty dolly to the rental truck. Loading up the empty boxes onto the metal contraption, I wiped the sweat off my forehead and adjusted the baseball hat that I had stuffed my hair into. This stupid work jumpsuit was hotter than Satan's ballsack and pretending to move these boxes so I could discreetly watch the warehouse where the girls were being held made me sweat up a fucking storm. *I hate these kinds of case jobs; give me a shitty coffee shop any day over pretending to be a stupid shipping worker.*

After a few more minutes, the last of the fake boxes were unloaded into the rented storage unit which conveniently faced the warehouse that was across the small patch of grass separating the two structures. Climbing into the truck, I returned it to its rental place and hopped onto my bike, too lazy to change out of my disguise. Ten minutes later, I pulled up to the compound's front gate.

"Can I help you?" The bushy-bearded, bald guy manning the gate gruffed out the question as he eyed my work outfit with a frown.

"I'm here to see Brooks," I sighed. I just wanted to get into the air conditioning, not sit here and bake while I waited for the gate nanny to approve me to enter their precious compound. He pulled out his cell and hit one of the buttons, pressing the plastic device to his ear. I huffed, turning my attention to the compound that stretched out in front of me while he contacted his babysitter. The main road wound in an S-pattern over the small hills, two side streets splitting off close to the entrance. One went to the left and led to a collection of small townhouses or apartments, while the other went to the right and was a turn-in to a parking lot for a seven bay garage where several civilians were getting work done on their cars.

Thankfully, none of them were paying attention to me as the doorman finally got off the phone. He eyed me a few more moments before finally letting me pass. I grumbled the entire five minutes it took me to get to the main clubhouse. Hopping off my bike, I headed inside choosing to ignore the stares my outfit was attracting.

"Oh, thank fucking hell for air conditioning," I moaned happily under my breath at the cool breeze that graced my sweaty, red face. "I could seriously kiss the inventor of central heating and air."

"I'll pretend to be that guy if it'll get me a kiss, baby," Brooks' whiskey-smooth voice sounded from directly behind me. "You certainly have some interesting work outfits. First you're a geriatric teacher, now you're a butchy plumber. What do I have to do to get you back in your cat burglar outfit? Cause that was sexy as hell." I chuckled, turning around.

"That would be my normal clothing, and I don't *like* wearing this shit, if you must know. I'm usually in shorts, not pants, because if you haven't noticed, this is the freaking desert and this"—I gestured with a wave toward the dark navy jumpsuit—"is fucking hot." I couldn't bring myself to regret my phrasing when Brooks' smile turned sinful.

"Then take it off," he whispered. I smirked, feeling myself get wetter with the heat burning in his eyes, but Garrett storming up to us interrupted anything I was about to say.

"Boss." His harsh voice was filled with warning making me raise a brow at him. He was in his usual attire that matched Brooks' outfit of jeans, shirt, and cut. His dirty brown hair was finger combed and slightly messy on top of his head. The sides of his hair were cut in a fade while his jaw was covered in a short beard that was a bit longer than scruff, but not as long as Brooks'. His tattooed arms and hands flexed as he saw his boss hovering over me, his harsh scowl centered on me. "What on Earth are you fucking wearing?" I rolled my eyes.

"I was working today, as you lot paid me to do." I gestured again at my outfit. "This is part of that. You should know that, Garrett, you've been around long enough." I don't know what came over me, but I flirtatiously backhanded his bicep as I called him out. His eyes dropped to where my hand had smacked him before raising a brow at me, his lips curling into a smug smile. *Ugh, asshole.*

"Yes, I have been around long enough." His words were thick with heat as he leaned forward, and his lips brushed against the crest of my ear with his next words. "Long enough to know you're not wearing any underwear beneath that get-up." I clenched my jaw at the arrogant smile that he angled at Brooks, whose eyebrows rose. His matching cocky grin focused on me, and I suddenly felt like a piece of meat in the middle of a cockfight.

"Fuck off, both of you." I pulled away, growling. "I'm not a prize to be won. If I want to fuck either of you, I will. So quit with the pissing contest, I don't like golden showers."

"Noted, baby." Brooks' smile made it obvious he was talking about the dislike of being peed on, not the rest of what I said. I rolled my eyes and walked away, heading straight for the bar. *I need a fucking drink.*

"No one came or went from the building during lunch hours, so either they eat within the building or they have electronic monitoring." I slid into the wooden stool, taking my hat off and let down my waves that had been sweatily plastered to my head all day. "Fuck, I need a shower."

"Did you get a count to how many people they had working?" Brooks questioned, sitting next to me.

"No, when I say there was no one, I literally mean no one." Angling on the stool, my knees brushed against his rough denim legs. I propped my head on my fist as I responded. "I was the only one around other than the one person working the front desk at the storage place." Slouching down in exhaustion, I ended up leaning into Garrett who had slipped behind me. His right hand braced on the counter next to me, fingers brushing against my elbow ever so lightly that I thought I was imagining it.

"Sorry," I muttered, leaning forward. Unfortunately, or fortunately depending on how you looked at it, Garrett followed. His muscled torso pressed into my back, making my heart beat erratically. Despite the heat coursing through me being between the two of them, my anger flared to life at the audacity of my stepbrother.

"We got the blueprints." Brooks pulled my attention back to him before I could snap at Garrett. "Stone's working on getting a security layout for you." I nodded, mentally checking off several of the items on my to-do list.

"Chase is in contact with some of his old buddies getting information on the auction, should hopefully know by Wednesday at the latest." I dropped my hand from under my chin before continuing. "I'll take the blueprints with me so I can work through routes and plans. When I have that all figured out, I'll bring them back."

"Actually." Brooks leaned forward, only this time his reasoning wasn't to hit on me. "Keep them away from here and don't talk to anyone outside of the three of us here at the club." I felt my heart sputter painfully, there was something going on here at the club.

"You have a rat," I surmised, my words whispered. Both Brooks' and Garrett's clenched jaws gave me all I needed. "You got it, boys." Garrett huffed a single laugh while Brooks smiled at me.

"Come on, I'll show you where they are." Brooks did his head tilt thing toward the hallways. I slid off the stool and started to follow, when Garrett grabbed my arm.

"You heading straight home after this?"

I scrunched up my eyes at him. "Why?" I dragged out the word, not in the mood to deal with his overprotective possessiveness.

"I need to know when you want to work on Harbold's files," he ground out, his jaw clamping shut. His shoulders were tensed, and he looked severely uncomfortable with having to offer up his help. Smirking, I patted his cheek.

"I'll let you know when I need you, bitch boy." He snarled at me before yanking out of my reach.

"Fuck you, Kiera. See if I'll help you in the future." He turned to storm away, only stopping when I snapped at him.

"Damn right you'll fucking help me. You cost me precious time on my final move against that fat fuck, so suck it up, Garrett, and be ready to jump when I say so." I whipped around, following a snickering Brooks down the hall, Garrett's grumbling inaudible due to the sound of my heart pounding in my ears. *Fucking asshole.*

Brooks led me to one of the last rooms in the dingy hall, a small space holding a dented metal desk, a couple of stained chairs, and one file cabinet sat in the corner. The walls were a discolored yellow, as if someone had smoked in here for years, and there was a giant, boot-sized hole in the wall. There were several rolls of paper lying on the desk, held closed by rubber bands.

"I'll hold off on looking through these till I'm at my house," I advised Brooks, bundling up the pile of papers, my eyes counting the number of rolls I had so I wouldn't misplace or lose one.

"Mhm," he hummed. His distracted tone had me looking over at him. His eyes were trailing slowly down my body despite being clothed in a frumpy jumpsuit.

Standing up fully, I cocked a brow at him. *If he wanted to play that game, I'd more than willingly be a participant.* I was glad I had left the hat on the bar and that the air conditioning had cooled my skin as I reached up to the zipper at the the neck of the scratchy navy material.

Keeping eye contact with Brooks, I sensually unzipped the jumpsuit, leaving me in my tank and a portion of my skin-tight shorts. The breeze in the office had my nipples stiffening against my top. No bra sat between my breasts and the white jersey material allowing the spider webs I had tattooed around my nipples to shadow through the shirt. Brooks' eyes zeroed in on the points, the bulge in his jeans growing larger the longer he stared. Bending over, I dragged the material down my legs, revealing my full leg sleeves and the shorts that barely covered my ass.

After shucking the jumpsuit, I took the few steps to stand in front of Brooks who was sitting in one of the chairs. I ran my fingers through his coarse, yet soft, golden blond hair, gripping tightly at the back of his head. His groan rumbled deep within his chest as I straddled him, the rough material of his jeans rubbing salaciously against my already dripping core.

"What were you saying about a test drive, Brooks?" I whispered against his ear as I ground against him. Fire and need coursed through my body as I felt him grinding against me. Calloused hands landed on my thighs skimming up until they gripped my ass tightly. "Don't mind if I do," I murmured before capturing his lips with mine. He moved with matching fervor. His hands slid down to my thighs before moving back to my ass; this time he dipped fingers under the thin spandex fabric to knead the flesh underneath.

I continued to grind against him, using his impressive erection to rub my clit. The sharp pulses of lightning that shot through me at the feeling had me shivering in his muscled arms. Releasing his hair, I tugged my tank over my head. One hand left my ass to cup my right breast, his beard rough against my flushed chest as he sucked on my nipple. The graze of his teeth had me moaning breathlessly, my hair brushing against my tattooed skin as my head fell back.

Brooks moved suddenly, scooping me up in his tanned arms and depositing me on the cold metal of the desktop. Yanking on my shorts, I propped myself up so he could pull them down my legs where he tossed them over to the corner of the room. Unbuttoning his jeans and belt, he shoved them down his hips before producing a condom from the top drawer of the desk. I snatched it away from him and after quickly opening it, rolled it down his thick cock. Brooks clutched the back of my neck and held me still with his other hand on my thigh. It took several rocking thrusts before he was seated fully inside me. I was panting with pent up desire by the time he started to move.

"You're so wet for me, baby." He tangled his hand in my hair, angling my face up. "Better make this one quick, don't want to have Warden come in guns blazing because I'm fucking you and he isn't." I moaned as he started moving in forceful drives.

"Let him see." I fisted his shirt tightly within my grasp. "Maybe he'll fucking stop being such a possessive asshole."

"You really are a fiery one, ain't 'cha?" Brooks' normally smooth voice was rough as he kissed me hard, his tongue tangling with mine. The grip on my hair was tight, holding my head steady and angled up to him. He pulled back, hand tightening on my thigh as he thrust harder. Faster. Wrenching more and more fervid cries from me.

Fuck, so good.

His grey-blue eyes darkened into two stormy irises, intensely focused on my breasts as they bounced with each thrust. A growl rumbled deep within his chest, his muscles tensing as he fought for control. Struggled against his urge to dominate me. Own me.

I was breathless. My release loomed ahead and I was going for it, knowing I'd be crashing into that blissful pool at full speed.

"Fuck." I could barely get the word out before stars flooded my eyes as I clamped down around Brooks. He continued his merciless pace, making the desk groan under our movements until he reached his own climax. Our heaving breaths filled the air, neither of us moving for a long moment as we stilled our racing hearts and unsteady breathing. He crushed his lips to me before slowly sliding out.

"Don't worry, baby," Brooks whispered against my lips. "Next time, I'll show you just how long an Ace can ride." I nipped his bottom lip sharply, resulting in him tugging my hair pulling my head away from him. "Naughty, Cat." His smile was sinful and domineering at the same time, his eyes glowing in triumph.

"I need to get going." I shoved him back, a matching smile curling my lips at his stumbling. *He might be the president, but I'm not someone who can be ruled.* I dressed quickly as he removed the condom and situated himself inside his jeans. Pulling the itchy material up over my legs, I decided to leave the top of the jumpsuit undone tying the arms around my hips.

"You're a walking temptation there, baby, with those tats on display," Brooks' warned, his head tilting toward my chest where the circular webs were shadows against the material. I cocked a brow at him.

"I dare anyone to fuck with me." I collected the blueprints from the ground as they had been shoved off in our quickie, before stepping up to him. He was tall, requiring me to look up at his ruggedly sexy face. "I will gladly fuck someone up if they try to start shit. I'm not someone to be used or abused without my permission." His eyes sparkled at my statement, his hand tangling in my hair once more as he kissed me without abandon.

"You're an Ace, baby, through and through." Despite not giving a shit about their club, my chest felt all tingly at his words. *The fuck is that shit?* I shoved the feeling away, locking it away with every other soft or fuzzy feeling I'd ever felt, focusing on the job ahead.

"I'm out of your little leather-wearing boy band's league, *Boss*," I mocked his road name with a cocked brow and smirk as I walked away from him. He hummed a skeptical response before opening the door for me; a small curl curved his lips up as I stepped out of the room.

"Whatever you say, *Cat*." The door shut in my face after he taunted my thief name.

Prick. I huffed a laugh heading back down towards the bar area ready to get the fuck off compound grounds.

STONE

We had rescheduled a new shipment pick up with our contact, making sure to change the normal date, location, and time. Nate and I had also decided that he and the other officers would do the ride, keeping the information between the four of us. Rubbing my hand over the short stubble on my scalp, I left the warehouse and headed toward the clubhouse. I was lost in thought when I ran into Kiera, literally. The blueprint rolls she had wrapped in her arms sprawled out on the dusty cement. She groaned to herself before kneeling down to pick up the rolls. I was distracted by her tatted skin when she called me out.

"You know you could fucking get down here and help me, Stone," she snapped, her mossy eyes filled with irritation as she looked up at me.

I could get used to her on her knees in front of me, I thought, *it'd put her in her place that way.*

"Fuck you very much, I don't kneel to anyone and certainly not to you. *My place* is wherever the fuck I say it is," she ground out, the irritation growing to rage.

Shit, I must have said that out loud.

"Not my fault you're digging yourself a deeper grave

every time you open your mouth," I bit out, refusing to help her. My arms crossed as I glared down at her.

"Get in line," she huffed standing up, the rolls secured under her arm. "You're not the only one who wants to put a bullet in my skull, and you certainly won't be the last."

"Why does that not surprise me?" I snapped. My eyes finally realized her tits weren't confined in a bra. *Fuck.* I tried to clamp down on the desire pulsing through me when I saw that her tits were also tatted up, but it was futile, and my cock went from zero to sixty in 0.2 seconds. "Why the fuck are you even here?" I pried my eyes away from her chest to find her smirking at me arrogantly.

"Well, I thought that was pretty obvious"—she waved her arm holding the blueprints—"but if you're really that much of a moron I don't think we need your help on this job," she snarked. I was starting to feel like Garrett with the amount of teeth grinding I was doing. I gave him shit, but I secretly found her feistiness sexy as hell too.

"I suggest you leave." I crowded her space. She was too much of a ticking time bomb, and when she finally went off and the consequences came down on her, I didn't want her anywhere near the club. "You might have Garrett wrapped around your little finger and Brooks distracted by that cunt of yours, but I know a threat when I see one."

"First of all, Garrett fucking hates me, so you're wrong on that front. Second, it's not my fault my pussy is fucking amazing and that your boss wants to come crawling back for another round. Finally, you can act reluctant all you want, but that fucking erection you're sporting says otherwise." She cocked a brow and started to walk around me toward her vehicle.

"You think you're such hot shit, Kiera, but you're not and one day all that shit you stir will come back on you,"

I shouted after her, her left hand shooting up in the air to flip me the bird. *Wait, did she say crawling back? Damn it, Boss.* I groaned. *He would be the one to think with his dick.* I stormed inside, cursing my reaction to her with each step. I needed to be focused on club business, not distracted by the target she could be marking us with.

Fucking fiery thief...

CHAPTER 5

APRIL 23RD
TUESDAY NIGHT
CHASE

I scratched the scruff on my jaw as I walked through the main hall of the large house. Memories of when I first met my kittycat flashed to the forefront of my mind, but not even the thought of our long night of chase and fuck could relieve the dark cloud that hovered over me at what I would have to tell Kiera. She was in the back room bent over the blueprints, absently nibbling on her pink lip.

Staring, I took in my kittycat when she was in her element. Her index finger on her right hand tapped rhythmically against the stone table top as she scribbled down notes with her left. Her long, wavy honey brown hair was messily braided over her left shoulder, the tail of it brushing the blueprints. She wore a pair of cut off denim shorts and a black tank where the sides were cut down to her rib cage showcasing her lacy red bra. I felt my mouth water at the sight, but I pushed it away, there were more pressing issues to handle despite the fact that I wanted to eat her right up. *Later*, I promised myself.

"Kittycat." I strode the rest of the way into the room. Her darkened moss-colored eyes flickered up to my face, brows drawing low in concern at my serious tone.

"What is it, my little assassin?" Her husky voice practically singing my nickname made my heart squeeze. *I don't want to do this.* I counted to three before addressing what I had learned.

"I found out about the auctions and the buyers." I leaned my hip against the table, my ever-present faux-suede jacket had been tossed over one of the leather recliners in the corner when I had gotten the call. The familiar softness it provided was missing and I found myself absently rubbing my bare arms as they crossed over my chest. My black shirt was tight against my torso, my leather holsters and the familiar weight of my guns providing the only comfort under this heavy cloud.

"And?" she asked, her eyes growing more worried. "Why are you so serious right now? You're never serious. Please don't tell me it's bad." Her eyes widened comically as a small pout curled her lip out. "I hope nuns aren't the buyers. Nuns are the buyers, aren't they? I hate nuns." I cracked a tiny smile, her attempts to soothe me making the dark cloud a little less grey and a little less substantial.

"No, my little kittycat, you're safe from your fear of clergy members. One of the main buyers," I hesitated to take in a reassuring breath, "is Frankie. He buys the girls to use as high-class, high-priced escorts in the Solace Hotel." Her face paled in alarm although two tiny splotches flushed in fury on her cheeks, her eyes stormy at the news.

"All right." She looked back toward the blueprints and her notes, absently bobbing her head in a nod. "Okay, that changes the plan." I tilted my head, the weight lifting off of my shoulders finally having told her. I wouldn't be able to hold back the bloodthirsty urge to shoot Frankie in the head if she had broken down. *She's stronger than that,* I chastised myself.

"What do you have in mind?" I could tell my voice was lighter, more cheery than before, the light-heartedness seeping back in when I saw the mischievous glint lighting her eyes. A manic grin curled her delicious lips.

"We're going to steal *all* of the girls."

APRIL 25TH
THURSDAY LATE AFTERNOON
KIERA

Abby was talking with a woman with a 'Property of Butch' patch on her leather jacket. No idea who Butch was, but I felt sorry for him because the way his girl was screeching at Abby was making my ears ring. I was leaning back against the bar, a lowball of whatever alcohol they keep around here swirling in my hand. My assassin was busy watching the warehouse, noting any guards or anything odd. He told me this morning to take a break from the job since I had been up all night planning, the prize of fucking over Frankie from a score fueling me forward. Since I didn't exactly socialize like a normal human being, I found myself at the compound waiting for Abby to finish listening to Miss Screechy Screecherson.

"You want more?" the boobilicious blonde bartender asked me, her smoky voice pulling me from facing the room to facing the bar. She held up the bottle of whatever I was drinking with a raised brow. I nodded, placing my glass back on the bar for her to fill. "What's your name? I'm Cheryl."

"Kiera." I sipped the liquor, the burn in my chest comforting me like a big fuzzy blankie. *Don't turn those judgy eyes on me; thieves like comfy things too.*

"So, you looking to be a hang-around? Or you looking to snag up one of the Aces and be an Old Lady?" she asked, her tone prying as she watched me. I raised a brow in response. "It's just that I've seen you around the three single officers recently." She shrugged. "You wouldn't be the first. But honey, let me tell you a little secret. None of those men will settle for just anyone."

"Why's that?" I found myself asking despite the fact that I literally gave zero fucks about Brooks, Garrett, or Stone.

"Well, Garrett"—she tilted her head in thought—"he likes to hit it and quit it and rarely does it with the same chick twice. Although, he doesn't go for the hang-arounds very often, usually drinks and sits in the corner all cranky."

I chuckled. *Sounds like Garrett.* My stomach tightened with the thought of my asshole stepbrother with anyone, but her words pulled me away from my troubling internal thoughts.

"Brooks is the player of the three. Tends to fuck whoever catches his eye and it's rare he stays with one for more than once or twice." I nodded, tucking this information away for later. For what? I didn't know, but my brain decided it was something I needed to remember.

"Stone, is well, Stone." She shrugged again. "I'm sure you get what I mean when I say that."

"Scares any possible women away with his scowly face?" I added with a smile.

"Better than being a snarky brat like this one woman I know." Stone's soft words were right behind me, his voice irritatingly sexy. Cheryl's face paled, and she turned her attention to wiping the bar and cleaning glasses, her eyes purposely avoiding the Aces' enforcer.

"You know you love me, jerkoff." I gave him a smirk as Cheryl choked at my blatantly disrespectful nickname. He growled at me, his lip pulling back as he crossed his arms.

"Why are you here? Brooks and Garrett are on a ride," he barked out, his hulking form trying to be intimidating by hovering over me. I pointed to Abby.

"That's my best bitch over there. Not everything revolves around the Aces, you know." I turned back around to see Cheryl looking at me like I was signing my own death warrant. *Which was probably true.* "Why didn't you go with the other two? Now the three musketeers are like the sad, broken up version of itself, like Guns 'N Roses or One Direction," I retorted. He growled before storming off into the back hallway.

"Wow," Cheryl breathed. "You're a special kind of stupid." I grinned but didn't say anything. Abby finally finished up with Butch's girl and sank onto the stool next to me.

"Holy shit," she groaned, rubbing her eyes. "Cher, get me the largest fucking glass you have back there."

I eyed Abby. The bruises on her arms from our attempted kidnapping had darkened to an ugly purple and blue but were slowly starting to fade. Her dark hair was thrown in a ponytail at the back of her head, her thin face flushed with anger. She wore dark jeans, a faded band t-shirt, and her 'Property of Tank' jacket. As soon as the boobilicious bartender had her drink set in front of her, she gulped down two large swallows before turning to me.

"So, how's it going?" Her rough voice was subdued, but I knew her sass was coming at some point.

"Good, Chase made me take a break from working so here I am." I flashed a cheeky smile at her. "How's the Old Lady life, ya old hag?" She punched me in the arm, making me laugh.

"Shut the fuck up, bitch." She smiled despite her attitude. "I should be asking you how you're doing in regards to certain club officers." *There's the sass*, I noted.

"I'm sure I don't know what you're referring to, ma'am," I said studiously pressing a hand to my chest. "I'm the most honorable woman around."

"That's the biggest load of horse shit I've ever heard." Abby rolled her eyes before continuing. "Seriously though, what's up with you and Brooks? And Stone. And Garrett." I scrunched my nose up.

"Nothing." I leaned forward to whisper in her ear. Brooks had said keep it between the guys, but Abby was too smart to believe otherwise. "They hired me on a job, very hush-hush." She hummed in understanding.

"That doesn't explain why Nate said it looked as though Brooks was about to eat you for dinner outside the other day," she called me out, a single brow cocked at me, silently demanding an answer. I just smiled and took a drink. She already knew or she wouldn't have brought it up, so I didn't feel the need to say anything. "You're playing with fire, Kiera." I rolled my eyes.

"He's a big softie. Besides, it didn't mean anything," I reasoned.

"He's the president of a motorcycle club for a reason, but I wasn't talking about Brooks." Her severe tone caught my attention. "I was talking about Garrett."

"What about him?" I was so confused. *Weren't we literally just talking about Brooks? How did Garrett come into this conversation? That sneaky bastard.*

"He's in love with you, Kiera."

I made a face. *Garrett, love me?* I honestly didn't think I'd heard anything funnier than that in a long time, but I contained the urge to laugh.

"No, he isn't. Garrett hates me," I explained. "I don't know if you've noticed, but he's only a possessive asshole because I'm family." She facepalmed and groaned.

"Sometimes, I think you're the smartest woman I've ever met"—I beamed at her praise—"but times like this, I think you're a dumb shit."

I deflated. *Am not*, I thought childishly.

"He's possessive because he wants you for himself. He either doesn't realize it, or he's ignoring it. It has nothing to do with your parents' marriage. And you fucking Brooks is a good way to light a block of C4 and watch it explode in your face."

"Whatever you say, crazy lady," I muttered taking another drink. *Garrett? Love? Certifiably insane is what that is.*

"You're impossible," she mumbled, throwing her hands up. "Fine, keep your head buried in the sand for all I care."

♠ ♠ ♠

An hour after shooting shit with Abby, I pulled into my wide driveway, shutting the bike off when I reached its proper home within the four stall garage. Chase's Audi was cool to the touch when I walked by meaning he had been home for a while. The smell of fragrant veggies and peppers filled the air of the mudroom as I hung up my leather jacket and took off my boots. I walked in on Chase softly singing along to the radio station he had playing through the home stereo system, his sexy, jean-covered ass shaking off beat to the upbeat pop song. He was hunched over the cutting board as he chopped through bell peppers at terrifying speed. Sometimes it was hard remembering such a bright and lively person was an assassin. *Well, until he sliced up food at the speed of light without cutting off a finger.*

"Kittycat!" he cheered when he turned to toss the chopped food into a prep bowl. His handsome smile lit up his face as his eyes danced merrily. "How was Abby?"

"She's good, was getting bitched at by another Old Lady whose voice was screeching something terrible," I told him as I walked by, leaning in for a quick, passionate kiss before sliding onto my bar stool across from Chase. "Tried to tell me some shit story about how Garrett's in love with me." I chuckled, expecting Chase to laugh with me, but he looked up from his chopping to raise a single brow.

"I can't say I find myself disagreeing with her." He smiled mischievously. "You two are just blind." I balked.

"Fucking excuse you? Blind about what?"

He laid the knife down and placed his hands flat on the counter, and my mind flashed back to when he had me trapped between him and the block of stone when we first met. My pussy throbbed thinking about it.

"The fact that you both actually give a shit about each other, other than in a familial way." I made a face, scrunching my nose. "Also, I know what you're thinking, and if you keep giving me those 'fuck me eyes,' I'll do just that." My blood sparked at his husky tone, his face shifted into a suggestive expression. I tilted my head up, leaning forward on my forearms.

"Promise, my little assassin?" My whispered words were heated. His pupils expanded significantly before stalking like a predator approaching its prey around the island. Before I could react, he lifted me out my seat and placed me roughly on the counter forcing his way to stand between my thighs. His steel eyes melted into two pools of liquid metal, his predatory smile sending shivers I didn't bother to hide down my spine.

"Is that what my kittycat wants?" he whispered wickedly, the scruff rough of his brushing my neck and jaw as he barely skimmed kisses against my quickly warming skin. Unable to speak, drowning in the desire and need that flooded my system, I tangled my hand into his hair and pulled his lips to mine.

I trembled under Chase's roving hands and rocking thrusts, his impressive length grinding against my clit through our clothes. Our tongues battled, only breaking apart long enough to yank our shirts off before moving back in. He moaned, shuddering, as I sealed my lips to his bare chest. Chase frantically and roughly ground against me when I bit down. Burning from the inside out, I made quick work of his button and zipper, unable to keep my hands off my assassin.

His calloused hands gently slid from my head, around my neck, and down to my breasts leaving fire in their wake. At the intimate touch, my nipples peaked, painfully begging for more. To my surprise, Chase pulled away from me leaving me breathless and needy on the smooth stone. I gaped at him as he chuckled, his manic smile made me quiver as his gaze shifted down my half dressed body. *Well, if he's not going to strip me, I'll do it my damn self*, I thought, reclining back against the counter to unbutton and shuffle my denim shorts off my legs leaving me bare to his roaming eyes. Hearing shuffling, I propped on my elbows to look down the length of my body, seeing him naked and shuffling around in the refrigerator and freezer.

"Hungry already, my little assassin?" I teased. Chase's lean muscled body turned to walk back to me. "We haven't even started yet." My smile changed into a strangled moan as the biting cold of an ice cube slid across my thigh. Sharp tingles spread across my skin as the frozen water melted against my hot body. My eyes fell shut as I lay back against the stone allowing Chase full freedom to do whatever he was planning, my greedy pussy already dripping onto the counter in anticipation.

"I am hungry, Kittycat," Chase murmured, but I was almost too lost among the sensations of the moving ice to hear him. "But not for food." Goosebumps pebbled on my skin as he moved the ice from my thighs up to my stomach, swirling around my belly button before caressing the curve of my tits.

"Fuck." I shivered, my voice trembling. The onslaught of sensations from the frigid ice compared to Chase's hot kisses and swirling tongue that pressed against my right hip made me dizzy with ecstacy. I hissed when the frozen block swirled around my pert nipple, both in pleasure and near pain, the temperature only serving to ratchet the heat within my veins.

I couldn't open my eyes as he trailed the ice to my other nipple, circling a few times before starting its trek back down my stomach. Quivering in anticipation, I subconsciously opened my legs. Chase's hitched breathing warmed my leaking pussy before the ice could reach it, and when it did, I was lost in a haze of painful lust and need. The intense shivers and tingles radiated from between my thighs making me arch back against the hard surface, especially when Chase swirled the ice around the entrance to my greedy pussy while sucking sharply on my throbbing clit. My release came quickly when he removed the ice and pumped two fingers in with deadly precision.

"What I'm hungry for," Chase whispered against my goosebump covered body that continued to be wracked from the aftershocks of my orgasm, "is something sweet with this pussy." Peeling my eyes open, I looked down at him. He held an open chocolate bar. Breaking a small piece off, he pressed it against my stomach. It melted almost immediately despite having ice covering my skin just minutes before. "Perfect treat," he hummed cheerfully before lapping up the pool, his eyes never leaving mine. Taking a larger piece, he pressed it against my stomach.

The chocolate continued to melt in a trail of dark sweetness across my skin up over my chest and neck, following the same trail as the ice that had long since melted and dried against the heat of my body. Chase's languid kisses and tongue followed the trail to nibble and lick my nipples and collarbone, the candy stopping right above my clit. When I whimpered in longing, Chase chuckled, finally obliging me by dragging the last bit of chocolate down my sensitive bundle of nerves and mixed it with my own juices. Our moans blended with the soft music that played through the speakers, filling the cavernous space as he proceeded to lick each drop of sugar from my body.

Unable to handle his torturous teasing, I tugged sharply on his hair, bringing his mouth to mine. Smoky sweet dark chocolate mingled with my own unique flavor. His fevered kisses picked up pace as he lined up against my entrance. I yanked his head back the way I knew he loved it as he sank into me all the way to the hilt. Our pleasured cries entwined echoing off the hard surfaces around us. His hips shifted back slightly before slamming home and ripping another scream from me, my pussy still adjusting to his size.

Rough nips. Heated licks. Sparking fire along my neck and jaw as he started to move in sharp, intoxicating thrusts. His name left my lips in a harsh moans and cries, my nails digging into his shoulders and holding him tightly to my bouncing tits. Tingles and waves of need built, making my moans falter until my second orgasm slammed down on me, Chase's rhythm slowing as I gripped his cock tightly in my waves of release.

Taking control, I nudged him back and snatched the chocolate off the counter before kneeling at his feet.

Breaking a small section off, I watched, mesmerized, as it melted against his cock. When it pooled and started to run down the side, I lapped it up, circling around the head before taking him deep. Salty mixed with sweet topped with a hint of smokiness as I sucked, my own juices dripping down my thigh. Tending to my own greedy pussy, I rubbed quick and hard circles around the tortured bud, letting Chase pump forward. Right as my body flooded with another wave of release ready to wrack my body, he pulled me to standing, pressing me against the counter, his bobbing cock rubbing tauntingly against my ass.

The smoky sweet smell of the chocolate filled my nose as I felt a piece run across my shoulder blades and work up to my neck, Chase's wet tongue quickly following the melted trail. I couldn't hold back the muffled moan as he held the half melted piece to my lips, letting it coat them before angling back for a kiss. Chase slid into my slick entrance as we devoured each other, my moans silenced by his demanding mouth.

I had to use the counter to keep my body from completely melting at his relentless pace. His hands gripped my waist in a tight grasp, my eyes rolling back at the rough way he handled me. The orgasm that had faded when he pulled me off my knees built to dangerous levels before finally exploding. Chase continued his merciless pace, faltering as he found his own release, fingers gripping tight enough to leave bruises. Our panting was harsh in the pop music playing overhead. A sweaty forehead pressed against my shoulder while my assassin attempted to calm his trembling limbs and thudding heart. When he was able to move, he slipped out, pressing a soft nipping kiss in the crook of my neck.

"Why did you let me ruin dinner by having dessert first,

Kittycat?" he teased, pulling his jeans up his trim hips. My legs still trembled, so I sank onto the wooden stool and looked over at him with a cheeky smile.

"Fuck you very much," I laughed. "I do believe you are the one who wanted something sweet."

"True," he hummed, nodding at nothing in particular. "But now I can make us dinner while watching you sit there, naked and absolutely edible, and we can continue this after we eat." He gave me another one of his wicked smiles. "Maybe on the kitchen table, and I can have more dessert."

Fuck yes with a definite *cherry on top.*

A.J. MACEY

CHAPTER 6

The dark night sky had just started giving way to the pinks, reds, and oranges of the sunrise. The air was cool, chilling my sweaty face as I lay on my back staring at the waves of colors. Rocks and gravel of the roof dug into my black long sleeve shirt. I had one more route to check on the blueprint vent plan before I could leave, and I wanted to see if I could catch when they did shift change since the black-clad security guards hadn't switched out since I got here over an hour and a half ago.

Heaving up to a sitting position, I grabbed my little notebook and attached pen before crawling back into the air vent. Instead of going left as I had earlier to cover over three-quarters of the building, I went to the right to finish up the last of the warehouse. I shuffled along silently, thankful that the rooms were massive enough to require such large vents. Unfortunately, they didn't seem to have the air conditioner on, so I was sweating up a storm in these stupid tin cans. *So far so good*. The vents matched the blueprints despite the building having been over ten years old.

The main issue was I still hadn't found where they were

keeping the girls and I had only seen a small handful of armed guards. *Where are you keeping them?* I mentally asked the guard right below me. Realizing he wasn't going to magically give me the answer, I crawled onward. After two more turns, I heard some quiet talking coming up through one of the vents. The words were inaudible from where I was above them, but the fact that there were more than one or two guards was a good sign so I continued on.

I clenched my jaw to keep from throwing up at the state the girls were in, all hooked to IVs lying haphazardly on the cement floor in a line. There were five in all, three of which were in clubbing type dresses while two were in jeans. The ones in dresses must have been picked up while they were out and brought here. I almost missed it, but I saw Maxine's "Property of Dagger" jacket pinned to the wall, an array of knives stuck in it like it was a dartboard, the leather shredded under the number of slashes in it.

Quickly jotting down everything I could see and all points of entry, I mentally tallied and crossed things off my to-do list. A good note from today's casing included finding out that there weren't any cameras in any of the rooms. *Makes my job easier*, I thought as I checked my watch, reading almost six in the morning. Going back to the spot where there were multiple guards, I waited. They looked exhausted, rubbing their eyes and slouching where they stood.

My patience was rewarded at six on the dot when a new group of guards, fifteen in all, entered the building through a nondescript side door that faced away from the storage unit. *Explains why we couldn't figure out their rotations.* I held steady in my spot for another ten minutes until I made sure all of the night guards had left before exiting the vent system and scaling down the back of the building.

**APRIL 26TH
FRIDAY EVENING
KIERA**

After receiving the call that Brooks and Garrett had
returned from their ride, Chase and I headed to update
the other three members of our makeshift band of merry
cohorts at the compound about what I had found. I was
tired and wanted to collapse into bed now that the sun
was set, but getting them the information was more
important. I enjoyed the feeling of the cooling night air
running through my hair as I neared the compound. *I
should take a vacation after this job is over*, I basked in the
idea, *just me and the beach somewhere with a large fucking
glass of booze and no asshole MC members or itchy, ugly
disguises.*

There was loud music pouring out of the bar's propped
open door, and rowdy voices filtered through the beat
of the song as patch members and scantily-clad women
entered and exited the building. The thudding steps from
my riding boots were drowned out by the level of noise
in the space. Chase had exited his Audi right after I had
gotten off my bike, taking up his usual position behind my
right shoulder as we entered the clubhouse. Scanning the
crowd, I purposely looked over the eyes wandering in our
direction until I spotted one of my men. I made my way
over to Brooks who was seated next to Garrett at the bar.
I had made it about two-thirds of the way there when a
tall, skinny man stepped into my path. Another member
flanked him, eyeing Chase with disdain.

"Hey there, sexy." The little pencil dick of a man leered at
me. "Haven't seen you here before. What do you say I give
you a night you won't forget?" I cocked a brow. *Oh wow,*

he's actually trying this shit right now.

"No thanks, I got more than enough great dick right here." I hitched a thumb at Chase who gave a cheeky smile and tossed an arm over my shoulder. The two members both glanced at Chase, cruel smiles curling their lips before Pencil Dick started talking again.

"Positive I can give you a better night than pretty boy back there." He jutted his chin toward my assassin. "Besides, we don't take too kindly to outsiders here."

"Cool, now can I pass?" I huffed, waving my hand in front of me so he would move which only made him step closer.

"The only place you'll be getting passed is from me to my friend." The dick in the background smirked at his friend's fucking *awful* line. I rolled my eyes, becoming increasingly tired of this shit.

"If I throw a stick, will you go get it? Because I don't need a bitch right now," I snapped which seemed to be the wrong thing to say because Pencil Dick snarled at me.

"Zero!" Brooks' smooth voice barked out over the music bringing even more attention to our stand-off from the people around us. Brooks walked around the dynamic dick duo, coming to stand to my left. "I suggest you leave my baby and my associate alone."

I kept my face flat at his endearment, when all I wanted to do was throw something at his stupidly sexy face. *I don't need a babysitter.* Pencil Dick and his friend immediately stepped back looking chastened keeping their eyes on their president.

"Sorry, Boss, didn't know she was your girl." Zero dipped his head in respect before moving on to a girl whose dress barely covered her girly bits. I rolled my eyes as I followed Brooks to the bar. I bit back a growl when I spotted another barely dressed woman flirting up

Garrett but pushed it back when he looked over at me. Abby and Chase's words echoed through my mind softly as I watched him watch me, and his vibrant green eyes darkened as he spotted Brooks' arm brushing against mine. His damned, kissable lips curled into a harsh frown before dismissing me to go back to the tramp next to him.

Love me?

Yeah, fucking right.

Without prompting, Cheryl placed my typical drink in front of me with a respectful nod before going back to filling drinks of the other members. I stood next to Brooks who had sunk back into his normal seat, my back pressing into Chase's chiseled chest. *I just fucking want to go to bed*, I grumbled internally.

"Didn't expect you here tonight, baby, not that I'm complaining," Brooks' words nearly shouted over the noise around us. I ignored Garrett's shoulders tensing at his words as I responded.

"I have news," I shouted back. Brooks' eyes lit up in understanding and he nudged Garrett. Leaning into his personal space, Brooks said something to him that I couldn't make out before walking off. My stepbrother didn't say anything to me as he got up, whispering something in the tramp's ear before starting toward the back office. Assuming we were supposed to follow, I caught up to him, my eyes tracing the muscles moving in his arms and shoulders as he walked. After another minute of stifling silence in the Aces' office, Brooks entered with Stone right behind him.

"I found the girls," I started once the door was shut, the much softer music allowing me to talk at a normal volume.

"I would certainly hope so, we told you exactly where they'd be," Garrett snapped, his words harsh as he glared at me. I bristled.

"I meant where within the warehouse, asshole." I unconsciously took a step toward him as my fingers curled into tight fists.

"How many?" Brooks asked, trying to diffuse the tension between us. I glared for a moment longer, Garrett's gaze unwavering as he glared back.

"Five"—I dragged my eyes from my asshole stepbrother to Brooks—"and fifteen guards. Shift change at six sharp. No cameras, no electronic monitoring of any kind in the building. Girls are sedated through IVs and kept together in the room next to where four guards are stationed. Only one or two sprinkled throughout the rest of the warehouse. I have their positions throughout the building marked down. They use the side door on the Southeast corner of the building which explains why we couldn't figure out their shift changes."

"How'd you get all this information?" Stone finally spoke, his eyes narrowed in suspicion. I huffed.

"I do what thieves are good at. I got onto the roof and snuck around the air vents." *That should be fucking obvious*. My exhaustion was making me irritable. Well, more irritable than normal.

"You went into the building?" Garrett nearly screamed. "Jesus fuck, Kiera! Do you have a fucking death wish?"

"Obviously, haven't you heard anything she says when she opens her damn mouth?" Stone sneered.

"Knock it off," Brooks snapped at his officers. "This is exactly what she's being paid to do, Garrett, so reel it in. Stone, get over your shit with her until this job is done and then you two can go back to hating each other, but we're on limited time right now."

"What about me?" Chase piped in cheerfully. "I want

something to do." The MC members looked at him like he had lost his marbles as he excitedly bounced on his toes. Brooks opened his mouth, but I cut him off.

"Now that we have the main information on the girls, I want you to see what you can find on Harbold and where he could have possibly moved his files," I instructed, knowing Chase's question wasn't directed at the Aces'. I was the only one he ever took directives from. Facing the guys again, I gave them a pointed look. "Are we done? I've been up since like three in the morning, I'm fucking tired, and I want to go to bed."

Brooks opened his mouth to respond when the sounds of screaming and shouting filled the air from out in the bar. Stone and Brooks bolted out of the room as Chase and I grabbed our weapons. Garrett blocked the door as I tried to follow.

"Stay here, both of you," he bit out. I felt my jaw fall open. *He can't be serious.*

"Like hell we're staying here!" I shouted in disbelief, but instead of arguing with me he shut the door quickly behind him, and the sound of a lock filled the office.

"Oh, my god," I huffed. "He just locked us in here. That fucking asshole," I fumed. I turned to Chase in anger. "Hold my shit." I shoved my gun at him, forcing him to awkwardly clutch it to his chest with hands full of his own weapons. Pulling out my lock picks, I got to work, and after a few quick wiggles, the janky lock opened.

The shouting had stopped. Now it was only tense silence and the sound of a man whose voice I didn't recognize arguing with Brooks. Walking silently, Chase and I weaved around people who were staring wide-eyed at the center of the room. When we finally reached a small opening near the back edge of the crowd, I spotted Brooks, backed by Stone, Garrett, and Nate, facing off with the stranger who was backed by three Alloy Kings' members. On second glance, I recognized the speaker as the Alloy Kings' Vice President Ron 'Savage' Sacher, his buzzed head and greying beard giving him away. He was bulkier and stockier than the Aces' officers except for Nate whose scary-looking muscles bulged under his clenched fists.

"Back off of your shipments and it won't result in any escalation," his deep voice commanded. Brooks rolled his eyes and crossed his arms, the perfect picture of indifference. I pulled my eyes away from the Alloy Kings' VP to scan the rest of the group, easily recognizing the other players. I felt my heart seize when I spotted a familiar face. Taking half a step to the left behind one of the watching club members, I moved out of his eyesight before he could spot me.

This was bad.

Very, very bad.

"Get off my compound before I decide to shoot you," Brooks drolled out. Ron just shrugged before waving his leather-wearing backup dancers toward the door.

"Then suffer the consequences." He chuckled giddily before following his members out of the clubhouse. No one spoke or moved until the rumbling of their bikes faded in the distance. The tense atmosphere faded but didn't dissipate as patch holders and hang-arounds went back to drinking and flirting. I turned my attention to Garrett, noticing his eyes were tight as he exhaled. He tried to hide it, and it probably wasn't noticeable to other people, but I knew him better than anyone. His hands trembled and his face was pale. Garrett was shaken up after seeing his ex-best friend. Stepping around the tall man I had hidden behind, I followed the officers back to the office.

"What the fuck!" Garrett lost it when he saw the open door, whipping around in search of me. Brooks and Stone glanced at each other in confusion while Nate only looked back at me with a small laugh. He had known me long enough to know that I wouldn't have stayed put. "Damn it, you little..." Garrett trailed off when he spotted me standing at the end of the line of people in the hall. Storming up to me, his calloused, tattooed fingers wrapped around my right forearm and pulled me into the very cramped office placing me between him and the desk.

"You're staying where I can fucking see you before you wander off and get yourself shot," he growled quietly in my ear, his hand still holding onto me. The metal of the desk was digging into my leg painfully, so I shifted till I was sitting atop it. His grip loosened but didn't release as he leaned against the side of the object. Chase's sparkling steel eyes caught mine, a brow raised as his gaze flickered toward Garrett before returning to me. I internally scoffed at his hinting. *Garrett does not love me.*

"Did you see what happened?" Brooks asked us, his gaze darting between me and Chase.

"Portion of it," I filled in, not giving away that I knew who each of the Alloy Kings were. "We have a problem," I started before Stone's attitude interrupted me.

"No shit, Sherlock, good job on your observation skills," he snarked.

Gritting my teeth, I glared daggers at him. *He keeps saying my mouth will get me killed, but he clearly needs to check what comes out of his own because he's going to end up pushing daisies before me at this rate.*

"Shut the fuck up," I spouted looking toward Garrett. "I'm assuming you saw who I did?"

"So, I wasn't just imagining things?" he questioned. I shook my head, scrunching up my face in sympathy. "Damn, well, that makes this a lot more complicated." I nodded, ignoring the way he was gently squeezing my arm in comfort, whether for himself or me, I didn't know.

"Want to share with the rest of us, love birds?" Stone sneered at us. Brooks sighed and rubbed his eyes at Stone's attitude. I swallowed the long, *long* string of obscenities I wanted to snap at him and focused on the question.

"The guy who wasn't wearing an Alloy Kings' cut is Jace Corden." I sighed before continuing. "He's another thief, but several years ago he became a hit man."

"All right, so?" Brooks asked, confused.

"He has no moral compass, so he'll kill or hurt anyone and everyone if the price is right," I urged. Brooks' brows drew low over his grey-blue eyes before looking over to Chase.

"What's the problem? Isn't that what you did?" Chase bristled from his spot to my left. Standing up straight from leaning back against the desktop, he squared up to Brooks.

"Excuse you, I'm nothing like that bloody fucking bastard," he huffed, highly offended, his hand pressing into his chest. "I don't kill kids, and I don't unnecessarily hurt or rape my marks before utterly slaughtering them."

"It's all right, my little assassin," I cooed, soothingly rubbing my hand down his soft jacket. "He didn't mean it like that." Chase puffed up his chest still glaring at the president before settling back into my hand, practically purring like a cat at my pets.

"Why do I feel like there's something you two aren't telling us?" Nate finally spoke, not recognizing the name. I grimaced. "That means it's really bad if you're making that face."

"He was my best friend." Garrett's rough and harsh voice cracked under the emotional strain of the past. "He was always after Kiera to the point of obsession. It got to the point we had a falling out…"

"Meaning you cut his face to hell and back," I corrected. The left side of Jace's face had been scarred, three large, jagged cuts going from above his eyebrow, down his cheek, and over his lips ending at his jaw. The rest of the officers' eyes widened as they realized the ugly scars on his face as well as the black patch over his eye had been given to him by their vice president.

"Because he was trying to force himself on you!" Garrett snarled at me. The feeling of Jace's hands roughly roving my body as I tried to fight him flashed to the front of my mind before I could shove them away. Sliding off the desk, I attempted to rip my arm out of Garrett's grasp, but he held steady.

"Fuck you, Garrett! Don't throw that fucked up shit in my face because I don't need your damn help remembering that day!" I shouted shoving his chest with my free hand, but in the cramped space he only stumbled the half step back into the wall.

"Enough!" Brooks yelled over all of us. "Did he see you, Kiera?" I shook my head, keeping my mouth shut so I wouldn't blow up. My eyes focused on Garrett who stared back. Taking a few deep breaths to keep my anger at the situation inside and not focusing it on Garrett and his assholey behavior, I calmed enough to resituate myself on the desk. As much as I pushed Garrett's buttons and wound up yelling at him, I was grateful he had been there that day, and I couldn't help but be thankful for what he had done.

A wave of exhaustion bared down on me at that moment, my eyes drooping in the weightiness of the urge to sleep. Their voices soothing around me made me slouch more and more until I was eventually leaning against something warm. My cheek rested against supple leather, the scent of grease, spice, and black currant filled my nose as I finally drifted off. A soft squeeze on my arm barely brought me back enough to hear a few harsh whispers.

"My kitten..." I slipped quickly back into a deep sleep, only this time I was accompanied by a memory I'd long since wanted to forget.

The summer air was hot as it lightly filtered through the open floor to ceiling windows, the gauzy white curtains billowing in the breeze. My sweats were rolled down until they rested snugly on my hips. The tank top I had on was form fitting, and I hoped I wouldn't see any of the usual faces. Except Garrett, I'm more than okay with him seeing me in a skin tight top.

Don't tell the asshole I said that though.

The cavernous halls and empty rooms that made up my wing of my father's house felt hollow, lonely. I nibbled my lip and thought, What should I do today? *Glancing at the large double wood doors at the end of my wing that were closed, I added sneaking out to see Abby or go poke around Vinny Russo's lavish estate down the way to my list, until I realized Abby was spending the day with her boyfriend Nate. Stealing from sleazeball Russo was also off the table when I remembered he was throwing some stupid party tonight that I was being forced to attend with Frankie and his new whore of a wife.*

The sound of the knob turning caught my attention, and I shot into my usual lounge chair to make it look like I wasn't about to do something I knew I would get in trouble for. I had just gotten the book I was reading open when the main person I wanted to punch in the face stepped through the door.

Frankie.

"Kiera." His husky voice was sharp as he called me like a dog. "I expect you to be ready for Vinny's party tonight at seven sharp. Wear the dress Barbie picked out for you," he commanded. I kept my head down, only glancing up at him under my lashes so he didn't lose his shit like he did last week.

His sharp suit was custom made and fitted, the open black jacket revealing a matching vest buttoned over a crisply ironed white dress shirt. He would have had a conniption if something was out of place, wrinkled, or anything less than perfect. Even his ungodly expensive Italian shoes were shiny enough that if I looked down at them, I would be able to see myself in perfect reflected detail. His light brown hair was slicked back flawlessly, not even one hair out of its cemented place, while his honey brown eyes were cold as they glared down at me. His golden tan skin was clean shaven, topping off the perfectionist air that he prided himself on.

"Yes, sir," I mumbled, counting the seconds until he left my portion of his gaudy mansion. He glared for a few more moments before turning on his heel and striding confidently out of the room. Unfortunately, I made the mistake of looking up before the door closed, my eyes landing on my second most hated person in this house.

Lorenzo Bianchi, my designated 'body guard.' Yeah right, more like prison keeper.

His blond hair was slicked back in the same fashion as my father, ice blue eyes centered on my face while the cruel slash of his mouth curled up in a mocking smirk. Bastard.

I sat completely still, my eyes back on my book without actually seeing any of the words until he finally followed my father out the door. Even after hearing the thud of the doors closing, I didn't look, fearing they would come back for another one of my forced 'sessions.'

At the thought of all the shit Frankie and Lorenzo required me to go through to keep from following my mother's gruesome fate into an unmarked grave in the middle of the Nevada desert, I slammed the book closed and chucked it across the room. Rage stirred within me, fueling the reservoir of fury I always felt sleeping within my chest to even higher levels. Turning in slow circles around the elegant sitting room, I wanted nothing more than to smash every lavish and expensive piece of art, furniture, and useless trinket until nothing was left but a room that reflected my turbulent emotions.

One day, I'll destroy this house of horrors, taking Frankie and Lorenzo and the long list of names of those who had earned a trip to Hell with it.

The door opening startled me, but when I saw Garrett's messily combed hair and sharp green eyes, I calmed. Jace's dark brown eyes sought mine out as he followed his best friend into my rooms. Garrett was dressed in his usual attire of dark jeans, tight shirt, and leather jacket, his black boots thudding loudly on the shiny tile floor. Jace used to wear something similar until recently, when he started wearing business-y type shit. Today, he was in a pair of ironed slacks and a ruby red dress shirt that was buttoned up to his collarbone, his tan neck peeking through the open collar.

"Hello, Kiera." Jace's rough and gravelly voice always put me slightly on edge. I wasn't quite sure why, he had never done anything to freak me out, but the way he said my name, like a tortured promise, had me standing straighter.

"Jace, Garrett," I muttered, turning to busy myself with something to do instead of staring at my stepbrother like some doe-eyed bimbo. That asshole didn't need to know that I found him sexy. He was already irritating enough.

"What are you doing?" Garrett demanded. His voice, in stark contrast to his best friend, melted me from the inside. So much so I was already starting to feel my underwear growing wet. I really should stop wearing these stupid things since I have to change them several times a day. Glancing over at him from my position in front of the fancy bar cart, I cocked a brow at him as I poured myself a very large glass of liquor.

"What are you going on about now?" I huffed taking a sip of the smooth, and probably more expensive than most people make in a year, liquor. Frankie always prided himself on being and having the best of the best.

"You have a party tonight with your father, and you're here fucking getting drunk," Garrett hissed stomping over to me, but before he could take the glass I jumped away being careful to not spill it.

"I've literally had one sip," I snapped, drinking another couple of gulps to purposely piss him off. "Also, I know I have a stupid party, your mother," I sneered, "even picked out my outfit."

"Fine!" he practically shouted. "Get drunk and be stupid before having to go parade around in front of your father's rich friends. I don't care," he growled before stomping away. The door slammed, echoing against the tile as he left. Realizing I was alone with Jace, I immediately clammed up. My senses went on high alert as he started leisurely around the room.

"Sorry 'bout that." He smiled. I had to force myself to not shiver at it. "He's just a little high strung today." Unable to *help myself, I scoffed.*

"He's always high strung," I mumbled into my glass, finishing the liquor, reveling in the pleasant burn that flared in my chest. Before I realized it, Jace was right in front of me, greedy eyes taking in my face.

"He doesn't deserve you." My breath caught at his possessive tone. His hands gripping my face kept me from taking a step back, and then his warm lips roughly pressed against mine. I pushed, kicked, punched, but everything I tried to do to keep his hands from wandering down my body was futile. Jace had always been faster than me.

The crystal glass slipped from my fingers in another frantic attempt to keep his touch away from me, his intrusive hands slipping under my tank and sweats. That fury I always had flared within me, and I screamed at him. I had no idea what came out of my mouth, but immediately after it did, Garrett came barrelling back into the room. Rage sharpened his green eyes as he tackled Jace. Garrett didn't shout or say anything as they fought, but Jace was ranting about how I was his and some other crazy shit I couldn't make sense of.

"For touching Kiera," Garrett whispered sharply when he had Jace secured under him, his hand reaching out to grab a pointed sliver of the glass. Before I realized what had happened, Jace's strangled screams filled the hollow space. Three jagged cuts marred his once abnormally perfect face. Clutching his damaged cheek, he ran. Garrett and I listened in silence to his fading footsteps. I was used to being the best so with him getting in my personal space, I felt a cold tingle of ice slide down my spine.

Garrett's tanned face was devoid of color except the two patches of red that betrayed the effort he'd used in beating Jace. Blood coated his hands and clothing as well as puddled on the marble tile. Jumping into action, I took my sweats off and started to wipe up his arms. I felt his gaze on my legs before dragging up to my face, but I didn't look at him as I cleaned up the blood. He had just saved me from Jace's unwelcomed advanced and yet, I knew that if I met his eyes, I would have wanted more. What did that say about me...

"Come on," I urged him, pushing away the thought. I was shaken up but determined. "Let's get this clean before Frankie can find out." We worked in silence until there was no trace of what happened except in our memories, Garrett taking the last of the physical remnants with him as he left.

A.J. MACEY

CHAPTER 7

Fucking Alloy Kings," I seethed, muttering under my breath. My body thrummed in excess rage as I watched the clean-up crew take Ricky, our most recent prospect, and wrap him in the body bag. Ricky had been tasked with watching the front gate last night, but when those fucking bastards came rolling through they didn't hesitate to put three bullets in his chest. I could barely stomach watching the security footage from the night before, and I'd added a few more boot holes into the office wall. Stone stood stoic and as still as his namesake to my left, while Garrett clenched his jaw and tightened his fists to my right. Nate had been charged with arranging our drops with our dealers, while we attempted to get a handle on the Alloy Kings issue.

Garrett had ridden Kiera's Harley back to her house last night, and Chase had driven her back home after she'd fallen asleep against Garrett. From what I had been told, she was still asleep after having been awake for almost 20 hours. Acid burned in my stomach at what my vice president and she had revealed last night. *Not only do we have to steal back Kevin's Old Lady, we need to protect our shipments, move against the Alloy Kings, keep Kiera's psychotic stalker attempted rapist away from her, and get those files from that one lawyer.*

Great.

Sighing, I let the crew continue their progress on clean-up and walked toward the nearest picnic table, my mind briefly flashing back to Kiera's fiery eyes as I checked her out that day we had taken a walk. Garrett was glancing at his cell, jaw ticking as he shoved it back into his pocket while Stone was scanning the area around us.

"Discussing our moves against the Alloy Kings or Kiera's job shouldn't be done here at the compound today," I stated quietly despite being out in the yard alone. "Any ideas where we could create a second 'homebase' for when we need it?"

"I can ask Kiera, her house is where she plans all her heists," Garrett suggested. I cocked a brow. *Is he offering this because it's the best for the club or because he wants to be near my baby?* "What?" he bit out.

"I don't trust her," Stone added grumpily.

"We know," Garrett and I said in unison before turning back to each other.

"We don't exactly have a better option seeing as how we all live here at the compound," Garrett snapped. "Unless you want to buy a house or have another idea, she's our saving grace."

"Would she even be okay with that?" I asked finding myself unable to disagree with the plan. *While Garrett would get to be closer to Kiera, so would I,* I thought.

"I don't see why not. Chase lives there, I can ask him." He pulled out his cell as I felt my brows go up.

"Chase lives there?" Stone seemed as confused as I did. Kiera didn't strike me as the type to have a live-in boyfriend, *or whatever the hell they are.*

"Yeah, moved in right after they first met," Garrett answered, distracted with his cell.

"You mean the day after he tried to kill her?" Stone growled. I rolled my eyes. I didn't understand what his issue was, she hadn't done anything to warrant his wrath. *Unless...* I stared at my enforcer realizing how blind I'd been. *He likes her too.*

"Are they a thing?" I found myself asking. Garrett scowled as he stared at me.

"I don't think so, but with her, who knows. I don't like to know everything about Kiera's sex life," he snarled as he held his phone to his ear. "Is Kiera awake? We need to use her house as a secondary clubhouse for the three of us." He waited as he listened, his stony face not giving away any details of what Chase was saying. "We'll be there shortly."

"All good?" I moved to standing, feeling an unusual excitement filling me at the prospect of going to Kiera's home. Without further talking, we left the compound on our bikes, Garrett leading the line. I eyed her enormous two-story house as we approached. The ride was barely fifteen minutes from the compound until we were pulling into her wide four-car driveway. The bright-red front door stood out against the sandstone and tan-colored face as we walked up to it.

The grand entryway with its two-story ceiling and curved staircase caught my attention. Our boots thudded loudly against the hard flooring. After walking deeper into the house, we came to an open kitchen that was remodeled to the nines while her living space held a large leather sectional and giant flat-screen TV. Chase's familiar face appeared from the main hall as he stepped into the brightly lit kitchen, the TV playing some cooking show I didn't recognize. The assassin was barefooted and wearing a pair of dark grey sweats. He wasn't wearing his normal jacket, only in a black shirt, and his shoulder holsters weren't strapped to his lean torso.

"Hello, boys," he greeted joyfully, his smile slightly manic as he eyed us. "Welcome." He gave a great wave of his arm around him.

"You've never been here?" Stone asked Garrett who shook his head, his scowl growing deeper.

"I don't know if you've noticed, but Kiera and I don't exactly get along," he said through clenched teeth glancing around him.

"Psh," Chase huffed flapping his hands in front of him, "don't be silly. You two are perfect together." His words were innocent enough, but I saw the mischievous glint in his grey eyes, nor did I miss Garrett's sliver of hope growing in his green ones. "Come on, make yourself at home. Kiera will be down in a minute; I just got her up."

"Are you always so happy?" Stone snapped. Thinking about it, those two were pretty much the exact opposite of each other. One was always seemingly cheerful and fell for Kiera immediately, while the other was grouchy and pushed as hard as possible to keep her away.

"Yes." Chase smiled again before going to the fridge. "Beer?" A round of yes's went up, and he passed around the cold bottles.

"So, are you and her an item?" Stone asked what had been burning in my mind since I found out they lived together. Chase laughed heartily as he opened his own beer.

"Not in the traditional sense," he explained, his eyes filled with love as he chuckled, "but I'm not exactly normal, so Kiera is it for me. But I know she'll take others." His knowing eyes landed on me as his lips curled in a tiny smile. *Busted...*

"Wait." Garrett shook his head in disbelief. "You're all right knowing that she'll fuck other guys?" Chase looked unruffled at the thought as he turned to Garrett.

"Of course, I want her to be happy. Besides, I like to watch. There's also the fact that Kiera will do whatever she wants to do, but I know she'll always have her special place for me right here in her little heart." He tapped his chest, his crazed smile growing wider. "She's my kittycat, and I'm her assassin." He crossed his heart in an x.

"Stop talking about me." Kiera's husky voice echoed down the hall. She rounded the corner looking grouchy, but that couldn't take away the fact she was in a pair of short-ass denim shorts, a loose tank that showed off her lacy bra, and her waves were tousled and messy like she had just woken up. *Or just been fucked.* My blood pounded at the thought remembering how it had felt to be wrapped by her tight pussy. "Great, just the faces I want to see when I first get up," she grumbled, stomping over quite adorably to the fridge. Pulling out an energy drink, she opened it and chugged until it was gone, Then burped loudly as she slammed the empty can on the marble counter. We all stared at her; she returned our gazes with narrowed eyes.

"Kittycat," Chase caught her attention. "Want to move this to the backroom?" She nodded, looking more and more awake as the seconds ticked by. Following behind her and Chase, we made our way down a side hall off the living room toward a nondescript door. She typed in the code on the small pad next to the frame and placed her fingerprint on the biometric scanner. The beep sounded followed quickly by a clunk of the door unlocking.

"Welcome, boys, to The Cat's inner sanctum." Chase practically skipped into the room in excitement while my baby followed at a more leisurely pace. I took in the room around me, noticing a large table with a stone top, but with the amount of papers on top it was hard to see. The walls were covered in corkboard and held glossy photos, papers, notes, with string connecting them, as well as a giant map of the city on the far wall. One common factor I found throughout the stuff tacked to the walls was her father, Frankie Casterelli, or information about his businesses.

"Holy shit," I muttered looking around. "You're really gunning for your father, aren't you?" She glared at me, her eyes sparking dangerously.

"That fucking piece of shit is going down even if it's the last thing I do," she growled. I held my hands up in surrender.

"I didn't doubt you, I was just asking. No need to claw me, baby." I paused as I grinned at her. "Unless you want to, of course." Garrett glared at me from his position on the other side of the table. My distraction worked, as she huffed out an eye roll before turning toward the table.

"Most of the plan is in place for the heist," she explained looking at the warehouse blueprints, "only need a run down on the guards and their security protocols."

"I should know by Tuesday," Stone added, his eyes focused on her notes. She nodded.

"Shouldn't have any issues with the heist," she said. "Chase and I need to go watch another shift change tonight and see if there is any difference between the day guards and the night time guards. We have their behavior, patterns, and rotations down, but I want to observe them a few more times throughout the next couple of days to identify anything that could pose a problem or any changes to their shit leading up to the auction." I had to admit, I was impressed. With her thoroughness and attention to detail, it wasn't hard to see why she was one of the best.

"We good to stay here and discuss some of our options for handling the shit with the Alloy Kings?" I ground out their name. She nodded as Chase practically ran out of the room and up the stairs. *He's very strange.*

"Yeah, but not in my workspace. You can have run of the living room and kitchen." We filed out into the spacious great room. "And if you go snooping, I will know because I have cameras recording 24/7 all over my house inside and out, so if I find out you went somewhere you shouldn't, I'll turn you into a female. Got it?" I cringed at that painful thought before nodding. "Good, I need to change before we go." After she exited the room, Chase rejoined us, his sweats changed out for jeans and his holsters now peeking out in their usual spot from under his jacket.

"Anyone hungry? There's lots of leftovers in the fridge, but if you want anything meaty you'll have to make it yourself." He pulled out a container of tupperware that looked like it was filled with some type of pasta dish.

"Do you eat meat?" Stone narrowed his eyes at Chase, not sure whether to take his statement seriously or not. Chase shook his head vehemently as he tossed the food in the microwave.

"Nope, I'm a vegetarian. Don't wear anything made from animals." He eyed our leather cuts as he petted his jacket absentmindedly. "Faux-suede, faux-fur. Animals are cute, innocent little creatures and I refuse to contribute to the slaughter of them."

"You literally kill people for a living," Stone scoffed,

crossing his arms. "How is that not worse than eating a cow?" Chase chuckled.

"People are assholes." He shrugged happily as if that answered all Stone's questions and left it at that as he started to scarf down the leftovers. After a few minutes of silence, Kiera re-entered the room dressed in her black pants, a black long-sleeve shirt, a matching beanie clutched in her gloved hand, and her hair braided over her shoulder. She had a black leather pouch strapped to her right thigh and her black gun poked out of the waistband of her pants on her left hip.

"You're left-handed?" I asked, dipping my head toward her gun, and she looked down at it before nodding. "You just keep getting weirder and weirder, baby." I smiled slyly at her to which she rolled her eyes.

"Stay out of trouble." Her sparkling eyes flickered between the three of us as she walked to the door leading out to the garage. "Don't make a mess of my house." Without further conversation, she went into the large garage with Chase right behind her.

"Nice house," I noted looking around after the garage door sounded signifying it was closing. "Maybe we should get one of these."

"I'm good at the compound," Stone bit out, curiously eyeing the house while looking uncomfortably stiff in Kiera's space. Glancing around, I spotted Garrett standing in front of the stone fireplace staring at a row of photos on the mantel. I walked over to him and examined the color pictures. Several of them were of Chase and Kiera together in different places around the world, both looking extremely happy with wide smiles and bright eyes. Next to those, was an older photo of a woman who looked almost exactly like Kiera, but had shorter, curlier hair. *Her mom*, I surmised tucking the question about what had happened to her in the back of my mind. Finally, the three pictures Garrett was staring at were the most surprising to me with how much they were at each other's throats.

One was of a teenage, non-tattooed Kiera standing in front of a similar aged Garrett, neither looking at the camera as if they didn't know it was being taken. Their attention was on each other, their usual scowls and glares prevalent on their faces, but even in the photograph I could see the love between them. Looking at the next one, it was of them a little bit older, a little after Garrett had been voted in the club. Kiera had a few tattoos, and Garrett was wearing his cut. They were seated on a patio somewhere. Kiera was looking out off to the side away from Garrett who was staring at her with a slight head tilt and no scowl, his sole focus on his stepsister. The third picture was recent based on Garrett's tattoos and haircut. This one was of him alone standing with his arms crossed over his chest in front of his bike. It was obvious he didn't know the photo had been taken since he was looking off to the side, and this is the photo that held Garrett's attention the most.

"We had just had a huge argument," his harsh voice whispered. "She had taken on a job I didn't want her doing and, Kiera being Kiera, she didn't want to listen and stormed off. I thought she had left at that point, but I didn't want to head back to the compound yet until I had calmed down. I didn't know she put these up here; I didn't even know she had them at all."

"You don't exactly ask nicely, Garrett," I countered. His jaw clenched. "You really care about her, don't you?" He hesitated, staring at the photo of them on the patio when he answered.

"Yeah, Boss. I do." His words were barely audible. "Have since I met her six years ago, but we've always been so hot-headed that all we'd do was go at it. I'm not going to lie, Chase was right when he said that her fiery attitude is hot." He looked over at me, his eyes hard. "I know you think so too. I also know that you two fucked each other the other day."

I grimaced. If I had realized how much he cared, I wouldn't have pursued her. *Yeah right, you always want what you can't have*, my brain whispered.

"Can you blame me?" I asked sheepishly, and he sighed.

"No, just," he paused, his jaw tightening, "don't hurt her, all right?" My brows went up at his resigned tone.

"Do you not think she cares about you, too?" I waved at the photos.

"Does it matter? She made it clear the other day that if she wanted to go for me, she would, like she had with you and Chase. Besides, she's had six years." He stared back at the photos, his hands clenching tightly into fists. "Let's just fucking get to work. I can't think about this anymore."

"Thank god, I thought I was going to have to call Oprah or Dr. Phil or some shit with your guys' sappy bullshit," Stone snapped behind us, his arms crossed as he glared at us. "Seriously, I didn't ever think I'd see the two of you going all soft over a woman, let alone the same woman. How about we focus on the shit that actually matters?" I rolled my eyes and took a seat at the island bar top.

"So," I started looking between my two officers, "we need to keep an eye on our shipments and dealers, figure out who the snitch is, prepare our counterattack on the Alloy Kings, deal with Corden, and get those files. All while hoping nothing goes awry with Kiera and Chase's heist getting Kevin's Old Lady back."

"Why would we need to get those files?" Stone narrowed his eyes, his lips curled in a snarl as he spoke. It was clear he didn't want to help Kiera with her personal vendetta. I held back my urge to roll my eyes at his stubbornness.

"Because one of our own fucked up," I explained, my sharp tone not wanting to argue this point.

"Why do we have to deal with Corden? If we take down the Alloy Kings, he should go scurrying back to take the next job." Stone leaned forward, his hands flattening against the shiny countertop. Garrett's fisted hands tightened the longer our enforcer talked.

"Because he's a threat. Not just to Kiera, but to us as well," Garrett bit out. The gravel in his voice was harsher than normal in his rage. "If he's willing to work with the Alloy Kings to take us on, he'll use whatever he learns from them and move on to another group willing to try and destroy us. He knows me, and now that he knows I'm an Ace he won't quit until he has Kiera, and he will gladly go through the club to get her."

"I knew she was a fucking threat," Stone growled, setting Garrett off. My VP launched off the stool squaring up with Stone who didn't back down from glaring.

"Enough!" I barked out, my single command echoing off the hard surfaces of Kiera's lavish house. "She's not a threat stop making her the enemy," I reasoned, focusing my attention on Stone. "Alloy Kings are our enemy right now, and Corden is with them meaning he's our enemy as well." Turning to Garrett I continued to chastise them. "You can't be jumping at everyone's throats when it comes to Kiera. She's a grown woman, and she doesn't need you protecting her honor."

"That's not what I'm doing," he scoffed, rolling his eyes, but in those green depths I saw the tiny spark of guilt. I continued to stare at him until he deflated. Grumbling incoherently, he sank onto his stool without further argument.

"Now." I rubbed my beard with my right hand, my brain wracking with thoughts and plans. "Any ideas?" We spent the next couple of hours going back and forth, discussing our options and possible next steps, and left before Chase and Kiera returned home.

APRIL 29TH
MONDAY AFTERNOON
KIERA

Stupid lumpy seat. My back was cramping as I shifted for the fifth time in as many minutes trying to relieve some of the tension. Staring at the large sandstone-colored building in front of me, I felt my lips curl into a scowl. The Solace Resort was almost 30 floors high, and the way the windows were placed made it look like vertical striations in the stone. My skin felt itchy being so close to one of Frankie's pride and joys, the other being the Solace Casino which was a similar building on the other side of the resort connected through a fancy-schmancy second-floor walkway.

I knew going after Cory Harbold would bring me closer to this wretched casino and resort, and I thought I was ready, but damn all I wanted to do was set the place on fire. *Don't worry, I won't, there're innocent people and other shit inside there, like money I could steal.* Checking my clock, I groaned when I realized his meeting with one of Frankie's underlings, Brian Chan, was running long. *Abby is so not going to be happy*, I grumbled internally.

Finally, ten minutes later, Harbold waddled out of the door and to his cock-eye parked Lamborghini. Staying at least four cars behind him, I followed in my beat-up sedan pulling into the coffee shop and parking at the back of the asphalt lot. After I ordered a straight black coffee, I held my head high as I made my way over to a glaring Abby.

"You're late. Again." She cocked a sassy brow at me. "Jesus, you're going to be late to your own funeral at this rate." I chuckled and sat at the table with her.

"Not my fault this time!" I huffed, my focus darting over to Harbold Law Office. "Someone's meeting ran long. I was actually on time!"

"Well, that's a damn miracle. Should the angels descend from heaven now to sing praise because you astoundedly materialized at the proper time?" Her voice was mocking as she raised a hand into the air like she was at church. "Praise Jesus, Kiera, for once in her goddamned life showed up on time. Hallelujah, can I get an Amen?"

"I'm pretty sure you're not supposed to say the Lord's name in vain, or some shit like that," I wheezed out in between my laughing because Abby, in her ripped up jeans and ratty band t-shirt, pretending to be a good church goer, was hilarious.

"Oh, shut the fuck up," she laughed back at me, taking a drink of her coffee. Realizing I had to try and act normal as well, I powered through a drink of my own.

"Seriously, bitch. Try this." Abby waved her coffee in my face, the black marker on the side of the cup taunting me. I scrunched up my face, but obliged her anyway knowing she wouldn't stop until I tried it. I mindlessly adjusted the itchy material of my turtleneck, sweating up a damn storm in the long sleeves and jeans in the desert sun. Cautiously, I took a sip of her drink which she had told me was caramel macchiato, whatever the hell that was, with extra caramel.

"Eh"—I smacked my lips together after swallowing the

sugar—"it's literally just liquid sugar; hurts my teeth. Besides, Chase would get on my ass about having too many sweets you know how he is about food." She rolled her eyes and took back her drink.

"Don't understand how you don't like it, but whatever. Also, don't blame Chase for his obsession with cooking since you're the one who got him started on it." She raised a challenging brow at me. I pinched my lips together and squinted at her.

"Why do you do that? I was perfectly content to blame him," I teased, unable to hold back my laugh. "He was looking forward to his retirement and wanted to learn something new, all I did was suggest it. He took that plunge all on his own." I took another sip of my black coffee, this time able to keep my face straight. I checked the time, four in the afternoon. Right as the clock hit the top of the hour Cory Harbold exited his office and waddled to his expensive sports car.

Kittycat: *On the move.*
Dipshit: *Got him, Kittycat.*

I tucked my phone away and downed the rest of my coffee. Abby still had most of hers left, so she carried the cup with her to the lot. We said goodbye and she headed out in her truck, Rocky, while I walked the rest of the way to my shitty piece of junk. The revving of two motorcycles caught my attention, setting my internal alarm bells off. I continued walking toward the car in an attempt to act normal since I was in disguise as the two Harleys pulled up next to my beater, both men wearing Alloy Kings MC cuts. *Fucking 1%ers,* I growled keeping my face cautious as I neared them.

"Miss Wright?" The VP of Alloy Kings asked, the alias I was using for this job rolling off his tongue easily. I hesitantly nodded at Ron 'Savage' slowly inching closer to my car. *Act like how a normal person would if confronted with criminals*, I commanded myself, *so* much easier said than done.

"Y-yes," I stuttered, looking at the other patch member and recognizing Vance 'Ironsides' McCall. "Can I help you?"

"Are you aware your friend is the wife of a very dangerous criminal?" Ron's voice was deceivingly concerned as if he actually gave a shit about my well-being. I barely held back the urge to roll my eyes, the Aces dealt in drugs and nothing else where as the Alloy Kings dealt in drugs, weapons, sex trafficking, and dirty work for other criminal organizations. I widened my eyes and pressed my hand against my chest.

"What do you mean?" *If I played along long enough, Ronnie boy here might give me something useful.*

"Her husband is a part of a motorcycle gang named The Aces." He awkwardly patted my shoulder in some strange movement of comfort. "I'm sorry to tell you this, but they deal in a lot of nasty business like drugs."

"Oh, my goodness," I breathed, "what should I do?"

"I suggest staying far away from them. They are dangerous, and sooner or later, they'll get what's coming to them." I bit back a retort and kept my face filled with fear. "Have you seen anything odd or shady going on with your friend or her husband?" *There it is*, I thought, *his ulterior motive.* I shook my head vehemently.

"No, I uh." I took a shaky breath. *Damn, I deserve an Oscar for this performance.* "I really only meet up with her for coffee. What kind of stuff should I look out for?"

"Any odd or suspicious behavior, like leaving at strange

hours or being gone for a few days. Spending a lot of time at this address." His sausage fingers held out a piece of paper with the address to the compound on it for me to take. "Have you been there before?"

"No, I don't typically travel to south Reno. My job's over in Sparks," I responded giving my cover of a music teacher in case they wanted to look into the paper trail, which would lead them to a small space I had leased in my alias where I hired a few music tutors to hold practices throughout the week. *The realism of the lie is in the details, people. Go on, write that down, I don't give these damn tips away for free, you know.*

"If anyone from their gang approaches you, or if your friend and her husband want you to go to that address, call me." He held out a business card that held the drawing of a crown, his legal name, and a number which I assumed went to a burner.

"I'll definitely do that." *Yeah fucking right.* I gave a trembling thanks and watched them leave on their bikes. I immediately got into my car and spent the couple hours mindless driving around and running menial tasks and errands in case they were watching. When I finally determined I had acted normal enough, I called Brooks.

"Hey, baby," he greeted warmly, his smooth voice sending pleasant shivers down my back.

"Hey, prick," I laughed out, finding the entire situation hilarious. "Apparently, you're over there doing some shady criminal shit and I'm supposed to be watching out so I don't get caught in the crossfire."

"Wow, hold up. What was that?" I rolled my eyes and said it again, slower this time in case he needed a bit more time to understand. "Where did you hear this from?"

"Ron 'Savage' decided to stop 'Miss Wright,' that'd be me

by the way, saying my friend, which would be Abby, and her husband were into some scary-criminal-motorcycle-gang thing and that poor, little me should call him if they tried to rope me in."

"You mean to tell me the vice president of our rival MC approached you in your disguise and warned you away from us?" I nodded at each of his points despite the fact he couldn't see me.

"Yes," I answered, slouching in the very uncomfortable driver seat of this car as I propped the old lady tennis shoes I was wearing on the dash. "I'm going to lay low tonight at the house. I'll come by tomorrow and we can figure out the rest of the plan."

"I can't believe the nerve of that bastard," Brooks snarled as I heard Garrett shouting shit at me in the background. "I'm going to kill him." I felt my brows furrow at his intense reaction. *I was used to this from Garrett, hell even once in a blue moon with Chase, but for Brooks to do it? Strange.*

"Brooks," I barked between Garrett's and his increasingly loud growling. "I can take care of myself. He didn't know it was me as The Cat or Kiera Casterelli, he only approached cause I was having coffee with Abby. If he or his buddy wanted to try something, I would have gladly shot them both in the face."

"Fine, fine," he huffed, "will Chase be there tonight?" I rolled my eyes, *I don't need a babysitter.*

"Not until later, he's going to be doing some more observing for a few hours. What are you guys up to?" I asked when there was a lot of noise in the background.

"Finishing up ride details. It's a short one this time, so we'll be back tomorrow when you get here." I heard the sound of bikes revving.

"All right, I'll see you tomorrow." I hung up before heading to the house, making sure to drive around in several circles. I found myself curled in bed a few hours later, exhausted and weirdly excited to see them tomorrow, and I finally drifted off.

CHAPTER 8

The bar's air conditioning felt good against my flushed skin from the quickly approaching summer weather. Cheryl was tending the bar despite the only ones here being me and her. She nodded at me and started to fill a glass as I made my way across the sticky floor. *Gross, doesn't anyone fucking mop around here?* Sliding into my usual stool, I grabbed the glass and took a long sip. I didn't have to wait long until one of my men waltzed into the room, unfortunately it was the very irritable enforcer, Stone.

"Why do I find myself seeing you around here more and more? You have a very nice house you could be at instead of in my space," he snapped, glaring down at me after having stormed to where I was seated.

"I'm glad you like my house, I'm very proud of it." I smiled brightly at him, or at least I hope that's how it looked, but based on his frown I didn't think I'd managed. "I need that shit you'd said would be ready today. I'm also supposed to be meeting with the other two Musketeers." I tilted my head, thinking. "Well, technically the Three Musketeers since you'll be there too, but you know what

I meant." I waved my right hand animatedly at the end of my statement. Stone finally took the stool next to me and scowled at Cheryl until a drink appeared. When it did, he looked at me like he didn't know what to do with me, so of course, I smiled nice and wide.

"You're weird," he muttered before taking a drink. I chuckled and sipped my own beverage.

"I'm a little weird, a little crazy. You know..." I shrugged and trailed off as I glanced over at him; his brows drew down and his head was tilted as if he was truly seeing me for the first time. His deep brown eyes were inquiring, his muscled arm resting on the bar top so he could turn toward me. Denim-clad legs rubbed against my thigh, sending shivers through me that I didn't bother hiding which had his brow raising.

"You really don't care that you're not normal, do you?" he asked in disbelief.

I scoffed, shaking my head. *Normal? Gross.*

"No, I like being me. I don't care if anyone else likes me, I don't exist for their entertainment," I answered truthfully, but deep down the ever-burning flame of fury pulsed at my words. I had been that before, but never again. "Besides, you guys aren't exactly normal here. You realize that, right? That's why you're called 1%ers."

"Touché." I felt my heart sputter when Stone cracked the tiniest smile. It transformed him from the surly bodyguard to a handsome man, one who didn't seem to have a chip on his shoulder or think everyone was out to get him.

I studied him as he took another drink, his ever observant eyes scanning the room and only briefly glancing at the club members who flitted in and out of the space. His light grey shirt was tight against his broad shoulders and barrelled chest which tapered to a trim waist. Stone was the bulkiest in the muscle department between the four guys who had caught my attention. Black jeans covering his thick legs were dusty from the desert outside, as were his black riding boots. His dark chocolate skin was smooth, unblemished and unadorned of tattoos or piercings. The shadow of black facial hair had the slightest hint of grey, and if I had to hazard a guess, I would say Stone was late 30s or early 40s, but when he had smiled he seemed to lose a decade.

"How old are you?" I found myself asking, and as soon as the question left my mouth I wanted to swallow it back up. *Well, can't do shit about it now.* His gaze darted back to me, calculating, as if my question was anything other than innocent.

"Thirty-one," he finally answered after a long pause. "You?"

"Twenty-two." I gave him a cheeky smile. *Big, bad Stone was making small talk with me.* I internally chuckled at the oddity of the conversation. His brows shot up when I answered him.

"Twenty-two and already a famous criminal?" He was shocked, his tone incredulous which wasn't surprising but slightly insulting. I bristled as he continued. "When did you start stealing?"

"I'll show you mine if you show me yours," I taunted. My double meaning was obvious in my seductive tone, but truthfully I only meant for my past since I didn't like to share unless I got some shit in return. *Like I said, I don't give shit away for free.*

"No thanks, thief." His semi-open demeanor slammed shut as soon as the question was out. His scowl was back in full force as he shot the rest of his alcohol, the glass crashing down against the bar top loudly in the quiet of the room. He stood, towering over me as he glared. "You can't flirt your way into my bed. You're an outsider and a threat to the club and that's exactly how it's going to stay."

"Who said I was trying to get anywhere near your dick? But whatever you say, *Grave*," I sneered his road name, not appreciating the fact that I was being made out to be a bad guy yet again. *I mean, I might be an asshole, but damn, I'm not that far into the evil front.* Before I realized he was moving, his hand clutched my jaw between his rough fingers to the point of near pain from the strength of his grip.

"Don't call me that again. You're not my Old Lady and you're not an Ace. You've done nothing to deserve the right to call me Grave. I've put up with all your shit until now, but this is where I draw the line," he ground out, fury making his eyes two ebony pools. I kept my face stoic as I looked at him, and turning my body to face him helped mask what my hands were doing.

"I suggest, Grave, you remove your hand." I stood, letting the rage consume me. "I would easily sever your femoral artery before you so much as blink," I hissed, the knife that I always carried open and cutting against his skin. The dark blood bubbled onto his black jeans in an almost invisible stain. "I will *gladly* stand by and watch you bleed to death if you don't back the fuck off." Our standoff only lasted a few more moments before he winced as I dug the knife in slightly. He released my jaw and his chest heaved in furious pants.

"Don't think I will forget this," he growled. I gave him a cruel smile.

"Then I suggest you don't ever forget that I will end anyone that tries to fuck with me. You can hate me all you fucking want, but you do not *ever* put your hands on me unless I say it's okay," I snarled. "Ace, no Ace, I will put anyone that's a threat to me six feet under." Pulling back, I wiped the bloody blade against my jeans before tucking it in its normal home, my eyes never leaving his steely gaze.

"Well," a familiar smooth voice sounded in the silent room. All eyes were wide as they watched us. Apparently, during our conversation the room had started to fill with patch holders ready to unwind with a drink or a good fuck from the several hang-arounds that had joined the crowd. "I guess I shouldn't leave you two children alone from now on," Brooks stated from his position a few feet away.

Garrett was standing behind his right shoulder, his fists curled in a white-knuckled grip. At me or his club's enforcer, I didn't know or particularly care. Abby's face was blank as she stared, but the way her body was taut with edginess, I knew she was concerned about how everything went down. Not for me, but for how it would echo within the club. There were clear lines drawn now between the Aces and me.

Fuck them.

"Back office," Brooks continued, his tone steely as he eyed us angrily. "Both of you. Now."

I kept my eyes trained on his enforcer in case he attempted to fight dirty. *I know I would.*

Murmurs and whispers broke out among the crowd as I followed Brooks down the hall, Garrett stayed between me and Stone as we filed down the dingy carpet. The office was cramped between the four of us, Stone standing as far from me as possible, while Garrett remained planted between us as we all faced Brooks.

"Jesus," Brooks huffed, his smooth tone pained as he rubbed his eyes. "I expected better from both of you. We absolutely can't have strife within the club with everything going on with the Alloy Kings." My brows dipped in confusion.

"What problems?" I asked as Stone glared over at me at my question. Garrett remained quiet.

"They're stealing shipments and are targeting us," Brooks explained briefly.

"Boss," Stone ground out between clenched teeth, "she shouldn't know club business. We don't know what her ultimate motives are. Hell," he started to raise his voice, "she could be working with Alloy Kings for all we know!"

"Oh, puh-lease"—I rolled my eyes—"like I'd ever work for fuckbag Ma-Gee over there. I hate Bryce Hill. He's a tool," I huffed out, thinking of the scrawny president of the Alloy Kings. All eyes trained on me in question. "What?" My single worded question showed my evident exasperation. "He tried to hire me in the past but attempted to fuck me over before I even did the job, so I told him to eat shit," I explained, looking around the room, Garrett seemed pissed while Brooks appeared contemplative.

"Did you know who we were before we were introduced?" Brooks asked. He was much more observant than I had initially given him credit for.

Fuck! I guess it was now or never. The question, though, was whether to play dumb and deny or go all in and act like it was no big deal... Maybe, I'd even gain a bit of that trust Stone always seemed to be going on about. *Well, here's go nothing*, I mentally grimaced. Let's hope I made the right choice.

"Of course I did." I shook my head in disbelief. "I know all criminals in the area. At the very least the names of the major players and where their main allegiance lies. How else do you think I knew your road names without you telling me?"

"You could have overheard," Garrett finally spoke, looking at me like I was some strange, fascinating creature.

"No, but that doesn't matter. Why the hell am I back here getting lectured like I'm in the principal's office? I told you before." I stared at Brooks, my eyes holding his grey-blues. "I will fuck up anyone who tries to start shit with me."

So much for a little earned trust. These fuckers expected too much from me without giving anything in return. They were going to learn today though. Brooks calls me baby, but we all know what they say about baby and corners.

"That doesn't mean you can do it within the club especially not in front of the other patch holders!" he shouted, his smooth voice filled with outrage. "You're here because you're on our payroll, meaning you follow our rules, meaning you don't disrespect the members!" I felt myself go numb, my emotions dulling until they were nonexistent. It was the only way to keep my sanity or for Brooks to keep his pretty face attached to his skull.

"Here's the thing, Brooks," I started, my fingers steepled in front of my mouth before angling toward him as if I was pointing. "Yes, I am getting paid for the job you want me to do, but do I have a 'Property of' patch on my back or the club's cut?" His head pulled back as he looked at me in confusion.

"No," Garrett finally spoke, his voice dead. He'd known me long enough to understand where this conversation was going.

"That's right." I smirked at him. "Have I been patched in?" Garrett's head shook no. "Go on rides?" Another no. "Hm," I hummed, my lips thinning as if I was thinking about the answers. "I guess that means I'm *not* an Ace and yeah, your first rule is Respect First." Their eyebrows raised in surprise that I knew their rules. "But in my world, respect is earned and none of you have earned jack shit from me."

"But," Brooks tried to cut me off, and I snapped. My intense emotions from the job and everything between the four of us finally caught up to me; my wrath burned like acid in my stomach and chest.

"But nothing, Brooks! Consider me officially off your payroll," I commanded. "I don't want your fucking money, not if it comes at the price of my freedom." I stepped forward, my chest brushing his. "No one rules me, *Boss*, and I sure as hell don't bow down to anyone. Not Stone, not my stepbrother, and certainly not to you." He looked as if he'd been slapped when I stepped back. Turning to Garrett, I saw that his mask was in place, but the pained strain deep within his green eyes flashed out at me.

"Fuck all of you. Figure your own shit out," I growled, turning and storming out of the room. I hadn't realized I was shouting until I stepped into the bar and all eyes landed on me. Keeping my head high, I strode out of the room and into the cooling night air.

♠ ♠ ♠

A few hours later after riding out my anger in a long cruise, I walked into my home. The lights were dimmed, but not off, so I was able to make my way through the large structure without issues. Grabbing a beer, I unlaced my riding boots and kicked them into the corner. My body thrummed with exhaustion mixed with the tail end of my anger. I didn't regret for one moment what I did, no one puts hands on me, but I couldn't help but feel down at the separation between them and Chase and me. It had felt good to work with someone closely. I usually would get the details for the job electronically, never face to face, before receiving the front half of the payment. I didn't interact in person, only electronically of course, with anyone until it was done when I got the rest of my money.

Doesn't matter, I told myself. I was going to do this job without the money solely so I could fuck over Frankie and his shitty escort service. That alone was enough of a payment. Chase had left me a note on the counter saying he'd be doing a couple more hours of surveillance on the warehouse tonight, so I took my beer and headed to the living room.

A strange sense of deja vu settled over me when my skin prickled. Something was off. Drawing my weapon, I slowly crept through the house. The sounds of paper rustling reached my ear in the silence of the house. It had come from the backroom where Chase and I would work and plan our jobs. Eyeing the intruder through the crack in the door, I watched him looking through my files, blueprints, notes, and other information I had tacked up around the room.

Son of a bitch. Shoving open the door, I saw red at the invasion and within a few moments and two shots later, the intruder was dead and bleeding over my floor. This was not what I wanted to deal with tonight. Walking over to him, I finally noticed the Alloy Kings MC cut and his wrinkled, tanned face that held a wash of grey stubble telling me it was one of their long-time patch holders, Trey 'Bandit' Marks. I pilfered through his pockets and found a crumpled piece of paper which held chicken scratch. When I finally deciphered what it said, I felt my teeth clamp shut.

Identify what The Cat knows about the auctions.
Set devices at Aces compound.

There was a checkmark next to my line, but his cellphone didn't have any outgoing calls or texts, which meant whatever he learned hadn't gotten out. *Good*, I thought ruefully. I leaned against the top of my table and dialed Chase's number.

"Kittycat," he purred cheerfully in the phone, "you have a good night?"

"There's an Alloy Kings club member growing cold on my floor and his blood is getting my house dirty, so not really." I heard shuffling in the background before the start of an engine rumbled.

"Someone broke in?" His voice buzzed with excitement. "Need me to call the Maintenance Man?" I looked back at Bandit, my head tilting on if I wanted the clean-up crew, a.k.a the Maintenance Man, to come out quite yet.

"Not yet, I need to call the Aces." I grumbled at the thought. "It was Trey Marks."

"Oh, took out a rival, huh? Fuck me, Kittycat, you get me all sorts of hot and bothered when you talk killing." I felt my blood pound at the thought of going at it with Chase, but I pushed it away. "I'll be home shortly, you call your guys." I hummed an agreement before hanging up. Taking a deep breath, I rang Garrett.

GARRETT

The tension between the three of us was at an all time high after Kiera had stormed out of the compound a few hours ago. No patch holders approached us. A few hang-arounds tried to cozy up to me, but I immediately shut them down. I noticed Brooks and Stone doing the same. I was trying to wrack my brain for another alternative to getting Kevin's Old Lady back since Kiera had said fuck the job, when my phone rang.

"Yes?" I bit out. Not bothering to look at the caller ID, I was shocked when Kiera's husky voice filled the speaker.

"I got something you're going to want to see." She sounded resigned, but still angry. *Not surprising, Kiera's always angry at something.*

"What is it, Kiera?" I ground out, not in the mood to deal with more shit. Brooks and Stone's focus had drifted to me when I spoke her name.

"Well, if you'd just fucking come over here you'd find out. Damn it, Gar," she muttered. Her voice sounded far away at the sentiment. I don't think she realized I was able to hear her. I wasn't exactly sure how I felt about her using the nickname Chase had given me. "Bring Brooks and Stone." The line went dead as she hung up on me.

"We've been summoned to Kiera's house," I informed them. Brooks looked cautious but intrigued, while Stone looked, well, like Stone. "Apparently, there's something we need to see." Without any more discussion, we left the compound on our bikes and rode toward Kiera's house. *It's a mansion*, I thought to myself as I started up the front walkway.

"Kiera?" I called out when I didn't spot her familiar dirty blonde head or tattooed body in her living space. I absently noticed that my photos still sat on the mantle and despite telling myself I didn't care, I couldn't help but be relieved.

"Back here," her voice filtered out of the room where she worked. First thing I noticed when we entered was her Glock on the top of the table, followed quickly by the dead person lying in a heap on the floor.

"Jesus." Brooks eyed the Alloy Kings member with an appraising eye. Stone's steely gaze was focused on Kiera who was casually bent over the table looking through the pile of papers on top.

"What happened?" I demanded. My relief was short-lived. Seething anger flooded my system when I fully processed that *my kitten* had to kill an Alloy King. She held out a crumpled piece of paper for me to take without looking toward us. I snatched the sheet away from her.

"What's that?" Brooks read the paper over my shoulder, his jaw ticking in anger as he read the to-do list. "They fucking wanted to blow up our compound? Damn bastards. How did they know you're The Cat?" Brooks asked, his hand rubbing his jaw.

"Money can buy everything, even information," Kiera offered blandly, seemingly unconcerned with the entire situation. Stone took the sheet from my hand and read through it multiple times. Before anyone could talk again, the sound of steps walking through the house caught our attention. Pulling out my gun, I held it by my side and eyed the door. I wouldn't hesitate to kill anyone who tried to come after Kiera.

"You can put that shit away, Garrett." She was watching me, her eyes burning in residual anger despite her calm outer shell. "It's just Chase." I didn't put the gun away until I confirmed it was indeed the assassin. He was clothed in his usual dark wash jeans, black shirt, and jacket. *How does he wear that shit in the middle of the Nevada desert?*

"Ah, good." He lit up when he saw us all in the room, his eyes not even darting to the dead guy on the floor. "The gang's all here!" Stone grumbled under his breath, but no one was paying attention to him, our focus on dealing with the threat of the Alloy Kings.

"Who is it?" Brooks walked up to the burly, middle-aged man who was staring at the ceiling with sightless brown eyes.

"Trey 'Bandit' Marks," Kiera supplied distractedly, not looking up from her paper as she scribbled down notes.

"Are you seriously not concerned with the fact you just shot someone?" Stone's voice was incredulous as he scowled at my stepsister. She briefly glanced at him before brushing him off, her eyes going back to her work.

"I told you, I won't hesitate to put anyone who's a threat six feet under. You don't come into my house, go through my shit, and expect to walk away." She shrugged as if it was the simplest thing in the world. Chase nodded enthusiastically before turning his bright eyes to us, excited by the idea of her killing.

"Have you killed before?" I clenched my jaw as Brooks took over the conversation. I knew he meant well, but I didn't want to think about the answer. Kiera shrugged again, content to be blasé about the entire thing.

"Does that matter? We have a dead Alloy King on my floor and a missing Old Lady, the only thing I want to focus on is stealing her back." My brows shot up. Kiera was acting weird. She never rescinded her promises; if she said she didn't want to be on the job anymore, she wouldn't be.

"What's your motive?" She glared at me when I spoke up, and I stared right back, my arms crossing in front of my chest. "Thought you didn't want to be on our payroll anymore?" Chase's brows drew down at that, meaning he hadn't known what had gone down. Stepping ever so slightly to Kiera, he showed which side of the line he was on, assassin and thief versus us, Aces MC officers.

"I don't want your damned money, but I'm still doing this fucking job," she snarled, her anger finally surfacing, but I couldn't understand where it was coming from or why she would even consider doing this job without being paid.

"Why?" I bit out, pushing her further to answer me. She started to shake, her eyes glowing in the bright light of the room. Chase's expression had alarm bells ringing in my head, his normal happy disposition melting into a wave of anger and sadness as he watched Kiera, so I pushed more. "Why, Kiera?"

She finally snapped.

"Because Frankie is one of the main buyers!" she shouted, shoving the papers and blueprints off the counter in a fit of rage. Understanding flooded me. Frankie was the only reason she would lose control. She always held a short fuse and would put up a fight quicker than hell, but she was *always* in control, unless her father was part of the conversation. Silence filled the space, Kiera glaring at the floor and the mess she had made like it was the source of all her problems.

"Fuck off all of you," she snapped when she saw the looks of pity from around the room. "I don't need you fucking feeling sorry for me. I just want to hit Frankie where it'll hurt the most, his merchandise and his money. Chase, call the Maintenance Man. The rest of you, get the fuck out of my house."

CHAPTER 9

APRIL 30TH
TUESDAY OVERNIGHT
KIERA

I was irritable and cranky as I stared at Cory Harbold's lavish estate. That asshole I shot earlier had stained my favorite pair of riding pants, so I had to give them over to the Maintenance Man and I had to reprint and rehang several sections of my wall in my workspace because of the blood splatter.

"Can't I just beat the shit out of Harbold for him to give me his files?" I grumbled the question to Chase who was lying on the ground next to me. He chuckled and lowered the binoculars so he could look at me. Despite the nighttime darkness, his steel eyes glowed as they watched me.

"As much as I love watching you kick ass, Kittycat, that probably wouldn't be the best option right now." He nudged my shoulder with his. "We need to stay under the radar until we go after Frankie." I grumbled gibberish under my breath and brought my own binoculars up to my face.

"Can we at least go in and snoop? That might make me feel better." I beamed. "I could take the batteries out of all his electronics, or steal his remotes so he'd have to get up to change the channel, maybe work off some of those extra pounds." Chase shoved his face into his elbow to quiet his laughing.

"You're such an asshole, Kittycat. I love it," he chimed cheerfully, pressing a soft kiss to my cheek. "Yes, we can go and sneak around. It'd make stealing the files easier if we knew exactly where they were."

"He doesn't have cameras right?" I stood and dusted the dry grass off my black outfit. Chase shook his head in the negative, and we pulled our black fabric guards up over the lower half of our faces to leave only our eyes visible. "No electronic security once we're inside, right? Only need to get past the floodlights and then through one of the doors?"

"Right," he agreed and followed suit as I started snaking through the yard to avoid the sporadically placed security lights. When we finally reached one of the side doors off the hallway where Harbold's game room and office were, I made quick work of the lock. Slipping into the dimmed area, with the only light source coming from the main kitchen and living area down the hall, Chase and I closed the door silently before making our way into Harbold's office.

We stayed silent, only using the hand signals we had created six months ago when he decided to join in on my heists. I started on the desk as he scoured the walls and bookshelves. It was an overly masculine office that was full of stuffy, shittily-made antiques and ugly pieces. I grimaced. *Not even a little baby thief would steal this shit.* Turning back to my main focus, I shuffled as quickly and quietly as I could through his drawers not finding anything useful.

I did, however, stumble across a mostly used tube of

lotion and crusty tissues. Retching, I pointed at the bottom drawer for Chase to come see. I could tell by this eyes that he was laughing at me. *Jerkface.* After a playful slap on my ass, he went back to the shelves. I struggled to push the thought of Cory Harbold jacking off at his desk as I moved to the filing cabinet. *So, so gross.*

We were finished with his office after a few minutes. Stepping into the hall quietly, we then slipped into the next room. There was a gaudy pool table at one end and a matching bar and stool set at the other. There weren't too many spots there could have been a safe or hiding place in the room meaning we were done in under a minute. Those were the only rooms on this end of the hallway, so Chase and I crept into the main living space and, after not seeing anyone, darted into the adjacent hallway.

Several rooms later, we made our way upstairs. First place I wanted to check was his master bedroom. If I were to hide something I didn't want someone to find, I'd put it where I could keep an eye on it where no one would go. *Because I mean seriously, who would get in bed with a total sleazeball like Cory Harbold? I repeat, gross. Don't be turning those judgy eyes on me, it has nothing to do with his weight. I wouldn't ever sleep with a lawyer, let alone with a mob boss' lawyer.*

I rolled my eyes at his giant circular waterbed with a mirror on the ceiling above it. *Oh my god, I feel like I've walked into a cheesy episode of Cribs.* Chase immediately went toward the bathroom as I headed to the walk-in closet. Buried amongst the expensive Italian suits, was a small safe. I mentally marked down the make and model, noting that four of the numbers were worn away. I was about to try different combinations, when the sound of Harbold's car could be heard from outside. Chase was hot on my heels as I hustled down the stairs and toward the door we had unlocked. We exited the building and blended into the black night when we entered the trees.

So close...

MAY 1ST
WEDNESDAY MIDDAY
STONE

Growling, I strode the several feet to Kiera's front door before ringing the bell. She had been ignoring my calls this morning, and at Brooks' command I was supposed to make nice since our cat fight had apparently been my fault. I internally rolled my eyes. *Not my fault she's a brat, a sexy brat, but still.* I checked my watch after a few minutes growing more and more irritated the longer I stood there. Finally, the thief answered the door. Her hair was down and slightly messy, brushing the front of her perky tits. I kept my eyes trained on her face despite the way her jean shorts that barely covered her ass taunted me. She leaned against the door frame and crossed her arms in front of her black tank.

"Why are you at my house, Stone? I'm not in the mood for another tussle unless it's rolling around in my bed, but we both know how you feel about that," she drolled out, her mossy eyes looking up at me. I struggled to keep my face blank at the images that flashed in my mind. *Fuck.* I ground my teeth before answering, hoping my rock hard cock wasn't too obvious in my jeans.

"I have that security information for you," I bit out.

Fix it, Brooks' commanding voice echoed through my head when all I wanted to do was snap at her, or fuck her until her attitude was nothing but moans, screams, and my name on her lips. Speaking of her luscious lips, they thinned as she stared at me, and after a few tense moments of her silence, she stepped aside and allowed me to pass. Waiting for her to lead the way, I stood still near her as she shut and locked the door. She brushed against my torso, her arm grazing my agonizingly hard cock on her way past me. *Fucking brat.*

"Let's go, Stone, don't exactly have all damned day," she called out when I didn't move, her cocked brow and sassy attitude focusing on me from the other end of the hall. I glared at her as I followed to her workroom. First thing to catch my eye was a large section of her notes on the wall had been taken down, and a giant stack of papers and a roll of string sat at the bottom of it on the floor.

"What happened to your stuff?" I pointed at the space, my brows furrowed, not able to imagine why she would take down her shit about Frankie when she was so intent to go after him.

"Asshole's blood got all over it, so the Maintenance Man had to take it," she growled staring at the pile of papers. "I'm not pleased with having to do all that damn work hanging it up again." She rubbed her face before leaning forward on the table. Her angle displayed her tattooed tits perfectly as well as the red lacy bra she was wearing. "My eyes are up here, Grave." Her smug smirk was firmly in place when I finally looked at her face.

"Fuck off, brat," I bit out. "The security for the girls is done by a third-party company usually only hired by the Alloy Kings and at the Solace." Her jaw clenched as her eyes flared in rage, but she stayed silent at the mention of her father's casino, so I continued, "I'm sure you saw the equipment they carry, but the gun and one taser is their standard gear set-up. They arrive together in a van for shift time after dispatching from their headquarters." I outlined the last bit of the security information for her, her hand racing across the page to take notes.

"That everything?" Her husky voice was distracted as she continued to write. I nodded, but she apparently didn't see me as she glared up at me from under her lashes with a single brow raise. "You listening, Enforcer?" she snarked.

"I fucking nodded. Maybe if you looked up once in a while you'd have seen that," I finally snapped at her, unable to stand her sexy attitude. She straightened before storming up to me.

"How's the leg today?" She raised a brow and poked the healing, bandaged wound she gave me on my inner thigh. The sharp stabbing pain that shot through my leg at the hit caused me to grimace. "Want me to give you more? Cause that's exactly where you're fucking headed."

I caught her jaw similar to how I had the other day, making sure to not grip as hard because I didn't, in fact, want more cuts. The pad of my thumb that drifted over her soft lips had my cock throbbing with the urge to have her on her knees in front of me, to feel her lips wrapped around it as I fucked her sassy mouth. Growling out loud, I shifted my thumb out of the way and smashed my lips to hers. She immediately smacked my hand away from her face, pulling back to narrow her sparkling eyes on me before yanking me from the front of my shirt to kiss me back.

Her movements were frantic, her hands roaming down my muscled chest to rub over my jeans. Her strokes wrought shivers through me, goosebumps raising as she moved her rough kisses across my jaw and down my neck. I reached up her top, pinching the front of her lacy bra and bringing the flesh underneath to stiff peaks. Her shuddered moans filled my ears, her breath hot against my skin. Unbuttoning her denim shorts, I was met with smooth, tanned skin, no underwear covering her bare pussy.

"Shit," I breathed, brushing against the slick folds, my fingers flicking against her clit roughly before sinking two into her soaking center. Her fevered forehead pressed against my neck as she gripped my shoulders tightly in attempts to stay standing. My movements pushed faster while her moans cracked in her pleasured fog. Capturing her mouth, I brushed my tongue against hers, forcefully silencing her.

Before she reached that final peak though, she pulled back, my coated fingers falling to my side. I stared down at her in confusion until she undid my jeans and dropped to her knees.

Oh, fuck yes.

Her mossy eyes burned when she looked at my erection. Silk honey tresses tangled between my fingers as I gripped it hard, ready for her pretty mouth to be wrapped around me. Looking up, she licked the bottom of my shaft before wrapping her luscious lips around me and taking my cock deep into her mouth.

Pulses of desire and need raced through my veins, pooling in my balls with each bob of her head, each stroke of her tongue against my throbbing vein. I had to grip onto the table top to stay upright, her twirling tongue and her cupped hand around my balls nearly bringing me to my knees. In the waves of lust that pulsed through me, her name fell in harsh whispers from my lips. Unable to help myself, I rocked forward. She didn't gag, taking my full length with each thrust until I was fulfilling my ultimate desire of fucking her mouth with her on her knees. My orgasm slammed down on me when she started to hum, the vibrations bringing me to release painfully hard at the back of her throat.

I yanked her to standing, pressing her up against the table, my tongue battling hers once more. Her teeth nipped my lips as I tasted my salty flavor on her tongue, but before I could return the favor, my cell started to ring. Growling, I tried to ignore it, but it was Brooks' ringtone and I couldn't ignore his calls. I pulled my jeans up until I was able to reach in and pull it out.

"What?" I barked out, angry that we were interrupted.

"You comin' back anytime soon? We're supposed to leave in five minutes." I groaned, rubbing my scalp. *I can't believe I forgot our ride this afternoon.* "You two make up yet?"

"Yeah, Boss. I'll be right there," I bit out before hanging up. Kiera's brow was cocked as she looked up at me, her unbuttoned shorts teasing me with a peek of her wet pussy.

"Club business?" she surmised, her arms crossed over her chest as she watched me situate myself.

"We have another ride," I muttered. Now that everything was said and done, my head was screaming at me for reacting solely to my body's urges. *God damn it, now I'm the one thinking with my dick.* My anger turned from being interrupted to the entire shit show as a whole. Making sure I had everything, I turned and immediately stomped away from the sexy brat.

"Fucking hell, Stone," she shouted out, her head sticking out of the back room. "Way to fucking say bye, jerkoff!" I gave a careless wave of my hand over my shoulder purposely ignoring the fact she'd literally just given me the best blow job of my entire life as I got on my bike.

Fucking fiery thief...

KIERA

That fucking bastard, I growled to myself. I stared, without seeing, at the notes I took from Stone's visit, angry with myself for falling into the sexual desire that had been building within me any time I was around the suspicious enforcer. Knowing him, he was probably just as angry. It would explain why the fuck he had walked off without any semblance of a farewell. *See if I'll fucking suck him off again*, I snapped mentally, *or do anything else with that fucking prick.*

Pushing away thoughts of the infuriating club officer, I focused on the writing in front of me. Tomorrow night was the heist, and I had to be focused, five girls were counting on me. Chase was currently out picking up the gear we would need to pull it off. We had decided the best way to get them out was to secure them in a harness and get them out through the air conditioning system since the vent was directly above them. I flipped through my notes and double checked we had the numbers of gear right: five harnesses, a low-riding board to wheel them out toward the roof—*you know what I'm talking about, the ones you rode in gym class in elementary school that hurt like a bitch when you ran over your own fingers*—and finally two pulley-belay systems to lower me down and lift them up within the room and on the side of the building.

Thank fuck the warehouse didn't have windows and that it was pretty much sound proofed. Otherwise, bringing the van to the building would be out of the question. This wasn't like our typical heists where I would go in and Chase would be a lookout. This required both of us since it was five fully grown adults not a piece of art, jewelry, or a file that I could carry by myself. Leaving the table, I stepped over to the map hitting the switch on the wall for it to roll up into its metal casing. The double door hidden behind the colorful city greeted me, the keypad lighting up green after I typed in the code.

The walk-in closet was large and two stories. Practice rope and pulley-belays hung from the ceiling, while mine and Chase's specially made harnesses were hung on hangers around the edge. Shelves held weapons, equipment, and more gear between the racks of safety straps. Grabbing the rolling cart next to the door, I started moving around the room in a clockwise circle. Harness for both of us, *check*, backup set of harnesses, *check*, rope, *check*, typical job instruments like lock picks, fake IDs, weapons, and extra ammo, *check*. After loading it onto the cart, I brought it out to the table. Quickly straightening up the scattered sheets, I cleaned the stone top so I could inspect all the gear before loading it into the bags.

Please let this go smoothly...

MAY 1ST
WEDNESDAY OVERNIGHT
BROOKS

The club members had long since gone home, the bar empty save for the officers, all of whom were tense and antsy. Tonight was the night. Kiera was going in the warehouse and we essentially just had to wait until they sent confirmation. As much as I told myself they'd be fine, I felt my foot bouncing anxiously and my fingers tapping against the bar top. Stone was swirling his lowball of whiskey, but didn't seem overly worried. But then again he was one of the best at concealing any type of emotion except for irritation, anger, or suspicion. Nate was fiddling with his beard, his signature sign that he was stressing.

Garrett, unsurprisingly, was the one panicking the most, by pacing in short passes before turning and coming back.

"Dude," I called out after what seemed like Garrett's twentieth pass. "She'll be all right. She has Chase with her, and she's the best for a reason. It'll be fine." Garrett threw a scalding look my way as he continued to pace. Nate nodded, his hand moving away from his beard after my words. Despite my words, I couldn't stop myself from glancing at the clock again. Stone huffed out a low chuckle.

"You all seemed worried. Guess you don't trust her as much as you thought you did," he challenged. Turning my attention to him, my eyes narrowed in response to his smug smile.

"We trust her just fine," I murmured, daring him to continue to push me. He let out a derisive snort and faced forward toward the wall of liquor behind the bar.

"Yeah, well, let's hope she doesn't fuck it all up," Stone muttered. He continued to grumble inaudibly under his breath before taking a large swig of his drink, no doubt going on about Kiera or some other petty nonsense. *He gives Garrett and me shit about how we're 'obsessed' with Kiera, and yet he always has to be the first to comment on her. Whiny, hypocritical bitch.*

"You know, Stone," I started, "for someone who seemingly dislikes Kiera, you sure do have a lot to say about her. Makes me wonder if you're trying to convince us or yourself that you don't like her. Either way, you're doing a piss poor job of it." He tensed under my prodding but didn't continue to argue his point, choosing to take another drink instead. Garrett growled under his breath as he continued his incessant pacing.

"I know she'll be all right, but that doesn't make the wait any easier," Garrett challenged. "You're not as calm and collected as you're playing off though, Boss, so don't sit there and lecture me."

"Yes, I'll admit I'm a tad uneasy," I admitted in a huff, hating that I had been called out. "But I'm not full-on panicking either. What could go wrong? They said there weren't any guards actually in the room and they'll both be armed. We only have to wait for"—I checked the clock on the wall over my shoulder, again—"another twenty minutes before we hear from them. It'll be fine," I urged, trying to calm him.

"I fucking hope so," he muttered, still pacing. Sighing, I turned to face the bar.

It's going to be a long twenty minutes.

KIERA

I felt sweat building at the back of my neck as I crawled through the vent, Chase right on my ass with half of the gear. The trek was slow going and a bit more difficult in my harness. Once again, I was thankful that the vents were so large that they allowed me room to maneuver when the harness got uncomfortable. The low-lying scooter was attached to a rope that connected to Chase's belt. It silently rolled behind him while we each carried a few harnesses for the girls and extra rope wrapped around my torso for the pulley-belay system Chase had strapped to his chest.

It was slightly after midnight, meaning halfway through the guards' shift when they started to take lunch. Their talking and eating would keep them busy long enough to hopefully get the girls out without any confrontation. I unwrapped the rope and handed it to Chase when we reached our destination, focusing on securing several harnesses together so I could take them all down at once. When the pulley was secured, I hooked the end and slowly started my descent into the large room. The smell was vomit-worthy since the girls hadn't been given chances to use a proper bathroom. *Thank fuck for my face guard.*

I unhooked the IV system from Maxine, making sure to grab her cut from the wall after placing her in the harness, and Chase pulled her up to the vent. I knew it was a major faux-pas for anyone else to touch the cut or 'Property of' jacket or having others wear it, but I figured the extenuating circumstances made it okay as I slipped it on the second girl.

By the fifth and final girl, sweat was dripping into my eyes and soaking my long-sleeve shirt as well as my beanie. *Who knew moving fully grown adults when they were like a giant sack of potatoes would be such a workout.* I huffed and secured the rope to her harness. I looked around the room, taking in the details of the space as Chase wheeled her to the roof where the others were. The room was unlit; only the very slim window near the top of the room let the moonlight filter in. The cement floors held a few cracks, while the walls were half finished drywall. *I should blow the fuck out of this place*, I thought to myself. *They wouldn't be able to use it again.*

The sound of the guards shuffling on the other side of the door let me know they were going to be finishing up lunch soon. My watch read 12:45 AM. *All right, 15 minutes to get the girls into the van and get the fuck out of here before they come check on them.* Pulling out my signature card, I dropped the white cardstock with my printed paw print on the ground. I quickly hooked myself to the rope when it reached me, Chase huffing and sweating as much as me in the air vent. Making sure to grab all of our gear, I shut the vent and followed my assassin to the roof access.

We went through the same process to get the girls down to the van, except this time Chase was on the ground and loading them up while I got them fastened to the pulley rope and down the side of the tall building. Once again checking to make sure I had all of our shit, I scaled down the building and disengaged the remote lock on the pulley anchor. Chase caught it, immediately throwing his hands in the air doing a little dance like he had scored a touchdown. Rolling my eyes, I couldn't help but smile at his ridiculousness.

We left the warehouse in a cloud of dust, all five girls safely secured in the back.

Thank fuck...

CHAPTER 10

MAY 2ND
THURSDAY EARLY MORNING
CHASE

Maxine was passed out in the backseat of the car, having woken up over an hour ago at the house. Kiera showed her the bathroom so she could shower and gave her a pair of clothes to change into before we would take her to the compound. Maxine was grateful, thanking us over and over to the point that my kittycat was severely uncomfortable. She wasn't used to so much attention since she preferred to stick to the shadows.

Speaking of, my little kittycat was staring out the window at the passing landscape, her eyes drooping with exhaustion. She was always tired and slept like a rock after our jobs, with me usually making the final drop and receiving payment, but she insisted on dropping Maxine off at the compound together. I think she just wanted to see a few certain officers, but I didn't mention it, as I didn't want to pop her bubble of success.

The front gate club member let us pass having known we were coming ahead of time, and the stillness around the compound meshed well with the early morning sunrise. I pulled up right outside the door of the clubhouse before waking Maxine. She immediately started to cry as she shot out of the car to her husband like one of my bullets. Brooks stood off to the side backed by Garrett and Stone; the first two appeared somewhat happy, although the latter was very clearly ignoring looking at Kiera as she stepped out of the car. She was wearing her lounge clothes—a pair of baggy sweats that hung low on her hips— and a small bit of one of my boxers she had stolen peeked out at the top under her tight black shirt.

"Thank you," Maxine's husband Kevin gushed. His furry mustache looked like a dark caterpillar on his upper lip, and I had a hard time not laughing as he talked. "Seriously, thank you so much. Whatever you guys need, whenever you need it, just let me know." He emphatically shook my hand, his calluses rough against my palm before turning and doing the same to a very uncomfortable Kiera. *My poor kittycat*, I chuckled looking over at her, *pretty sure she'd rather face her fear of nuns than be here right now*. Kevin and Maxine went inside the bar and left the five of us standing in an awkward silence.

"Your money was transferred to your account," Brooks said, looking down at our girl. Her exhausted brain was slow to respond as she furrowed her brows.

"What?" she asked after a few minutes. "I don't understand."

"Wow," Stone huffed rolling his eyes. His attitude was starting to grate on my nerves. I understood running from feelings you didn't like, well I knew about it, I didn't actually *know* since I really didn't hate anything, but his rudeness was pushing me in that direction.

"Leave my kittycat alone." I curled my left arm around her, pulling her sagging body to me. She leaned against me as a crutch to hold herself upright. "She just did you a favor with the intention of not getting paid, might I add, and she's tired, so keep your shit to yourself." I buried my face in her hair to keep myself from getting angry. Kiera didn't like when I wasn't my usual happy-go-lucky self. She tended to worry then, and I didn't want her to do something silly like that.

"I don't want your money." I assumed Kiera directed her words toward Brooks, but I wasn't sure as my eyes were closed while I nuzzled her, her shampoo's berry scent filling my nose. "I told you that."

"Well, too damn bad," Garrett bit out, "you did the job so we paid you. Why did you even come if you were so tired?" His question was filled with enough exasperation to have me peeking over at him. His green eyes were centered on my kittycat's tired face, his jaw ticking in irritation.

"Fuck off, Garrett." Her words were slurred. "I should... punch you... asshole. Fuck, so tired..." she trailed off and leaned more and more into me. I immediately opened the car door right behind her and guided her into the passenger seat. Closing the door after buckling her in, I turned to the Aces' officers. Every single one of them wore melancholy expressions as they stared at Kiera, knowing this was the end of the job, so me being me, I decided to stick my nose into the middle of it.

"You know you guys don't have to be so sad," I added cheerfully, "you're more than welcome around the house any time. Besides, pretty sure she'll be around, but you know you could always see if she wanted to come to one of your parties." I hummed, poking Brooks in the forearm that snugly crossed his chest in rapid succession. Brooks eyes lit up in laughter, getting what I was hinting at while Stone stormed off, his jaw tensing, but he couldn't hide the erection in his jeans. Garrett ground his teeth, staring longingly at Kiera. He was the only one she hadn't claimed, and I could read the hurt on his face plain as day. A plan forming in my head had me smiling slyly at him.

"What?" he barked when he saw me looking at him. "Why are you making that face, assassin?" I just smiled wider before walking around the car and getting in. "Chase?" he called out as I sank into the driver's seat. His brows furrowed as he watched me pull away, and Brooks chuckled and patting him on the shoulder. He seemed to know I was up to something. *Good*, I thought to myself, *by the end of the weekend my kittycat and Garrett will finally have to address their long-time-coming desire.*

MAY 3RD
FRIDAY NIGHT
KIERA

I turned my bike off and remained seated on it as I eyed the door to the bar. It was once again propped open, loud music and rowdy voices filtering out into the warm night air. I was only here at Chase's urging, some bullshit story about how I needed to tell Garrett that we were moving in on Harbold's files tomorrow night. *Don't see why I couldn't have just texted him that, but whatever.* My hair was down and unbraided for the first time here at the compound, tousled and windblown from my ride in. I decided to say fuck it and rode in my short shorts and regular band tee that I had cut to show off my sides down to my waist. *Because this is the desert and it gets hot as fuck here.*

Attempting to not bump into anyone, I curved around couples and people, scanning the crowd for my asshole stepbrother. More glances turned my way than before due to the confrontation with Stone. Maxine and Kevin were among the crowd, and Kevin immediately darted over to me.

"Kiera." He shook my hand like he had the day before.

"I just wanted to thank you again." He leaned forward to whisper in my ear. "It'll help take off some of the heat if it looks like a member accepts you, so go with it. Call me Dagger." I nodded slightly, signifying I understood as I shook his hand.

"No problem, Dagger. Anytime." I nodded and gave a tiny wave to Maxine who waved obnoxiously at me, her smile bright. *Glad to see she is doing better.* I turned back to sweeping the crowd. Before I could find Garrett though, Brooks stepped in front of me.

"Hey, baby"—he smirked down at me—"you lookin' for someone in particular?" I cocked a brow, and the feeling that he already knew the answer crept over me. *What are you and Chase up to?* I mentally asked him. *Damn troublemakers.*

"Yeah, Garrett. Seen him?" I decided to play along, suspicion pushed to the back burner as he hitched a thumb toward one of the chairs off to the side. Narrowing my eyes at the president, I inched around him and walked in the direction in which he pointed. I felt my chest tighten sharply and I ground my teeth. That same tramp that had been hitting on him the other day was straddling his lap. His hand rested on her thigh while the other held a lowball of alcohol. I took calming breaths to try and see through the red wave of rage at her practically smothering him with her breasts as her fingers tangled in his hair. I closed the distance between us with purposeful strides, but I might have been stomping. *Who knows.*

"Garrett," I bit out, feeling my heart beating painfully fast within my chest. His hard green eyes moved from her face, as she had been talking in some ditzy fucking girly voice, to me. *I'm not jealous at all. Yeah, yeah, turn those judgy eyes on me since I'm clearly a fucking big green monster right now.*

"What?" His harsh tone matched my short one, and I focused in on his hands as he made no moves to dislodge her. I ground my teeth some more before answering.

"I need to talk to you." The tramp finally turned her attention on me, and her bright baby blues watched me as her bubblegum pink gloss covered lips tilted down.

"He's busy, bitch," she snapped. Her ditzy voice rang in my ears as Garrett's brows rose sharply in irritation at her words. *Oh, hell no, she did not just call me that.* I stormed up to her and grabbed a fistful of her bleached blonde hair.

"I suggest you watch what you fucking say to me," I hissed in her face. "I also suggest you find someone else to fuck because this Ace is mine." I pulled her by her hair, and she flopped ungracefully onto the gross floor flashing an ungodly amount of weirdly shaved pussy before trying to come after me, but Garrett was faster. Stepping between us, he faced Princess Prissy No-Pants.

"Bambi, I need to have a conversation with her," he mumbled before grabbing my arm and dragging me down the hall.

"Bambi? Seriously?" I huffed. *Pretty sure I rolled my eyes hard enough for them to pop out of my head and roll down the street.* "I thought you would have better taste than that." Garrett stayed quiet until shoving me into one of the back bedrooms.

"What the ever loving fuck was that?" he growled, getting in my face as I had done to Bambi. *Cue the shudder. I mean seriously, who names their kid that? Crazy people, that's who.* "I was fucking busy!" His arm went out wide in the general direction of the door. I tried, really tried, to bite back my retort, but that stupid green monster I attempted to ignore, the one that liked to lurk in the background when it came to Garrett, barrelled forward.

"Fine, go back to Bambi, I'm sure Brooks would be up for another round with me since you're *so* busy," I sneered, my chest heaving hard as I shoved him away from me and walked toward the door. Before I could make it there, Garrett slammed into me, pressing me back against the door, his seething face only a breath away. I opened my mouth to snap at him when he silenced me with a raw, passionate kiss filled with years of pent-up cravings, loathing, and temptation.

Growling, his hands roughly cupped my face, fingers tangling in my hair as our kiss filled with battling tongues and nipping bites. My palms rubbed against the taut planes of his chest and sculpted abdomen. His shirt was soft under my fingers, but all I wanted in that moment was his skin against mine. Not giving a shit about the rules surrounding the cut, I shoved it down off his shoulders until I could toss it off to the side. I ran my hands up his tattooed torso reveling in the warmth that radiated from his tanned skin.

His hands slid down my neck and over my breasts before ending on my hips. Gripping tightly, he started to walk us back toward the king sized bed in the middle of the room. He sat slowly, kissing and biting my jaw and neck until he was situated right in front of my chest. Hands skimming over my skin pushed up and bunched my shirt around my ribs for me to take off, and as soon as it was gone he immediately bit my left breast over the fabric of my bra. The sharp feeling of his teeth had me grasping his shoulders to stay standing and a breathy moan escaped me. Stripping me out of my bra, Garrett yanked his shirt over his head baring a chiseled chest and inked skin.

"I think I make a better lap playmate than that fucking tramp out there," I murmured, situating myself across Garrett's powerful thighs in the same position Bambi had been and wrapping my hands into his hair. My breasts brushed lightly against his scruff making me shiver.

"You think so?" Garrett stared up at me, his rough hands running down my back agonizingly slow until he reached my ass. I knew my arousal was soaking my shorts, but I couldn't bring myself to care when all I wanted in that moment was for Garrett to fuck me. His damned, kissable lips curled into a devilish smirk right before he slapped my ass, the sharp sting melting into a warm pool of pleasure.

"I should fucking punish you for interrupting me." His harsh whispers caused his hot breath to wash over me, leaving goosebumps over my breasts in its wake, my nipples peaking against his strong chest. Another slap came right after and I couldn't contain the soft moan that fell from my lips. His green eyes darkened as his pupils blew out wide, the smirk growing. "Liked that didn't you, Kitten? Stand up." My pussy quivered at the question and at the command. *Fuck yeah, I did.* Following his directive, I placed my booted feet on the carpet.

"Strip," he ordered. My skin flushed under the heated, yet leisurely, perusal as I bent at the waist to untie my boots, his eyes drinking me in. Kicking them off, I kept eye contact as I unbuttoned and slid the shorts down my legs. Power surged through me at the control at which I held Garrett's attention. He shifted back further onto the bed until his calves rested against the edge of the mattress. Crooking a finger at me, he commanded me forward.

"Get that sexy ass over here." He patted his lap, but he stopped me before I could straddle him once more.

I allowed him to move me, and he had me lying on my stomach over his legs, my knees resting on the ratty comforter with my ass perfectly angled up in front of him. A rough, calloused hand grabbed the back of my thigh lightly before sliding to my ass as his right arm rested on my back and gripped my hip tightly.

"You've given me a lot of shit over the years, Kiera," he ground out, desire thick in his words. I couldn't see him directly, only out of the corner of my eye, and at the way he was eyeing me I felt a drip of my own wetness start to slide down my thigh and onto his jeans. "You don't know how many times I've envisioned you splayed over my lap like this so I could punish you for your fucking feisty mouth and your damned sexy attitude."

Without warning, his hand left my ass and came down in a stinging slap. I clenched my thighs together to keep from leaking anymore; my moan sounded slutty even to my own ears. Another slap, his right hand coming to my hair, tangling into the tresses in a tight, but not painful grip.

Fuck me. I felt my eyes roll back at the position. I didn't do submissive, but something about Garrett's rugged, domineering personality had me aching for more.

"Don't fucking close those legs," he demanded, delivering another slap, and the moan I released was even louder. When I was lost in the sensation of his punishment and not doing as he commanded, he pulled on my hair to angle my head up off the bed.

"Open your legs," he growled, tattooed fingers brushing against my wet thighs as I shifted my knees. "God damn," he groaned feeling the near steady stream pouring from my greedy pussy, "you fucking love this, don't you?" I couldn't form an answer as he cupped my cunt and rubbed circles on my throbbing clit and slick entrance. He released the grip on my hair to bring another hit to my already tortured ass, his left hand never moving between my legs.

"Fuck," I mumbled in my lustful haze. At my response, he slipped in two fingers, his thumb rubbing over the tight bud of my ass. Wanton moans swiftly turned to cries of pleasure as he pushed me closer to the edge. One last spank sent me flying over into that blissful release, my eyes blackening for a split second with the intensity of my orgasm.

"Get up," he commanded and withdrew his hand, much to my disappointment. My body trembled as I maneuvered myself off his lap, and a wet spot soaked his jeans on his left thigh. His eyes held mine prisoner when I was finally standing in front of him. I nibbled my lip in excitement. *My turn to get him out of his clothes.* Placing my hands on his thighs, I leaned forward until I was brushing his lips with mine.

"Now, you strip," I whispered stepping back until he was standing. Taking his spot, I sank onto the bed while he took off his boots. He unbuckled his belt and unzipped his jeans, and I watched as his cock was immediately freed from under the fabric of his briefs. *Holy. Fuck.* I clenched my thighs together as another pulse of wetness dripped from me. *His cock is pierced.*

"What did I say about those legs, kitten?" he demanded, bending over to pry my legs apart. "I want to see your fucking pussy soaking for me." His stare bore into mine as he stood once more, daring me to disobey. Cocking a brow, I did just that, slowly bringing them together. I smiled innocently at him as his eyes blazed in response to my blatant disobedience.

"What are you going to do about it, Garrett?" I taunted.

Stalking forward once more, he wrapped my hair around his hand and held me in place while his free hand went to my breast. I continued to watch him as I waited for what he was going to do in punishment. Kissing me hard, he distracted me long enough to pinch my nipple sharply. Lightning shot through me, my thighs opening almost immediately in response. My eyes rolled back when he shifted from pinching to rolling the aching peak between his fingers.

"Keep those fucking thighs open or I'll leave you wanting and panting and go back out to the bar." I snarled, biting his lip hard. "You little..." he breathed, but his eyes were on fire with craving despite the pain. His tongue darted out to lap up the tiny bead of blood that had welled up from my bite.

"Don't you dare fucking leave me in here," I ground out, my chest heaving as the anger of his threat fueled my lustful haze even more. "The only thing you better be planning on doing is fucking me until I can't walk, got it?" *He isn't the only one who could make demands.*

"That I can do," he growled, capturing my lips again, his jeans rough against my thighs. He stood and ripped the obstructing piece of clothing down his legs before kneeling between mine. His scruff brushed against my sensitive skin as he pressed hot kisses down my neck, making sure to shower both breasts in attention before pushing me until I was lying back against the bed. My skin was on fire under his mouth as he trailed down my stomach to lick up my slit before immediately dipping into my entrance. Stars burst in front of my eyes at his ministrations, the roughness of his facial hair a delicious contrast to the sensual licks. Swirling tongue. Teasing nips peppered my greedy pussy. I nearly lost myself to the pleasure washing through my body.

I tangled my fingers in his hair, his groans mixing with my broken cries. Tugging, I pulled Garrett up until he was hovering over me so I could capture his lips. I could taste myself on his lips and tongue. Reaching into the shoddy night stand, he yanked out a condom. When he ripped the wrapper open with his teeth, I grabbed the slippery material out before rolling it onto his impressively sized cock. He lined up and pushed into me in one smooth motion, but despite being incredibly wet, the sudden stretching had me clawing at the bed as I cried out. *Fuck.* I pressed my head back into the comforter as I adjusted to his size and the bumps of his Jacob's ladder.

"God damn, Kitten," Garrett's harsh murmurs filled my ear as he slid out and back in agonizingly slow. I was panting, each rung of his piercing left me trembling as he continued his torturous pace. Untangling my fingers from the bed, I gripped his ass tightly to bring him fully inside me. Garrett took my hint, his pace quickening as he nipped sharply at my neck.

Painful tingles built through my lower back, spreading with each thrust toward my pussy, and my voice cracked with the intense build-up to my orgasm. Sitting back, Garrett grabbed one leg and hitched it over his shoulder. His fervent gaze locked on my face and body as he hit deeper bringing me even closer to that edge. When the build-up became almost too much to handle, fire burning my veins and electricity running over my skin in powerful waves, his hand cupped my breast and rolled the sore nipple between rough fingers.

"Garrett." His name broke on my lips as I descended at lightning speed into release, my greedy pussy clamping around him. His piercings rubbing just right to bring quivers to my body.

Withdrawing, he gripped my hips tightly and flipped me onto my stomach. He stood at the edge of the bed, pulling my trembling hips back to meet his cock. I cried out as he pushed back in, the sensitivity from my orgasm still lingering.

"Fuck," he ground out, propping his foot onto the bed as he pounded into me. I started to press my chest and face into the bed, unable to hold myself up at the surges of searing pleasure, but Garrett wrapped my hair around his hand and pulled my head up and back. His other hand went to my shoulder and neck, holding me in place as he drove into my still dripping pussy. This time when my orgasm came, there was no intense build-up. I shattered against him when he brought a hand down on my ass in a stinging slap. Waves of desire flooded my system as I milked him of his own release. Whimpering, I collapsed onto the bed, Garrett following suit on his back after tossing the condom.

Neither of us spoke for a long while; the sound of the music and other patch holders talking filtered lightly into the room from down the hall despite the closed door. I looked over at Garrett after propping up on my elbows, my gaze tracing the tattoos I don't think I'd ever seen. Black, greys, and colors swirled together in one giant collection of art, but one piece in particular caught my eye. Moving closer, I felt my brows furrow as I stared at it, my sex-addled brain not processing what I was seeing.

A little black kitty paw print.

Right over his heart.

Feeling his gaze on me, I pulled my eyes from the tattoo to look at him. He watched me watch him for a long moment before I spoke.

"Is that..." My eyes darted back to the tattoo. "Is that what I think that is?" Emotions I didn't know how to handle blossomed in my chest, that stupid green monster of jealousy and envy purring at the sight as he nodded.

He had the symbol I leave at all my heists tattooed.

My paw print permanently marked his chest.

I couldn't believe my eyes. His skin was hot against my fingertips and his heart thudded quickly under my touch when I reached out. Chase and Abby's words whispered in my mind, and my chest crushed under the weight of the surge of emotions. I grinned.

"Does that mean you're mine now?" I teased. He huffed an exasperated laugh.

"That would be the first thing your mind goes to." My heart skipped in my chest as he smiled down at me. "If that's what you want, then yes." His smile faded as his jaw clenched. "I can't... I can't promise that I won't get jealous of Chase, Brooks, or Stone, but Kiera..." The desperation in his voice had me inhaling sharply. "I've waited for this for years, and I'll take you any way you'll let me." My smile curled into a sinful smirk at the words despite knowing that's not how he meant them, but I couldn't help myself.

"Oh, really?" I whispered. "That better be a promise." His eyes smoldered as he nodded. "Then, yes." His brows furrowed.

"What?" He was confused, and to be honest, it was quite adorable. I rolled onto my back and pointed at my left hip.

"Yes, that's what I want," I admitted quietly, trying to quell the emotions that continued to build. *I don't do emotions very well, if you couldn't tell. Don't turn those judgy eyes on me, people.* He sat up, eyes scanning down my body until they rested at the tattoo I pointed to. A little spade symbol in black ink, just like the one on his cut.

"When?" he murmured, a rough finger tracing the tattoo.

"It was my first tattoo," I confessed, opting to look at his hand instead of his eyes. I wasn't sure I was ready to see all the emotions swirling in those green depths.

"Me too." His fingers captured my chin so I would look at him, and he smiled down at me. "You're very uncomfortable right now, aren't you?"

I burst out laughing with a nod. "I'm getting all itchy," I joked, loving that he knew me well enough to understand that I hated emotions. *Love? Did I just say that?* I pushed the thought away. "I think we have lots of time to make up for," I whispered, feeling my pussy throb in need of attention. "So get your ass over here because I'm pretty sure I can still walk." With that, he surged forward and wrapped me in his inked arms; the wicked glint in his eyes had me dripping anticipation.

Fuck yes...

GARRETT

I sighed. My feelings and thoughts about what happened were all jumbled. I was happy as fuck, and yet, scared as hell. I'd been dreaming of this exact moment for so many years but never really allowed my heart to believe that it would happen. Now that it had, what did it mean? I knew she said she wanted me as much as I want her, but for how long? How long until I piss her off again, pushing her too far, and she turns me away? I didn't know if my heart could take it.

I have got to be realistic about this and about Kiera, she has always been a short fuse and when it comes to her, I was a lit match. *That's not exactly the best of combos,* I grimaced. Not to mention I had a job to do, and I couldn't let my feelings for her cloud my judgement. I also couldn't let her walk all over me with that snarky attitude of hers.

Fuck! This definitely could get messy, I groaned quietly as I rubbed my eyes with my left hand. I had always been protective of her, she's always been *my kitten*, but now? We were in uncharted territory. Part of me said I should just take the gift of last night and move on. As I looked at her though, so peaceful, so beautiful, I knew that I could never give her up. She was *finally* mine. This was my time to finally love Kiera the way I'd always wanted.

Oh, I was still going to show her who's boss. I was still going spank her ass and own that sweet fucking pussy of hers but at least this time, it wouldn't just be in my dreams. My cock ticked to life as I thought about all the ways I was going to own her body when I felt a small hand slide up my chest coming to rest on the paw print over my heart. I pulled Kiera closer to me, her head resting in the crook of my arm as I inhaled her signature scent of berries and grease, now laced with a hint of our sex.

I stared down at her delicate features and vowed to always be a place of peace and comfort for her. Her safe place where she could be herself and to not worry about the things that I knew haunted her dreams. My throat constricted as I tried to swallow down the emotion that held my heart in a vise-like grip. *What the fuck is happening to me?* Kiera happened... is happening and in this moment, I knew that all my bluster about showing her who's boss was bullshit because this girl right here, she owned *me*. She'd owned me from the first moment I laid eyes on her and now that she was finally in my arms, I didn't give a fuck who knew it.

CHAPTER 11

Sooooo," Chase cheerfully dragged the word out, his tone nosy in my earpiece, "how was the compound last night?" I rolled my eyes; the little bastard knew the answer to that already. Brooks even had the balls to smile and thumbs up Garrett and me when I had left early this morning.

"You know very well how it was, my little assassin," I murmured, unlocking the same door Chase and I had entered through the other day. "Can I ask why you and Brooks were trying so hard to throw us at each other?" He chuckled giddily.

"Because, as I said before"—his statement was smug, and if I didn't give a shit about him, I would have smacked that self-satisfied smile I knew he was wearing right off his handsome face—"you two were just blind. Now though, you've gotten past that ridiculous set of blinders you were both wearing. Besides, Brooks and I have been talking."

I groaned. *That certainly wasn't a good thing.*

"Don't sound so pained, Kittycat, turns out he likes to watch too!" He sounded absolutely excited about the prospect. "Now, all we have to do is get Stone to stop being a little bastard."

"Stone isn't exactly little," I mumbled under my breath. Chase's laugh filled my ear, and I rolled my eyes again and slipped into Harbold's bedroom, walking straight to his closet.

"You know what I meant, Kittycat," he playfully scolded. "You think you might be happy with the four of us?" I furrowed my brows at his question, my fingers typing in strings of numbers in different combinations until the light switched green.

"What do you mean?" I asked, my voice strained as I reached into the deep safe and scooped out the very large stack of papers and files to secure in my backpack. Pulling a white business card with a black paw print on it, I left it in the safe before locking it.

"Well, we could be yours and then you would be our girl. No hang-arounds or other girls, just us," he explained as I strapped the bag across my back making sure to secure the clips across my chest.

"Like, as in a relationship?" I questioned, finally making my way out of Harbold's house, my boots nearly silent on the staircase.

"Yeah, we'd date you and you'd date us. Obviously, Stone will come around eventually." Chase sounded completely sure of that fact while I still had reservations on the suspicious enforcer.

"Did you and Brooks have this conversation already?" He hummed as my eyes adjusted to the darkness of the night before I started across the yard.

"Brooks, Garrett, and I did this morning while you were on your way home," Chase admitted shamelessly as if they hadn't been discussing a major portion of my life without me, but I bit down on the urge to snap at him because, knowing Chase, he was just doing what he did best, besides killing, trying to keep me happy.

"How about we have a discussion all together before I make my final decision, okay?" I asked him directly, pulling the ear piece out of my ear. He nodded happily before pressing his lips greedily to mine. "Let's get out of here before he comes back from his stupid party."

We took off silently, closing the quarter-mile distance between the estate and the waiting car and bike quickly in a jog. Before leaving, we both slipped into the car to scan through the files. I handed off half of the stack to Chase who immediately started to flip through the various pages. I found the dirt I was looking for on Frankie, his long list of crimes, where all his money was, and essentially how his entire empire was run, but unfortunately, I found something else. Something that made my blood run cold.

"Chase"—I tapped his arm and shoved the file into his hands—"Alloy Kings are on Frankie's payroll. They not only supply the girls for his escort ring and all his dark web porn, but they provide muscle and move his drugs and weapons while Frankie cleans their money through his casino." His lips pulled into a deep frown as he realized the implication. The Aces weren't just going up against a rival MC, they were taking on an entire underground mob empire. The Aces might be good and have numbers on their side, but they would get absolutely slaughtered going against them unprepared.

"You take all the files and head to the compound, get your guys, and we'll meet at the house. I'll head there and pull anything and everything we have on the Alloy Kings." I nodded in agreement as I stuffed the papers back into my bag. After giving Chase a passionate kiss, I slipped out of the car, hopped on the bike, and made my way straight to the Aces' acreage.

"Hey, Kiera," Kevin greeted since he was was working the front gate of the compound. "Brooks and them are at the back garage warehouse, you know where it is?" I shook my head, too focused on what we learned to mentally pull up the Aces' compound map. Kevin gave me directions, and I immediately sped to the location where a large metal building greeted me on the crest of a hill. Pulling up outside the door, I got off my bike and strode inside; anticipation for the long upcoming battle that I knew was on the horizon burned like acid in my stomach.

"Brooks! Garrett! Stone! Where you at?" I shouted out strolling around the large shelves full of motorcycle parts and piles of half-disassembled bikes.

"Back right corner!" Brooks' smooth voice echoed slightly throughout the metal building. I made a beeline for them, and by the time I reached them, I was panting. "Jesus, you look like you've seen a ghost, baby."

"We've got a problem," I huffed trying to catch my breath. "Is there anyone here? Any cameras or mics?" All three immediately straightened, faces falling into severe expressions with hard eyes and ticked jaws. Brooks shook his head. "I got Harbold's files."

"I would certainly hope so since you're a famous thief." Not even Stone's attitude could phase me. I just stared at him until he was done with his unnecessary commentary.

"That means it's bad," Garrett murmured, worry filling his emerald eyes as he looked at me.

"The Alloy Kings are on Frankie's payroll, essentially in a partnership with the mob," I admitted solemnly. Their eyes flared in understanding quickly; Stone's hand rubbed over his buzzed scalp while Garrett ground his teeth.

Brooks looked at me in contemplation.

"You have a plan, don't you?" His smooth tone soothed the frantic thoughts whipping around in my head about the situation. I gave him a conceited smile. *He knows me so well.*

"Not yet, but you bet your ass I will." I tilted my head toward the door. "Let's get to the house. Chase is pulling files as we speak." Within five minutes, we were on the road to the house, but what we came up to had me pushing my bike to its limit.

Flames engulfed the rubble that had once been my house. What wasn't burning in the fire was blown wide in shattered fragments. My stomach fell as my heart nearly stopped when I didn't see Chase anywhere, his Audi engulfed in the raging inferno. I didn't even stop to prop my bike up, letting it fall to the wayside as I ran toward the destruction.

"Chase!" I screamed, but an iron grip wrapped around me to keep me from running headlong into the fire.

"Baby." Brooks' voice was pained as he held me to his chest. My own screams drowned out all noise as I felt myself burn from the inside out at the sight of the fire and my home that had been blown to hell. *My little assassin...*

I don't know how long I struggled against Brooks until I finally stopped, my voice having given up long ago under the volume of my screaming cries. My body numbed from feeling and emotions as I stood stoic in the president's arms. Garrett and Stone handled the police and the fire department; after they had shown up and battled the out of control blaze, the fire died out.

The other two MC officers, despite the protests of the fire department and police, scoured the rubble, but came back empty handed, faces solemn as they looked at me.

Brooks' arms fell to his sides when he realized I wasn't going to run directly into a fiery death in a wave of despair, and he made a call. Within a half hour, over two dozen Aces members arrived to help the police canvas the large blast radius.

According to the detonations expert for the Aces, Rider Frost a.k.a. Blast, numerous well-placed pipe bombs and explosives were activated after the house had been doused in an accelerant. After the canvassing was complete, and the authorities as well as the MC members left, the sun had started to rise in the distance. Not even the growing light on the horizon could warm the ice that had solidified in my chest. The night had passed by in a numb haze, but finally, the three club officers gave me the news I had been hoping for.

No sign of Chase within the bomb site or in the remnants of my burned home.

At that pinprick sized amount of hope, my fury sparked, burning brighter and hotter than the fire that had destroyed the place I'd called home for the last four years. Resolution filled me as I stepped forward to the cooled rubble. Kneeling one leg down, I grabbed a handful of the ash and crumbled it, letting the wind blow the dust away.

"What are you going to do?" Stone's voice was quiet behind me as I felt the three of them creating a half circle behind me.

Staring out at the ruin in front of me, I answered, "I'm going to kill them. I'm going to kill them all."

MAY 5TH
SUNDAY MORNING
BROOKS

Leaning back against the office desk, I watched Kiera. My baby had been silent since we left her house, her face as flat as stone, but her eyes were what caught my attention. They burned and smoldered in silent fury, waiting to be unleashed on those who had targeted her and had taken her assassin. Her grave declaration echoing in my mind, I had no doubt she would do just that, but she didn't have to do it alone. I looked around the room at my fellow officers. Garrett and Stone appeared as angry as I was at the blatant attack on *our girl*. Nate came in, his face drawn in tension.

"It was definitely Alloy Kings, but no one knows where Chase would be at. They have dozens of shell companies and safe houses," Nate explained, pity filling his eyes as he looked at one of his oldest friends.

"Not to mention the fact it could be any one of Frank's properties," Garrett growled, running a hand over the back of his neck. "What's our next move, Boss?" I hesitated, looking over to Kiera.

"Do you have anything you need to do?" I questioned quietly, unsure of how she would react right now. She was a ticking time bomb and we all knew it. Her brown-green eyes that glowed in anger centered on me.

"Yes, I need to stop at The Bank." Her voice was flat, dead.

I furrowed my brows. *The bank? Whatever money she needed she could use from the club,* I thought.

She must have read my facial expression because she started to shake her head. "Not that kind of bank. I'll need a large vehicle." My curiosity growing with her request, I turned my attention to Nate who nodded before heading back out of the office to pull one of our crash vehicles out of the garage.

We filed out in a single line, down the hall and into the morning sun. Nate pulled up a moment later in a large

SUV. Switching places with Nate, Kiera got into the driver's seat while Garrett and Stone slid into the back seat.

"Keep me updated," I whispered to my Road Captain. "See if this is related to the snitch we have within the club."

He nodded as I climbed into the passenger seat. The drive was silent, not even the radio played as we headed wherever my baby needed to take us to. Over a half hour later, we entered Carson City, driving through the main portion of the city until we were on the outskirts pulling into a bank parking lot. Instead of parking in the front, she pulled around to the rear of the building and backed into the spot in front of a nondescript door.

"I thought it wasn't a normal bank?" I tilted my head in confusion.

"It's not," she muttered, her furious eyes staring at the building. "Come on, boys. I'll need all of you." Exiting the car, we walked all the way back around to the glass front doors. A bald man with plastic frame glasses looked up from his position behind the counter. His teeth were bright white against his dark skin as he smiled.

"Ah, Ms. Kitty," he exclaimed, his voice rising in excitement as he addressed Kiera. I had to force myself not to question the blatant alias. "Need to make a withdrawal?" She nodded.

"I also need to visit the backroom, Dwight." She smiled at the bank worker whose tag read: Dwight Abrams, Manager. My curiosity continued to grow as he nodded and led us to a side hallway and down a long staircase.

Jesus, we have to be down at least three floors at this point, I thought as I let my gaze wander around the concrete room at the base of the stairs. All four walls held thick vault doors, all of which were behind barred enclosures. Stone was looking around the place in appreciation as Garrett eyed Kiera.

"Which vault this visit?" Dwight pulled out a set of keys as Kiera did the same. She smiled wickedly; the Devil himself would cower in fear at the look.

"All of them." Even Dwight's eyes widened as he stepped up to the first wall.

"Are we to expect you back again after this visit?" His question's double meaning was clear—are you going to live long enough to come back?

"I would like to think so, I just have some business to tend to, Dwight. No need to fret about me." Her words were polite as she unlocked all of the barred gates and the manager stepped up to the first vault. Dwight dipped his head, spinning in the combination for the lock and turning his own key in the thick door.

"Of course, Miss Kitty. The Bank just wants to make sure its proprietress will be around in the future." The vault unlocked with a loud clunk before he moved to the next three doors.

I studied Kiera; her chin raised high as if she sat on a throne. *Although my baby's crown would be made of gold and the most expensive jewels she could get her little thief hands on, it would also be dipped in the blood of her enemies.* It just occurred to me that he had said proprietress, meaning this bank's existence was owed to Kiera, and whatever was held in these vaults was hers and hers alone.

"Let me know if you need anything else, but it looks like you're in good hands." Dwight dipped his head flashing a wolf-in-sheep's-clothing smile to the rest of us before starting back up the stairs. We stood in stoic silence until we heard the door at the top of the stairs shut.

"What is this place, Kiera?" Garrett demanded quietly as he stepped up to her, his hand resting on her lower back bringing her attention to him. Her smile was cruel, as if she really did wear a bloody crown of stolen jewels atop a throne of bones. Hitting a button on the wall that I hadn't noticed before, all the vault doors swung open in a hiss of hydraulic air.

"They wanted a battle," she murmured, her words manic and crazed. Her furious eyes flared brighter as her lips curled in a snarl. "I'll bring them a war."

Looking around, I felt my jaw drop. The first vault was large and filled to the brim with guns, ammunition, and wickedly sharp knives. The second held even deadlier equipment like explosives, grenades, and... *are those rocket launchers?* I couldn't believe my eyes as I turned once more, greeted with a vault of gear-like harnesses, pulleys, rope, and a large rack of different sized black or desert camo clothing. Finally, the last vault was filled with what I had expected from The Cat: money, file cabinets, and stolen goods including famous paintings, jewels, and artifacts.

"Jesus," I breathed making another circle. Stone was stunned into silence, for once not snarking on every single thing Kiera did, while Garrett looked at her as if he'd never seen her before.

"When..." I stuttered attempting to get my brain to work. "How?" She chuckled; the sound wasn't pleasant but as cold and biting as the arctic ice.

"There's a lot about me you don't know, Brooks." She eyed me predatorily, deadly. This wasn't the baby I had come to know, this was someone dark and lethal, someone any smart person ought to be afraid of. "You'll learn, of course, but to start"—she waved her hand out—"this is one of my stashes."

"One? One of your stashes?" Stone finally spoke, his question littered with surprise.

"You think I'd be stupid enough to leave all my shit at my house?" she sassed him, a brow raising. "Fuck no. I knew years ago I would go after Frankie, and when I did"—she nodded after pausing, seeing a plan in her head that the rest of us couldn't—"I would bring all of Hell with me."

What had Frankie done to her to burn her so badly? I found myself asking quietly in my head as I watched my baby. This wasn't the kind of anger from being burned, I realized. No, this was the kind of loathing one had after years of staring down evil itself before walking away carrying only scars she could see.

"How long have you planned to go after Frankie 'Smokes'?" Stone asked.

My baby's eyes darkened into that depth of rage at the question. Silence reigned as we waited for her answer, Garrett's jaw clenching, but he couldn't hide the pity in his expression. He knew what had happened to her, and based on his facial expression as he looked at her, it was very, *very* bad. Garrett didn't pity, ever, until her.

"Since I was seven," she finally whispered. Striding into the first vault, she piled up a duffle with guns and ammunition, effectively ending the conversation.

Frankie 'Smokes' Casterelli's death just moved to one of my top things to deal with.

Right after getting back Chase and fucking over the Alloy Kings.

It's going to be a long ride...

CHAPTER 12

MAY 5TH
SUNDAY EVENING
KIERA

For the fifth time since leaving The Bank, I double checked my pocket to ensure the flash drive was still there. Not that I didn't have more copies, but I didn't want to have to go back to dig it out of the vault. We unloaded the vehicle into one of the unmarked buildings at the edge of the property that was never used. Nate returned the SUV to its usual home after we finished. We would be back later to separate the gear between the four officer houses, each of which were equipped with hidden rooms to hide the weapons and other miscellaneous gear I had loaded up. I didn't have a plan yet on how to get Chase back and hit the Alloy Kings where it hurts, but when I did, I wanted everything I could possibly need at my disposal.

Sipping the glass of alcohol Cheryl had placed in front of me, I sank into my usual stool at the bar. I sat without seeing, but I felt the gazes on me from the club members and the hang-arounds, their eyes lingering on my thigh holsters. I wasn't holding back at this point; the Alloy Kings had gone too far, so I had loaded up on my weapons not giving a fuck how I looked to anyone else.

Brooks sank into the seat on my left while Stone took

the right. Garrett opted to stand, his hand going to my shoulder and neck like he had the night we fucked, but my mind was solely out for blood, unable to focus on any sexual desires. It was only a few minutes of solemn, tense silence between the four of us until my phone dinged, but the sounds of shouts behind us pulled me away from checking it.

"Brooks Abbott!" a familiar smarmy voice called out and, turning on the stool, I spotted Alloy Kings President Bryce Hill backed by his VP Ronnie boy and that bastard Jace Corden who was attempting to glance around Garrett as he stepped in front of me. "My, my it's been a long time, 'asn't it?"

"What do you want?" Brooks questioned dully from his seat, his forearm resting on the bar as he took a drink. Shifting to standing, the three officers created a wall between them and me.

"We'd like to offer you a little trade," Bryce tittered. "You see, we have something you might like. A certain assassin..." At the mention of Chase, I shot out of my chair. Garrett barely held me back from shooting the three of them in the knees.

"Ah"—Ron's eyes lit up in recognition—"I never would have guessed, *Miss Wright*," he sneered my alias. The club members' eyes flickered to me in confusion, but I didn't attempt to quell their curiosity, my entire focus on what they had to bring up about *my assassin*.

"As I was saying," Bryce took over, "we want to trade you the assassin."

"For what in return?" Stone scoffed his question, clearly not up for whatever game they were attempting to play.

"Her," Jace finally spoke, his rough,deep voice bringing back memories I had to fight to push away. His bright brown eye centered on me as he stepped forward, the black material of his eye patch scuffed up in the light. "The assassin for my Kiera. Or if you prefer, The Cat." Murmurs and whispers ran through the crowd at my identity. Garrett pulled me tighter against him at Jace's predatory smile. Brooks stepped forward and angled himself in front of me.

"She's not yours, Corden," he ground out. His brow went up, attention shifting back to Garrett and me.

"I see my girl's mentioned me then." His wicked smile was crooked from his facial scarring. "Glad I was memorable." I bit back the urge to throw up. "But that's not the conversation right now. You want the assassin? You give us the girl. You have until tomorrow evening to make your decision." Without any more conversation, they left, Jace smirking at me once more on his way out.

The bar was silent as everyone stared at me, understanding filling their eyes. Garrett squeezed me once before releasing. Now that the confrontation was done, I pulled out my phone to check it.

Dipshit: *Deer*

My heart clenched painfully at the message, but I had no idea what Chase meant. Grabbing Brooks' sleeve, I dragged him down the hall to the office. Garrett and Stone followed quickly, their faces filled with confusion at my abrupt movement. As soon as the door shut, I started to pace, my mind running through what he could have meant. It wasn't a term of endearment, and it didn't make sense as a location.

"Hey, Boss." Nate's voice filtered in from the door frame. "The boys want to talk to you about everything." His voice was grave, meaning they weren't happy with me being in the middle of this shit show, but right now I didn't care. Brooks sighed before directing me toward the door not bothering to ask why I dragged him back here. The talking in the room quieted as we entered, the tension and accusing eyes on us. Brooks addressed the room, but I wasn't focusing on what he said, Chase's message holding my entire focus. Finally looking up, I glanced around the room for any semblance of a clue when my eyes landed on *her*.

Deer.

Bambi.

"Brooks," I bit out in the middle of his statement. "I know who our snitch is." He immediately stopped talking to look at me, his eyes burning. Shoving the phone in his hand, I stormed over to the bleached blonde bimbo who attempted to dart toward the door, but I was faster. I grabbed her hair and dragged her to the middle of the room.

"You little fucking cunt," I angrily spouted out as I tossed her onto the ground. Without hesitation, I had the sweet satisfaction of her nose crunching under my fist. I saw red.

My house was destroyed because of her.

The Aces had lost a shipment because of her.

My assassin had been *taken from me* because of her.

I continued to throw punches, and the feeling of her nails on my arms didn't phase me as I felt her blood splatter my face. After what felt like an eternity in a single second, Garrett's harsh voice pulled me back to myself, Stone's angry face appearing in my vision as he yanked her beaten and broken body to standing.

"Kitten!" Garrett shouted as I punched her once more in the stomach. "We'll get him back, Kitten." His hand soothingly rubbed circles on my back as I heaved in sharp breaths. The fucking snitch spit blood at my feet, her knees giving out. The only reason she didn't fall to the ground was Stone's excessively tight grip on her arms.

"Fuck you, bitch," she slurred through the blood that poured down her face. Brooks immediately stepped in front of her, my phone extended toward me, another text had come in. A GPS pin showing Chase's location.

"Why did you betray the club?" Brooks' smooth voice demanded in outrage. She glared at him, and when she didn't answer, he grabbed her bloody face in a vise-like grip. She screamed an answer.

"I didn't know! I didn't know he was an Alloy King! I was just out with some guy and drank too much," she half-sobbed half-laughed, the shock making her delirious. "I swear it was an accident!" I glanced at Garrett who was looking at her in disgust, his jaw ticking at her confession. Brooks and Stone glared harshly at her as she spoke, no pity or forgiveness within any of the officers' eyes.

"Get her the fuck out of here," Brooks commanded Stone before addressing her once more. "You're burned in the underworld from this point onward. If I think you've so much as blinked in our, her, or the club's direction, I will gladly hand you over to my baby and let her deal with you as she sees fit. Trust me though"—he crowded her space—"she will make you wish you had been killed long before she buries you out back. Got it?"

Stone dragged her out of the bar immediately after Brooks had finished talking. Garrett directed me through the hall and out the back door, taking me toward the side building we had deposited our stash in earlier.

"Stay here"—he kissed my forehead—"we'll be in to figure out a plan after we talk with the guys."

I stood still, nodding, the numbness leeching my emotions away. As soon as the door was shut, I couldn't wait. I packed as much as I could carry in terms of guns, ammo, knives, and even a smoke grenade on my person before pulling up the GPS pin. It was a small shack only ten minutes from here. Leaving a note on the desk, I left the building and the compound heading straight for the Alloy Kings and *my assassin.*

♠ ♠ ♠

Parking half a mile away, I situated my bike under the debris of a few fallen trees, the broken splintered bark covering the shiny surface of my black bike. I stuck to whatever landscape I came across and made my way to the small, two bedroom ranch where they were keeping Chase. Based on the floor plans I could scour on my way over, there was a kitchen, cramped living room, bathroom, and one bedroom upstairs, while the second bedroom was downstairs, a small hall door separating the stairs from the room.

There were two men walking in a rotation around the edge of the yard, one in the front while the other paced the back. Dropping behind a bush, I waited for the man patrolling the front yard to come close. Sliding out the large knife I had stuffed in my boot holster, I calmed the torrent of emotions that swirled within me as I got into position remembering everything Chase had taught me. When the man came, I shifted quickly around the bush and, before he could make as much as a whimper, he lay in a pool of his own blood on the desert dirt. I continued silently around the house; the other guard was bored as hell and too busy messing with his phone to see me coming.

Two down. Unknown number to go.

Peeking in through one of the dusty windows I scanned the room. There were three guards in the main floor that I could see.

"Why the fuck are we even doing this stupid shit?" one of the men scoffed. "We aren't damn babysitters, even if Chains and that fancy bastard Corden say we need to watch him. This is complete bullshit and we better be fucking paid extra for having to drive all the way here."

I zeroed in on the mention of Jace and Bryce Hill's road name, staying stone still in my spot as they continued to bitch about the situation.

"Who even bloody cares about this wanker downstairs?" This Alloy King had a choppy British accent, his face was covered in a variety of tattoos that shifted as he talked. "I just say we take him outside and shoot the arsehole." I bit back a growl at his threat. *Over my dead fucking body, you expat bastard*, I thought, *I think I'll kill you first.*

"Both of you, knock it off." The third one finally called an end to the complaints in a gruff command. "Metal, you're with me," he directed to the non-expat, his thumb hitching to another area of the house. Standing up, the two of them went into the kitchen leaving the third alone.

Seizing the moment when the British asshole turned away from the entrance to this hell hole of a house, I bolted in. I plunged the knife into his throat, reveling in the feeling of his esophagus giving way to my blade. Unfortunately, he was more of a fighter than the two outside and kicked the rickety coffee table, resulting in a loud thump. The noise must have alerted the other two Alloy Kings because they came rushing in as he bled out all over the ratty carpet. Throwing several punches, I somehow avoided getting shot, but I didn't escape getting kicked in the ribs.

Fucking bastard, that hurt!

Fuck it. I pulled out my Glock and figured the time for subtlety was over. My anger started to burn in the background, the numbness that had blanketed over me slowly receding as I quickly put two bullets in each of them. Rolling my shoulders back, I straightened my shirt and eyed the room until I spotted the door to the basement. Channeling my inner-Chase, I strode silently and confidently down the stairs into the basement. There were two voices talking loudly on the other side about what they should do.

"Fuck, man, I don't know!" the first one shouted. "Check out in the hall and see if you can see anything." I pressed my back against the wall by the opening of the door in the small alcove between the stairs and the basement bedroom. A surly-looking man peeked his head out and looked around not seeing me in the shadows of the darkened hall.

"I don't see anything odd," he spouted to his partner in the room. "The guys could just be watching a movie upstairs. I'll go check real quick." Sliding out of the room he shut the door behind him. I silently followed him up several steps before slicing his throat. The only sound in the house was the thud of him falling against the carpeted stairs, his meaty hands clutching his wounded neck in a useless attempt to stop the bleeding.

Making sure my faceguard was secure and that my braid wasn't falling out, I closed the distance between me and the room where Chase was. A whoosh of the air conditioning kicking on brushed against the top of my head shifting the uncovered strands of hair. I closed my eyes and took a deep, centering breath. The numbness took control. Focus. Rage would only hinder me when I entered the room. I needed to let the rage fuel my actions but keep my mind clear. The severity of what I'd done was not even a blip on my radar because getting Chase back was my only goal. When I felt centered enough, I readied my gun and opened the door.

I was faster than the man standing to the left of Chase who was tied to a chair, getting the jump on him trying to wrestle his weapon out of his hand. He shouted obscenities as I elbowed his jaw and smashed his hand against the wall. The plaster dented and cracked under the force of the hits. The gun he was holding dropped to the ground in a thud. Kicking out, I caught him in the knee which gave me space to unload three bullets into his torso. Fuck. I growled at the fact he was still alive, only one of my two shots hitting a vital organ while the other hit his shoulder. Jumping forward, I stomped on the hand going for his discarded weapon. The sound of bones crunching beneath the tread was drowned out by his girly screams.

"How?" he coughed, blood starting to fill his mouth. I smiled, feeling that dark part of me that I tried to keep contained, the one Frankie instilled in me long ago, come forward.

"You planned for a thief," I murmured, my voice sounding crazed to my own ears. "Not an assassin." Immediately following my words, I placed another round between his eyes. Now that they were dead and the job was done, the emotions flooded in. Anger. Despair. *Fear.* I tucked my gun away and slid the knife into its sheath as I dropped in front of Chase.

"My little assassin," I whispered, my words cracking under the emotions surging through me. Tears pricked my eyes as I pulled the strip of duct tape over his mouth. His eyes were bright and cheery, a hint of lust burning in his molten depths.

"I knew you'd figure it out." He was giddy, completely unperturbed that he was still tied to a chair in a rival safehouse. "I'm just glad they were really shitty kidnappers; didn't even find the phone I had tucked in my waistband. Can you believe that?" He scoffed as if he was really blown away by their stupidity.

"I don't give two fucks, Chase Yarwood, if they were the stupidest or the smartest kidnappers. All that matters is that I've got you. Fuck, I love you so much." I cupped his shaggy face tightly between my palms. The scruff had grown slightly without him trimming it as he did every morning. Pressing my lips to his, I drank him in. He wasn't injured that I could see, no cuts or bruises, and that's when it all became too much, and a few tears leaked from my eyes.

"Aw, Kittycat," he practically purred, "don't cry. You know I'll always come back to you, my love." He nuzzled my hair as he spoke, and my attention moved to his wrists and ankles where I cut the ropes freeing him from his prison. "I'll call the Maintenance Man to come out while we head back to the compound."

"Let's go." I nodded, my tears drying as he made the call. Within five minutes, we were on the dusty road back to the Aces.

MAY 5TH
SUNDAY NIGHT
GARRETT

I sighed. Stone was silent behind me and Brooks didn't look too concerned about the members after having spoken to them. It took the last half hour to convince them, but once they understood Kiera wasn't here to cause any trouble within the club, only to help, they backed off on their complaints. The door to the storage building opened quietly, but the silence inside the room was what had me pausing.

No Kiera.

Missing weapons.

"What the fuck!" I shouted as I barrelled into the room. Spotting a piece of scrap paper with Kiera's girly handwriting, I scooped it up.

I'll be back.

That was it, nothing else. I growled and shoved the note into Brooks' hands before storming out of the building and back toward the bar. None of us had gotten the GPS coordinates from Kiera's phone, so we couldn't leave to go searching for her and Chase. The party in the bar was toned down more than normal, the music barely on while most of the patch holders kept their distance from hang-arounds, not wanting to be caught with anyone who could betray the club. I paced in front of the counter after snatching a glass of whiskey from Cheryl. Brooks and Stone were only a few steps behind me, both looking just as worried.

"I can't believe her." I ground my teeth together. *That little...*

"I can. Did you really expect her to stand by and wait when she knew where he was?" Brooks countered, taking a seat at the bar. "She isn't exactly the patient type." I rolled my eyes.

"Trust me, she actually is the patient type, but what she doesn't understand is the difference between having balls and being stupid." I felt my heart sputter to a stop when the talking throughout the bar silenced.

Kiera confidently strode through the door, Chase looking as happy as ever right behind her. She was armed to the teeth, blood spattered across her tanned face. Her hands were covered in dried red stains and her knuckles were cracked and bleeding. She held her head high as she walked through the room and came directly up to us. She even had the balls to smirk at me.

"I told you'd I'd be back." She chuckled, her mood significantly improved since earlier. Chase patted Stone and Brooks sharply on the back as he smiled, his hand taking mine to shake.

"Ah, yay, the gang's here! I sure did miss you guys," he parroted. "Those Alloy Kings were a bunch of idiots. I mean, seriously, they didn't even try to have a conversation with me! You'd think after being rude enough to take me from my own house they'd oblige me by answering my questions while I waited for my rescue, but no," he huffed. "Little bastards just decided to duct tape my mouth shut instead." We were silent as we stared at them.

"Jesus." Brooks shook his head to come out of his stupor. "Did you seriously go after him all by yourself?" She nodded and shrugged.

"They took what's mine." She said it as if that perfectly explained her running head first into a deadly situation alone. I felt my blood boil.

"Are you out of your fucking mind?" I growled, getting in her face. The closer I moved in the more I noticed how much blood was actually covering her. "What about going after a rival's safehouse, *by yourself*," I emphasized the last part, "sounded like it would be a good idea, Kiera?" Her lips curled into a scowl as she glared at me.

"I knew I could do it," she snapped. "You're welcome, by the way. The Alloy Kings are now down seven members." A gasp could be heard from one of the patch holders at her words, and Stone eyed her in appreciation while Brooks seemed surprised. I knew she could handle herself, but fuck, I didn't want her to get hurt.

"You didn't have to do it by yourself," I hissed, my anger burning at the fact that she had left and she might never have come back. *I just got her, I can't lose her now.* "You have people at your back, but you're too fucking stubborn and hard-headed to see past your own damned selfishness." Her eyes flared, not in anger this time, but an emotion I didn't think I'd ever seen in her eyes, hurt. Instead of snapping at me or fighting me like she usually did, she turned without another word and walked out of the bar.

"Nice, Gar," Chase chastised, his words exasperated. "I think she's been through enough the last few days. She can handle herself, and she doesn't really need you fucking hounding her right now." It rubbed me the wrong way that he was lecturing me.

Grinding my teeth, I snapped back. "I fucking know that"—I took a half step closer to him—"but that doesn't change the fact that what she did was reckless and stupid. She went in without a plan and without backup up against an unknown number of people. One of these days, her actions are going to get her killed. How are you going to handle that then, huh?" Chase stayed silent, but I saw in his grey eyes that he couldn't fathom a life without Kiera in it. Sighing, I followed Kiera's path and stepped out into the desert evening.

If I were Kiera, where would I go? Turning my head slightly, I eyed the face of the building. I curled around the side of the clubhouse and came to the fire escape. Climbing up the rusty ladder, I found Kiera sitting on top of the center building on the roof where the main heating and air unit was. I grasped the edge of the little structure and heaved myself up. My kitten was sitting with her knees bent in front of her, her tattooed arms wrapped around them as she looked out at the compound's grounds and the outside stretch of Nevada landscape. I sank into the same position she sat in, and memories of us doing this when we were younger and she needed to escape Frankie's house flooded me, only this time she wasn't a broken teenager, but a fierce woman.

"I see you found me," she murmured, eyes staying on the night covered desert. I smiled slightly as a single laugh fell from my lips.

"I'll always find you, Kiera," I admitted quietly. "I didn't mean to yell at you..."

"Yes you did, Garrett," she cut me off, but her words weren't harsh as she smiled slightly. "That's what we're good at." Her eyes flicked to me, lit with a teasing glint as she smiled. My chest crushed under the thought of losing her. "I'm... I'm sorry," she stuttered in a barely audible whisper. "I'm not used to having people to lean on and, to be quite honest to answer your question earlier, I wasn't thinking. I just acted. I know it was dumb, and looking back, I'm surprised I didn't get anything more than the bruised ribs."

"Let me see." I shifted, my fingers coming to the hem of her blood covered shirt and lifting it up. A darkening boot print was splayed on her ribs. Bruised, but not broken. "It's probably a good thing *you* killed them and not me, because I would have been far more brutal. No one gets to hurt you and get away with it." She chuckled, her mossy eyes finally returning to normal after the fucking shit show of the last 24 hours.

"I'll make sure to hand over anyone who does." She

paused dramatically. "If there's anything left of them after I'm done with them."

Scooting closer, I curled my kitten in my left arm to bring her between my legs. Her warm muscled back pressed against my chest as her hair tickled my jaw. I propped myself up with my right hand behind me and held her to me as we watched the world around us for a while, no one but us and the Nevada desert. My mind drifted back to the first time we ever did this.

"Garrett Oliver Newlyn," my mother snapped, smacking the side of my head sharply. "Get your damn shoes on, we're going to be late." I grumbled to myself but complied knowing she'd throw her empty bottle at me if I didn't. I laced up my boots quickly, surprised she was even sober enough to go to dinner with this fucking tool she'd been seeing. I glanced over at her; she was wearing an expensive dress and a shiny strand of pearls. How the fuck did she afford that after pissing the money away on her last batch of heroine and booze? *I pushed back the question and focused on tying my second boot.*

We climbed into the beat up sedan that barely ran half the time and started down the road, heading toward another part of town I never spent any time in. Where the hell are we going? *I internally groaned seeing the worn down houses turn to posh estates and mansions finally figuring out she'd been pegging a rich dude for his money. I kept my mouth shut knowing she would make me walk home if I said anything, and I didn't want to call any of the patch holders at the club for a ride since I had just started hanging around recently. We pulled into a fucking giant driveway to an even more massive house approximately twenty minutes later.*

"He has a daughter," my mom informed me as we got out of the car. "She's around your age. Be nice," she hissed. I rolled my eyes, of course she would keep that information to herself until the last possible fucking moment. I schooled my face into a bland mask as she rang the doorbell. I could hear the ringing echo through the house. How fucking big is this stupid place?

"Hello, Barbie," a man greeted. He was polished to perfection in his suit and gelled hair, complete opposite to me in my ripped up jeans and barely combed mess of dirty brown hair atop my head. I wanted to roll my eyes at the nickname he gave her, mainly because when she was dolled up like she was now she looked like the hooker she was. She tittered at him kissing her on the cheek, and his cold brown eyes centered on me judging everything about me. "You must be Garrett," he added dismissively before holding out his hand for me to shake. I stared at it with no intention to return it, but my mom's sharp elbow in my side reminded me to try and be polite.

After he released my hand, he moved out of the door way allowing us to enter, and my eyes darted around the space in distaste. Everything was either marble, polished to a high shine, or a deep, stained wood. How the fuck did my shit mom end up with a man as well-off as this? Another man with blond hair that was gelled in a similar style to my mom's latest victim strode into the room. What's up with all the gel on these rich bastards? He was followed by a thin girl who looked to be a year or two younger than me with dirty blonde hair that was braided over her shoulder. She wore a pair of nice slacks and a white blouse that made her tan skin stand out. She kept her head bowed slightly staying at least five feet away from the blond who stared at her harshly. Her eyes were a dark green mixed with a honeyed brown that reminded me of moss as she glanced up at me from under her lashes. Her gaze warmed as they worked their way down my tight shirt and jeans, but she didn't say anything or make any moves to introduce herself.

"Barbie, Garrett, I would like to introduce my daughter Kiera and her bodyguard Lorenzo," the man, Frank, if I remembered correctly, introduced the two. I shook the bodyguard's hand first. As I stared at his face, something about him put me off, he seemed slimy. Pushing the odd thought away, I held my hand out for Kiera whose lips thinned as she stared at it. "Kiera," Frank's tone went from friendly to ice cold in a second, and her jaw ticked on the side he wouldn't be able to see as she slipped a calloused hand into mine. How would the pampered daughter of a rich man earn so many callouses?

"Kiera, this is Barbie," Frank continued his introductions, his eyes frigid as he stared down his daughter who quietly huffed before shaking my mother's hand.

"Pleasure to meet you, Ms. Newlyn," Kiera said, her voice low and husky. The throaty quality caught my attention, and I felt myself needing to shift to keep from sporting a boner in a room full of new people.

"Please," my mother started, shaking Kiera's hand gently, "call me Barbie." I couldn't hold back the eye roll this time. When my gaze focused back on Kiera, she had a curious expression trained on me, but since we were surrounded by people, neither of us spoke to each other. Frank and my mother continued to talk as he led her into an adjacent hall, their voices fading until it was silent. The creepy bodyguard continued to glance between Kiera and the direction his boss went before he finally made up his decision to follow, but not before speaking to Kiera.

"Stay out of trouble," he murmured, his lips curled into

a cruel smile. My brows furrowed at the tone of menace within his voice. Either he really was creepy or she was a troublemaker. She glared back, her fingers twitching at her sides.

"All right," she ground out, her mossy eyes spitting fire at the bodyguard who chuckled again, taking half a step forward to her.

"Wouldn't want you to be punished for disobeying your father, now would you?" he questioned softly. Alarm bells rang within my mind at her paling face, but before either of us could respond, Lorenzo strode confidently out of the room. I watched him leave and when I turned to look at Kiera, I found myself alone. What the... I didn't even hear her move.

Unsure of what came over me, I started toward the direction she originally came from and at the end of the short hall, I saw a pair of black pants and a tanned arm curving around another hall through a set of double wood doors. I followed, my curiosity piqued by the girl whose fiery eyes burned at her father and bodyguard, yet stayed silent at their demands.

The set of rooms was empty when I entered, but an open set of balcony doors caught my attention. The white curtains billowed in the breeze as I walked past. She wasn't out here, but I looked up in time to see a tanned foot disappear over the edge of the roof above. Glancing around the face of the mansion, I found nearly invisible foot and hand holds within the stone. I knew I should have stopped, but something about the girl called to me, I just wasn't sure if it was her fiery spirit I saw in her eyes or the fact that she was beautiful.

Either way, I followed her up and found her perched on the very top of the flat roof, her lean body standing near one of the other edges of the space. I felt my heart race. Is she going to jump? *I started toward her quickly.*

"Hey," I called out. Her head whipped to me before she scowled deeply.

"What?" she barked, her arms crossing her torso and calling attention to her perky tits.

I had to force myself to keep looking at her face. The closer I got the more I realized she was different up here than she was down in the entryway. She didn't bow her head, and she didn't cower. Instead, her eyes centered on my face as she watched me carefully.

"Why the fuck did you follow me?"

My brows shot up at the vulgar language. I wouldn't have expected a rich girl to have the balls to talk the way the guys around the compound did.

"Fuck you very much," she snapped taking half a step towards me, "I'm not just some fucking rich girl." I realized I had said my internal thought out loud, but I ended up rolling my eyes instead of apologizing. She had her own wing to the house, she was the very definition of rich girl.

"Whatever you say," I countered finally glancing around me. The estate's acreage spread for a long distance before finally giving way to the Nevada landscape and more lavish homes, but I noted this was the largest house within the immediate vicinity.

"Go fucking bother Frankie and your mother and leave me be," she bit out sinking to the pebbly surface of the roof. "I like my time away from people." She glared up at me like I was impeding that. Which technically I was, but I couldn't help it. I stared down at her; her honeyed hair was wavy on top of her head as her thin arms curled around her knees, holding them tightly to her chest. Her eyes stayed focused on the landscape intent on ignoring me.

"Well, I certainly don't want to be around my mother or your asshole of a dad," I pushed seeing how she would respond to my insults. She scoffed, her own eyes rolling at the statement before glancing at me in suspicion as I sank down next to her, following her lead and wrapping my knees up in my arms

"What do you want from me?" she murmured intensely, her eyes narrowing. I stared at her flawless skin—smooth with only the lightest bit of shadowed freckles across the bridge of her nose. Her luscious pink lips curled down in a cute frown, but her eyes held my attention the most. Filled with fire, haunted ghosts, and within the swirling depths a huge pool of anger simmered and a hint of something akin to fear threaded through the furious flames. What would she have to be angry about? What would she fear up here in her posh ivory tower?

"Nothing," I answered honestly, shrugging one shoulder. "I'm only here because my mother dragged me along to meet the guy she's been fucking." Kiera stared a little while longer, but she must have realized I was telling the truth before looking back out across the yard.

"All right. You can stay up here," she muttered, "just stay quiet. I like my time away from fucking prissy wives, fat cat men, and lavish parties."

I nodded, lost in thought as we watched the sun start to set, neither of us wanting to go back inside to our waiting parents.

I could get used to this...

CHAPTER 13

Chase's gunpowder and musk smell filled my nose as he shifted under me, his scruff scratchy against my scalp as he nuzzled me in his sleep. My right arm was draped over his sculpted upper body, his arms tight around me. I barely opened my eyes to see the morning sun filtering into the spare bedroom of Brooks' home. Being warm and comfortable in the arms of my assassin, I tried to go back to sleep after having been up until the wee hours of the morning with Garrett, but Chase had other ideas. His hands started to knead my back and sides in leisurely caresses. I tilted my head back and peered up at him. His eyes were two molten pools of steel filled with crazed lust.

"Good morning, my little kittycat," he murmured quietly. His whispers were rough with sleepiness. I smiled and trailed my forefinger down his nose before poking the end of it with a soft 'boop.'

"Morning." My voice cracked as I stretched, my muscles trembling under the movement. Chase took the opportunity to skim his calloused palms over my stomach toward my chest, the shirt I'd stolen from Brooks to sleep in bunching up around my ribs. With a soft smile at me

Chase pressed his lips to mine in a gentle kiss, the heat emanating from his body seeping into me. I cupped his scratchy jaw as he rolled to cover me, his trim waist and boxer-covered hips settling between my thighs. His cock was hard and pressing deliciously against me, and my body and blood buzzed at the feeling, finally waking from their sleepy state.

Grinding against me, Chase pulled a soft moan from me as he rolled over my sensitive pussy. I nipped his lower lip. Tangled my fingers into his hair. A groan rumbled deep in his chest as I tugged at his hair, the sharp pull causing him to surge his hips once more. His kisses trailed languidly toward my jaw and to my neck. Turning my head, my eyes focused on the door to the room that was almost all the way closed. A sharp bite made my pussy tighten in response, and my eyelids fluttered shut.

"Oh, shit." Brooks' smooth voice filled the room as he stood in the now open door. "My bad." He went to leave and close the door when Chase called out.

"Where you going?"

Brooks' grey-blue eyes focused on Chase's steel ones as he stopped moving out of the room. Chase waved a hand signifying for the president to come in. Brooks' brows furrowed, but he didn't protest as he stepped in and closed the door softly behind him. I watched him stare as Chase returned his attentions to my neck. The bulge in Brooks' jeans grew the longer he watched, his eyes darkening into stormy depths as he looked at me. I crooked a finger at him, my greedy pussy reveling in the thought of having both of them.

Shucking his cut over a chair in the corner, he let his riding boots thud softly against the hardwood flooring when he closed the distance between us. He kneeled on the ground next to the bed, his fingers tangling into my hair as Chase shifted down the bed. Brooks' eyes lit up when he saw the shirt I was wearing.

"You look good in my clothes, baby," he murmured, his lips barely brushing against mine, "but you look even better out of them." He helped get the old t-shirt over my head before returning his hand to my hair and delivering a rough kiss that had me shivering under Chase who had moved down to kiss my left breast. My heart was thundering in my chest at their attention, and my hands wandered over hard muscles and taut planes. Chase's tongue swirled and flicked around my nipple as Brooks palmed my other breast, the rough pad of his thumb barely brushing over the stiff peak.

Brooks finally pulled back from our kiss, his eyes tracking Chase's nip at my stomach on his way down to my hips. Leaning forward, I pressed my lips to Brooks' pulsing neck, my tongue darting out against his warm skin. I kept my attention on Brooks while Chase slid my thong down my legs, I assumed to toss it over his shoulder. A shuddering moan ripped from my throat when my assassin sucked hard on my clit, and a graze of teeth on the bundle of nerves had my back arching against Brooks' hand.

My eyes fluttered open when I felt Brooks pull away from me, his attention on untying his riding boots. Standing, he pulled his shirt over his head, a swath of tanned skin greeting me. A large chest tattoo shifted and moved with his powerful muscles as he unbuttoned his dark wash jeans. His torso was bulky and defined, but not as cut as Chase's. My mouth watered at the sight of his tented briefs, his thick cock clearly outlined in the light grey fabric. I glanced down at Chase who had paused in his sensuous ministrations; his lips curled in a wicked smile as he eyed Brooks' masculine form.

Through some silent communication between the two of them, they switched places. Chase kneeled where Brooks had been next to the bed, his lips and tongue coated in my dripping arousal. Moaning against his mouth, I drank the taste of myself as we battled for dominance. Brooks' hands rested on both of my thighs, running up until his thumb brushed against my sensitive clit. Two fingers circled my entrance torturously slow before slipping in as my right hand wrapped around Chase's hard cock inside his boxers. I groaned painfully when Brooks continued to tease.

"More," I begged, my voice breathless as Chase rocked forward against my grip in a shuddering pulse. At my command, Brooks obliged, pushing in and curling until the tips of his fingers hit me at just the right spot. I lightly tugged on Chase as I opened my mouth. Taking the hint, he took his boxers off and pressed the head of his throbbing cock against my lips. I licked the bead of pre-cum from his head before I sank my mouth around him. Lost in my own pleasure at Brooks' fingers, I couldn't tell which one of them was moaning, but it fueled me onward pushing me to take Chase fully at an urgent pace. Brooks' tongue lapped at my clit and around his fingers, and the sudden heat of his mouth had my pace faltering.

I pulled back from Chase as my orgasm slammed down on me, my hand tightening around him and Brooks' hair that I had grasped in my fist. My screams were swallowed up as Chase descended, his tongue brushing against mine. When the aftershocks finally subsided, I focused on what was happening around me. Chase was passing a condom to Brooks, both of them talking in inaudible whispers. Propping myself up on my elbows, I narrowed my eyes at them. *Damn troublemakers*, I thought, *but fucking sexy troublemakers.*

"Roll on your side," Brooks murmured sinfully smooth in my ear. He crawled on the bed and nestled himself behind me. Once I was lying on my right side, I watched Chase sink into the chair, his hand fisted around his cock stroking leisurely. My skin burned under his perusal as Brooks' hand hooked my leg over his hip so my flooded pussy was bared to my assassin. Without much fanfare, Brooks' thick cock lined up before pushing in with short rocks. My eyes rolled back when he was finally seated fully within me, my head leaning back against Brooks' warm bicep. Moaning in pleasure, he thrust in. Quicker. Harder.

Chase's pained, yet gleeful groan had me opening my eyes from my lustful haze to look at him. He pumped his own erection in matching strokes to Brooks' tantalizing rhythm. The tingles and sharp sparks of another release started in my lower belly, growing to encompass my torso before gripping my greedy pussy as Brooks grunted behind me. Right as I was about to fall into that blissful release, a calloused hand gripped tightly enough around my throat to heighten the intoxicating waves of pleasure. I exploded. *Fuck.* My orgasm pulsed through me in shuddering, electric surges. The sexy MC president released my throat before slipping out, his rough beard and tiny nip on my shoulder had me shivering against his muscled chest. The scraping of the chair and soft footsteps barely registered in the lusty haze I was drowning in.

"Stand up for a minute, Kittycat," Chase urged, his quiet words filled with glee as he watched me move. Following his instructions, Brooks lay down on the bed, the condom on his impressive erection slick from my pussy. I glanced between the two of them ignoring the feeling of my wetness dripping down my thigh. "Here's what I want you to do, Kittycat," Chase whispered sinfully as he leaned into my back, fingers lightly brushing my ass leaving goosebumps in their wake. "I want you to ride him and while you're full of his cock, I'm going to fuck that sexy ass of yours. How does that sound?" I shivered at the thought, my greedy pussy clenching tightly as I nodded, my brain unable to form a coherent thought through my lusty fog.

I gazed down at Brooks as I crawled up onto his prone body, my hands braced against his chest as I rose above him. Lining up, I sank down slowly, allowing myself to stretch and accommodate him once more. A wave of hunger flooded me when he was fully inside me, and Chase's words echoed in my mind. I rocked a few times against Brooks, and he groaned and palmed my breasts. The bed dipped behind me. Chase's warm hand pressed against my shoulder blades until I was folded over Brooks' chest. The sound of Chase's travel sized tube of lube opening that he always carried sent a shiver down my spine. A slow, cocky smile spread across Brooks' lips and I melted further. I felt him withdraw before he bounced me on his hips. Gasping at the sharp pulse of pleasure, I bent my head to close the distance between our lips.

My attention was split between Brooks' domineering kisses and the feeling of Chase's slippery finger massaging the tight ring of my ass. I couldn't hold back the rocking of my hips as he started to work on stretching me out. My eyes rolled back when he added another finger, and the feeling of Brooks shifting slightly inside me had me whimpering. After a few more thrusts, Chase's hand disappeared replaced with a lubed cock. Exhaling, I relaxed against the sudden invasion, leaning back into Chase's slow and rocking movements. A shudder ripped through me. I melted into a puddle of pure need between them as they started to move in tandem. Hands roved my heated flesh. My eyes sealed shut as they worked my body in slow, but purposeful movements.

They shifted their rhythm. Moving harder. Faster. My moans turned into urgent cries, tingles rippling through every part of me. I clawed at the bedding, my nerves feeling like a thousand strikes of lightning the closer I came to my release. Chase's nails digging and dragging down my back in a sharp scratch was the final push, causing shockwaves of desire to pulse through me as I clamped down on them. Their pace didn't slow, bringing me quickly back up to that peak of pleasure before throwing me over once more. The feeling of fullness had me shouting their names.

Chase was the first to falter, his thrusts pausing as he reached his own climax. Nipping at my sweat coated back, he pulled out, his eyes searing my skin as I sat up. I braced myself against Brooks' barreled chest and took over riding him, my braided hair brushing against my peaked nipple. Rough hands squeezed my breasts tightly, but not to the point of pain, the flood of sensations building up slowly toward my fifth and final orgasm. Brooks' broken and hitched breathing had me riding him harder, driving both of us to the edge of shattering. Chase's strong arm wrapped around one side of my body, fingers rubbing against my clit in time with my bounces. Brooks cried out, his body tensing under my fingers as he came, but I didn't stop, and several moments later I followed him into that blissful pool. My arms gave out under my wracking body. I lay against Brooks' torso, my breasts thudding with the rapid beat of my heart.

"I don't think I can move," I murmured, my voice rough

from the extent I had used it during our threesome.

Chuckling, Chase assisted my trembling body up and off Brooks' sweat sheened chest, my back braced against his strong torso. Our panting breaths filled the room as we basked in our post-sex exhaustion.

"Nap time?" I joked, and both men broke out in laughter, but unfortunately Brooks shifted to a sitting position.

"I have some shit to take care of today, but before I do that, have either of you been around the compound yet?" I felt Chase shake his head.

"I know from maps, but we haven't been around it yet. You planning on being a gracious host and showing us around, *Boss*?" I cheeked, a smartass smile curling my lips as I teased him.

"Stone is right, you are a brat." He chuckled, giving me a quick kiss before starting to get dressed. "But yes, if you guys want. I'd understand if you'd rather do nothing all day though, it's been a rough couple of days." I laughed as Chase bounced on the mattress behind me in excitement. Moving, he started to clap his hands, his eyes lit up with mirth at the idea of a look around The Aces' Motorcycle Club compound.

"I guess that's a yes," I translated Chase's childlike behavior for Brooks as I started to pull on a fresh pair of clothes I had gotten from my stash at The Bank.

After a few minutes, we were all dressed and out in Brooks' small kitchen. I scoured his cabinets for something to eat, but all I really wanted in that moment was an energy drink. *Barely any sleep followed by an absolutely fuck-tastic threesome was not a good way to start the day energized*. I pouted as I closed the last cabinet door.

"Here"—Brooks' tanned hand appeared in my eyesight

with a large can of my favorite energy drink—"I figured you would want one." I stared at the can, my brain not processing that he'd done something sweet for me. Coming out of my stupor, I squeezed him tightly, his laugh barely audible under the pressure of my arms. I let go and snatched the can away and ripped it open, the bubbles of the drink burning my throat as I chugged. Burping when I was finished, I sighed, already feeling its magic working on my tired body and mind. "Wow, note to self keep that on hand," Brooks teased.

"Oh, yeah," Chase agreed his head bobbing in a jubilant agreement, "pretty sure she keeps them in business with how much of it she drinks." Very maturely, I stuck my tongue out at them. "I'll be back, I'm going to go brush my teeth and all that fun morning stuff."

My assassin left us alone in Brooks' smaller kitchen, the basic wooden cabinets bathed in the sun streaming through the windows. Leaning against the laminate counters, I watched the president flit about preparing his own breakfast. Well, more like lunch now since it was nearing noon. He wasn't wearing his cut which allowed me to stare shamelessly at his back muscles as they shifted and moved under his plain grey shirt. His jeans hugged his legs just right, molding perfectly to his sculpted ass. If we had more time, I would go for round two right here in the kitchen not caring that the blinds were wide open.

I don't really have much modesty, clearly.

"So," he started. Turning, he leaned back against the counter with his plate clutched in one hand as he ate his sandwich with the other. "How are you, really, after going after Chase?" I sighed, my good mood seeping away at the topic.

"It's done and over with, that's all that matters," I

muttered, not wanting to talk about this.

"Where'd you learn all that kind of stuff?" He seem determined to learn more about me. Swallowing the urge to snap, I answered him.

"What stuff? The thieving?" I looked over at him when he didn't answer, his blond hair flopping as he nodded since his mouth was full. "I don't really think I learned it from anyone, I just started doing it when I was little. A pickpocket here, an unlocked door there. Sort of grew from there." I shrugged.

"What about the killing stuff?"

"I trained for fighting with Garrett and Jace," I ground out the bastard's name, "when I was a teenager, and I kept it up when I was on my own. Then Chase came along. He taught me everything he knows, and I taught him everything I know."

"Kiera," Brooks whispered, his grey-blue eyes glued to my face. "Why are you going after Frankie?" I snarled at my father's name, though I wasn't overly surprised he came up. They were willing to go into a war against him, and they would find out eventually.

But damn, I didn't want to talk about it.

"One day, Brooks, you'll learn everything he's truly capable of. The rumors and the whispers are only a portion of what he can truly do," I admitted quietly. Panic clawed its way into my throat, but I continued, "Just know everything that's coming to him is more than well deserved."

Stormy eyes watched me, a tiny thread of pity in their depths, but Brooks didn't push any further. I turned my head from him to look out the front window. The yard outside was small, but not ridiculously so as it lined up against a sidewalk and paved street. There were four small houses on either side of the street, several of which had motorcycles or cars parked in the driveways. A feather light touch caught my attention. When I glanced over, Brooks stood looking down at me.

"You good?"

I nodded, unable to talk otherwise everything I tried so hard to push down would bubble out, and once that dam was opened there was no fucking way to stop it.

"All right, come here." He nudged me into his warm chest, a corded arm curling around my shoulders in a soft hug. Inhaling, I took in his leather, grease, and citrus scent. Chase skipped into the room before I could bury my nose in Brooks' chest to enjoy his smell more.

"Did you break Kiera?" Chase deadpanned at seeing me wrapped up in a hug. I laughed lightly at first at his stoic question and before I knew it, tears streamed down my cheeks as I laughed uncontrollably. Because of Chase, I was able to mask my tears of painful memories with tears of laughter and exhaustion. Chase was scarily accurate at reading my moods, and he always knew what to say in any situation to help me feel better. In the past, he had been sent to kill me, but looking back now? I think he was sent to save me. And he did, more than I ever truly realized.

"Thanks for that, Chase," I teased once I was able to stop laughing.

"For what?" he asked, his eyes soft as he stared down at me. I felt Brooks shift toward the door to open it, a light laugh trailing behind him at Chase's antics.

"For being you," I mouthed unwilling to say something so mushy out loud. I might like Brooks, hell, I might even trust him a little bit, but that sentiment was only for my little assassin to hear. Chase simply winked at me and walked out of the house followed by Brooks. I stood there a moment, lost in thought about how much my life had changed since I broke free of Frankie's hellish house of horrors. *Soon*, I thought, *I'll be free of Frankie for good.*

I hope he's ready for me, because I'm coming and I'm not alone.

CHAPTER 14

MAY 6TH
MONDAY MIDDAY
CHASE

"Come on, Kittycat. I want to go see the compound," I urged bouncing lightly on my toes as I tugged on Kiera's arm in excitement. Kiera chuckled, her mossy eyes lighting with happiness from the dreary depths they had just been in. They didn't know it, but I had been eavesdropping on their conversation and it took me a few extra moments to collect my anger at the mention of Frankie 'Smokes' before stepping back out into the kitchen. Training my attention back on Brooks' front yard, I found my focus darting between the compound as Brooks explained the area and the two of them, giddily noting that they stood close enough for their arms to brush.

"The compound's about 50-55 acres. We're currently in the southeast residential area where most of the single members and the officers live with the exception of Nate and Abby who live over in the family residential area." He pointed to a section of houses on the other side of a five bay garage and what looked like a large park/picnic area. "It's not required to live on the compound, but it's usually cheaper and the sense of community helps. There's another patch of houses toward the front in the north residential area where the prospects and hang-arounds are. That garage there is the members' garage, and the park is where most of the club events happen since there's usually grilling involved." We continued down the path heading toward the main clubhouse, and my gaze darted around the property in interest.

"You've been at the main clubhouse which is the bar, extra rooms, our public office, and essentially the central hub. Kiera, you've been to our back warehouse." He pointed to the large metal building out to the left in the distance. "That's where all the old bikes and parts go for disassembly and storage for use in our garages which is that building right there." He indicated a seven bay garage not too far off the front entrance which was directly in front of us down a long winding road. "Which is for the public to come in and get work done. There's a few other random buildings on the outskirts of the property, but they don't really have much other than acting as supply storage for the bar or other random shit."

"So cool!" I squealed, my lips curled in a broad smile. My mind turned from the space around us, to the topic of The Aces as a club. "How do you get to be a member?" I glanced over at Brooks as I asked, his brows raising sharply as he looked back in surprise. I chuckled at his expression. *He's so easy to shock.*

"You want to be an Ace, Chase?" My chuckle turned into a full-bellied laugh.

"That rhymed," I chimed. Looking down at Kiera, my body immediately sparked at her tiny smile. "Do I have to be a member if we do that thing we talked about?" I beamed when I saw the tiny smile fall into thin line.

"I don't think so, at least not fully. It's a different

situation than we've had before, so we'd have to see how the guys handle it," Brooks offered as his head tilted in thought. My kittycat groaned slightly as she rolled her eyes. *She can play hard to get all she wants*, I hummed, *I know damn well what her pretty ass wants.*

"Hello," she interjected with a wave of her hand. "Do I not get a say?" Brooks smirked down at her with a knowing expression thinking the same thing I had. Shaking my head fiercely, I answered ridiculous question.

"Nope, you're ours and we're yours, Kittycat. You're stuck with us," I teased, but deep down a niggle of something bloomed in my chest as Brooks curled her under his arm. My blood sparked at Brooks' golden tan and sculpted muscles as they rippled around Kiera's thin shoulders. I watched them carefully, intent on keeping Kiera as happy as possible.

She leaned into him subconsciously as her tan cheeks heated in a tiny flush. Despite her play at not wanting this, her eyes lit up and her step held a bit more pep as it did when she was excited. Glancing at Brooks, I found him focusing solely on Kiera. His smile was genuine and it seemed for a moment that he had forgotten that I was even there. I let my mind wander about the seemingly laid back president before me. Since we had our talk a couple of weeks ago about sharing, Brooks' demeanor toward me had shifted.

He was more open, less 'Boss' like, and more treating me as an equal instead of the crazy sidekick to Kiera's thief crew. He smiled and laughed more, as I was witnessing right now. Hell, he had even started to joke around me more instead of being the 'cool, level-headed' leader of a motorcycle gang. There was a looseness to him now and, if I was honest, it was sexy. I liked this Brooks. This was the Brooks that Kiera needed, and what Kiera needed was what I wanted to get for her. That warming sensation in my chest grew, and I found myself not only enjoying the change in him, but I appreciated seeing a man make the woman I loved feel safe and happy. My cock throbbed at the swirling thoughts. *Hm...* I thought as I discreetly adjusted my growing erection. *Maybe I wouldn't be opposed to him being stuck with us either.*

"We can talk whenever we find Garrett, how about that? Cause he'll skin me alive if he isn't included," Brooks added with a laugh.

As we turned down the walkway toward the bar, I tucked the intriguing train of thought away for future pondering. *I have a much more important surprise to think about*, I internally squealed. The desert weather was cooler than it had been as we strolled, the clouds keeping the sun covered.

"What are you going to do now that your house is gone?" Brooks asked.

Speaking of... I felt my lip curl in a smug smile unable to keep it hidden.

"Buy a new one?" Kiera shrugged, her statement going up like a question. "I had that one custom built for my work room and practice space, so probably get something temporary." Her eyes narrowed on me in suspicion. "Why are you looking like that, my little assassin?"

I pantomimed zipping my lips closed before throwing away the key, and her eyes burned in response making me giddy. I loved when she got fired up, and surprising her was one of the fastest ways to do that.

"You'll find out in a little while," I taunted.

Her eyes narrowed further on me, but I didn't give anything away. She huffed and started to storm away, but not before I heard her mumbling under her breath.

"Damn troublemaker."

Damn straight, kittycat.

KIERA

I was lost in thought as we entered the bar. My curiosity burning at Chase's suspicious behavior, but I pushed it away to take in my surroundings. Garrett and Stone were talking with Nate while Abby was shooting the shit with a few other Old Ladies I didn't recognize. The nosy looks they directed at me and the appraising eyes they gave Chase did not escape my notice.

"Kiera!" Abby waved me over to the group of women who were eyeing me. Obliging her, I walked over despite the three sets of gazes watching me shrewdly. "Kiera, I want you to meet a few of the other Ladies, this is Leah." Dark blue eyes took me in as the woman looked up at me from her short height. Her pale skin practically glowed in the dark ambiance of the bar. Her reddish brown hair was slightly wavy and pulled into a low ponytail over her very thin shoulder. *Damn, she's tiny, I could probably count the ribs on this chick.*

"Haley." This woman was my height with golden yellow skin and lean muscles like housewives that do pilates have. She played with her black shiny hair that brushed the tops her shoulders, twirling it around her finger. Her dark brown, almond judgy eyes were surrounded in a hazy kohl liner and mascara, her lipstick a bright pink making her stand out.

"And Olivia." The last woman was taller than me and voluptuous. *Pretty sure she'd smack herself in her face if she so much as took a sharp step with those giant tits.*

She would have been pretty with light green eyes and ashy blonde hair if it hadn't been for the absolutely *awful* orange spray tan that covered her skin. "Ladies, this is my girl Kiera." I smiled slightly, uncomfortable at being the center of attention.

"The one who beat the shit out of Bambi," Haley murmured, her soft tone filled with judgement, but I held back on the urge to snap.

"Yeah, well..." I shrugged slightly. "She was in bed with the Alloy Kings, so I don't regret it," I admitted honestly, trying really hard to keep my attitude on a leash. If the guys really wanted to attempt this relationship, I would need to *try* and get along with them. *Well, at least try to be polite... whatever the hell that is.*

"Is it true you took out a dozen Alloy King members in a rampage?" Olivia prodded, her green eyes narrowing on me.

I chuckled, my mind immediately going to the show Archer and the rampage episode. *If you know what I'm imagining, I know you're giggling too.* Shaking my head, I set the record straight.

"Not a dozen, just seven," I said without a hint of regret. Their brows cocked, looking at me like I was a shiny new toy to play with.

"Yeah, she's not exactly the most personable woman," Abby teased trying to reduce the tension between them and me. She might be loyal to Nate and the club, but I knew she'd pick me over these bitches if push came to shove. I rolled my eyes, unable to stop a small smile from curling at the edges of my lips. *She's not wrong.*

"Are you Boss's girl or are you Warden's?" Leah rounded out the trio. Her question irked me the most as she eyed my men with greedy eyes despite the fact she wore a

'Property of' jacket.

"Both." I smiled sweetly as their faces scrunched with disgust. "The assassin over there is mine too," I tacked on the end, my voice catching the attention of the officers. Nate shook his head, a small smile curling his lips while my guys all smirked. Well, almost all. Stone just looked, well, like Stone—mouth turned down in a frown, arms crossed, and some slight confusion showing in his expression.

"Wow." Haley's voice was filled with both judgment and disgust, but I couldn't bring myself to give a shit since I wasn't here for her to like me. "Do you rotate days or do you just take turns?" she snarked, looking way too proud of her mean girl comment. My sweet smile turned into a wicked grin as I answered.

"At the same time." They balked at my response as well as at my farewell to Abby as I gave a slight wave. "Bye, bitch." She had been trying not to laugh, but at my goodbye she burst out laughing. I couldn't hold back the snicker as I made my way to the guys.

"Nice to see you making friends," Nate chastised playfully. He'd known me long enough to know that I didn't take shit.

I only smiled at him and took the glass of alcohol Cheryl had put out for me. *Did she ever sleep or did she just live behind the bar?* Stone rolled his eyes and glared at the wall intent on ignoring me, while my guys chuckled.

"I'm going to get started on that task, Boss. I'll catch everyone later," Nate excused himself leaving the bar with Abby in tow. The three Old Ladies watched us with prying eyes to which Chase gave a little wave. At his attention, they blushed and turned back toward each other.

"We ready to go?" Chase piped up, his eyes glowing

again with that sly glint. I sipped my drink reveling in the smooth burn and once again trying to figure out what he had planned. Stone grumbled under his breath, but the other MC officers nodded and placed their empty glasses on the bar.

"Where are we going?" I questioned, finishing my own drink. Chase smiled innocently and zipped his lips. I huffed but followed them anyway. The same vehicle I had used when we went to The Bank was out front, and Garrett held the front passenger seat open for me. With a quick kiss on my head from him, I sank into the seat before he closed the door. Chase buckled into the front seat while the officers smashed into the back row.

"I don't see why I had to fucking come along for this field trip," Stone bit out, his broad shoulders scrunched together against the window.

Chase sniffed, his hand waving in the air. "Because you're part of the group whether you accept it or not." He hummed to the pop station he had changed to as we pulled out of the compound.

Staring out at the landscape, I watched the Nevada desert pass quickly until we turned off the main road ten minutes later. My brows furrowed and I sat forward in the seat, the belt locking against my chest as I scanned the area in front of the car.

"Where are you taking us, my little assassin?" I murmured distractedly. Before I realized what happened, a swath of dark cloth was over my eyes obstructing my eyesight. "What the fuck!" I twisted against Garrett's arms as he held the fabric in place.

"It's ok, Kiera." He laughed at me from the back seat. "Just a few more minutes, I promise."

I sighed and crossed my arms like a petulant child. *I hate surprises.*

"It's a good surprise, don't worry."

I rolled my eyes. *Of course he would know what I was thinking, sneaky bastard.* But I complied with their shenanigans and waited until the car came to a stop.

"Ready, baby?" Brooks' smooth voice was excited, nearly as giddy as Chase who I could hear doing a little dance in the driver's seat.

I quickly agreed, and the makeshift blindfold was removed leaving me to blink several times to get my eyes to adjust. When they did, I inhaled sharply.

"What the..." I trailed off as I stared. The surprise was a giant house. *No, scratch that, it's a fucking mansion!* We were parked in a circular, paver-covered drive; stucco walls and manicured bushes lined the outside where a large double gate was closed. In the middle of the drive was a little garden with green and red desert flowers and bushes. As I stepped out of the SUV the sound of running water met my ears, but I couldn't place where it was coming from so I turned my attention back to the mansion in front of me.

It was a light beige-yellow with a Spanish tiled roof. There were two stories and an expansive green front lawn on either side of the drive. The landscape was luscious as I made my way up the wide walkway to the front door which was a beautiful cherry stained double door under a large glass roof that expanded over the path. Windows sparkled in the daylight as the clouds started to pull away. Both the left and right side of the front of the house had second floor balconies and wrought iron railings.

My breath hitched when we walked in. A large stone fireplace was the first thing I saw followed quickly by matching cherrywood stained ceiling beams and a wide staircase off to the left. The living room was large and held another fireplace as well as furniture that was reminiscent of the pieces I had had at the old house, but these looked brand new. The dining room held a very long dining table with over eight chairs, but it could fit at least ten to twelve. *Jesus.* I was floating on cloud nine as I moved into the gourmet kitchen that was outfitted with the best of the best in appliances, counterspace, and cabinets. The last bit of the main floor included a bar room with yet another fireplace and a wall that could be opened to the patio that sat under a second floor balcony. The backyard held a pool, hot tub, and fountain as well as a giant green patch before ending at a garden feature with lots of stone walls and flowers.

The guys trailed after me just as stunned and silent as we headed to the second floor. Another glass door wall that could be folded up like the one downstairs filled the hall before splitting into two sides, each of which held two bedrooms as well as a master in mirrored fashion. The master ensuite on both sides faced the front and had double doors to their respective balconies. The bathrooms were to die for with large soaking tubs in front of a picture window, a walk-in shower, vanity, and dual sinks. The last portion of the master bedroom included an enormous walk-in closet. The remaining bedrooms on the second floor were all huge and each had their own bathrooms attached.

"I don't understand." I turned in another circle in the spare bedroom we stood in. "When did you do this?" Chase was bouncing on his toes as he looked at me.

"I had it built for you!" He scooped me up in his arms, his nose going to my hair. "There's a basement too, outfitted with all of the specifications I know you were wanting." I felt tears well up at the enormity of his gift. "Do you like it, Kittycat?"

"Chase, it's beautiful." I hugged him tightly, my chest squeezing painfully under the swell of my emotions.

"When did you start having this built?" Stone questioned, his tone disbelieving. "This had to take months." Chase released me and nodded.

"Six months, to be exact." He smiled at me as the weight of his words settled on me.

"You started it right after we met?" I smiled, my love for him growing as he nodded.

"Crazy people." Stone rolled his eyes as he insulted us under his breath. I glared at him.

"Fuck off, Stone. Don't be a dick just because someone else is actually capable of thoughtful gestures," I lectured, my hands going on my hips. "Why is it so big?" I turned my question to Chase.

"I figured it would be good to have extra room." His eyes twinkled as he waved toward the MC officers. "Turns out I was right! They can each have a room!" Brooks and Garrett both looked surprised at his offer.

"Really?" Stone grumbled some more. "You four are seriously considering doing the polyamorous relationship thing?"

I looked at the others who all nodded, their eyes trained on me. I had my reservations about how everything would work, but thinking about them being with someone else made my stomach turn, so I nodded too.

"Yeah, I guess we are." I smiled when their faces lit up.

"You want to do this too?" Chase poked Stone in the arm. "Don't think you've snuck under the radar in the 'I'm attracted to Kiera' party."

Stone glared, but didn't object, his lips thinning as he

nodded his head ever so slightly as if he was reluctant to do so.

"Fine," he bit out, "but I'm not doing any of that sex sharing thing."

I chuckled but agreed, because multiple partners and Stone didn't belong in the same sentence. *Not yet anyway*, my brain whispered mischievously.

MAY 7TH
TUESDAY AFTERNOON
STONE

I was running through the list of shit we had to get done on the sheet of paper in front of me when the assassin sank into the barstool to my left. His faux-suede jacket shifted quietly around the set of guns I knew he always carried. I kept my eyes focused on my paper as he waited patiently for his drink; Cheryl was getting used to both him and Kiera being around the compound more and more frequently.

Speaking of the brat, my brain had been battling back and forth for the last 24 hours on the fact that I had agreed to their relationship shit. One half was fucking delighted about it, thinking I'd get to fuck her whenever I wanted without worrying about pissing my fellow officers off, while the other half... well, it was screaming at me that it was a distraction that I didn't need at the beginning of this war that was about to go down with the Alloy Kings. A battle was coming, and soon, so right now was just a waiting game for a side to strike first. *Us*, I mentally tallied since Kiera had already done a good deal of damage to their numbers when she went for Chase. *Which, if I'm honest, was ridiculously hot.* Just thinking about it made me rock hard.

Chase seemed to be content to sit in silence as I

continued with my list; this time I added in things we would possibly need for an advance on their compound and shipments. Knowing they were working in partnership with the mob changed the game slightly. We had to be cautious of what shipment we took in case the Alloy Kings weren't the only ones that could be at the drop point. I knew full well that we would be backing Kiera in her attack against Frankie, so being smart now was important. With Frankie entering my thoughts, I stopped writing and turned to Chase.

"What did Frankie 'Smokes' do to Kiera to earn being blacklisted?"

Chase's demeanor slammed closed in a wave of anger. Seeing his eyes burn in fury as his muscles tensed had me leaning away from him. *He's a scary motherfucker when he wants to be.*

"You'll learn soon enough, Stone," he ground out, his lips curling into a snarl. Whatever it was had to be bad if it had someone like Chase reacting in such a way. "But I'm not going to discuss that with you right now."

I wasn't pleased, but I tucked the urge to push for the answer away for later when we focused on Frankie instead of the Alloy Kings. *Eye on the ball, Stone*, I lectured myself, *Alloy Kings are top priority*.

"All right, where is she anyway?" I found myself asking. As soon as the topic of Frankie was done, Chase's anger melted back into his cheery self. Chase finished his sip before answering.

"Walking around the compound." He looked at me with a small curl of his lips. "She likes to know a place like the back of her own hand. She has maps of the compound in her files, and Brooks gave us a rundown, but she wanted to check everything out for herself. She'll probably do that for the next week or so noting any security weaknesses, so be prepared for an ass-chewing if there's anything blatantly weak in security around the compound."

"Great," I huffed. But truthfully, it couldn't hurt to know what needed to be addressed with what was about to come down. I had been considering bringing up with Brooks that any of the families with children should be moved to temporary housing in case anything happened. The thought was interrupted when the alarm suddenly sounded. Chase slammed the rest of his drink before casually pulling his matching guns from their holsters. I had already grabbed my own weapon from its holster at my lower back as Cheryl dragged the several Old Ladies and hang-arounds in the bar to the safe room making sure to secure the door behind them.

"Stone!" Nate's booming voice called out as he entered from the back door with Garrett and Brooks in tow. "Where's Kiera?" My heart dropped as I realized she had been walking around the compound.

"Was she alone?" I questioned Chase. His eyes hardened, and he nodded as he started toward the front door of the bar. "Hold up." I latched onto his arm before turning to Brooks and Nate who were checking the compound cameras on their phones.

"Alloy Kings at the southeast storage building," Brooks ground out, his jaw ticking as he flicked to the southeast cameras. "Fucking shit! They've got some kind of humvee."

"Damn it," Nate boomed. He stuffed his phone into his pocket before checking his magazine. Brooks' face paled, his eyes still glued to his phone.

"What?" Garrett asked sharply. Chase, Garrett, and I all collected around the phone. My eyes couldn't process what I was seeing right away, but when they did I felt my blood boil. Kiera was wrestling against three Alloy Kings as they carried her toward the large vehicle, while the remaining group was fighting with Aces who had swarmed the area.

"God damn it!" Garrett shouted. He ran toward the front of the bar and out to one of the club's old SUVs still parked in one of the front stalls of the lot. Opening the back hatch, we piled in, Nate climbing into the driver's seat, while Chase went to the passenger seat and made sure to roll down his window. Brooks, Garrett, and I held on tightly to the grip handles we had custom installed as Nate barrelled the SUV toward the battle.

The sound of gunshots and shouting echoed against the buildings as we approached. Our numbers seemed to be evenly matched since no bodies littered the ground, but there were several who appeared injured as they bled against the dusty cement. My eyes scanned for Kiera; her screaming curses could be heard over the rest of the fighting. Finally, I spotted her after the third pass. She was being hoisted into the open back of the humvee, her braid messy and sticking to half her face as blood poured from an injury I couldn't see.

Nate squealed the SUV to a stop only narrowly missing several of our own members. As soon as the vehicle was slow enough to exit we jumped out, Chase following suit from his seat up front. Garrett was the fastest behind Chase as they sprinted toward Kiera. Brooks ended up taking on two rivals who were overpowering one of our members. I had almost caught up to Garrett, when a shot rang out followed by a scream. Rider, our demolition expert, was clutching a bleeding wound in his shin, but before the Alloy King could put another one in his chest or head I changed course and tackled him to the ground.

Grappling with him, I was able to get his gun away from him, knocking him out with a hit to his head from the handle of my own gun. My attention switched to Rider, and I ripped my cut off before shucking the shirt I was wearing to tie a makeshift tourniquet around his leg to slow the bleeding.

"Go!" He waved me off after the tie was on, the blood flow slowing to a trickle before stopping. "I got this." He leaned back against the tree near him with the Alloy Kings' gun in his free hand. The sound of the humvee revving pulled my attention, but Chase and Garrett were busy each with their own rival. The Alloy Kings started to retreat to their two remaining vehicles after the humvee cleared the fence. Sprinting over to them, I shot the one Garrett was struggling with in the side right as Brooks tackled the one Chase was up against. Unfortunately, the guy was able to maneuver away from the president and jump on the retreating vehicle.

That was it, their attack was over. Two Alloy Kings were lying on the ground bleeding or unconscious, while our patch holders immediately started helping the injured. Thankfully, no one had been killed.

"Where is she?" Garrett demanded, looking around for Kiera's honey brown waves that were nowhere to be seen in the group. "Fuck! They have her. Nate!" He ran toward the SUV as he shouted at the Road Captain who was wiping a sweaty brow. "Driver, now." Garrett, Brooks, Chase and I shot back into the vehicle, peeling out to follow the humvee tracks so quickly that it squealed.

I'm going to fucking kill them...

CHAPTER 15

The weather was warm, but not uncomfortably so. The sun filtering between the clouds provided shade. I had originally thought to bring my notebook and the attached pen for this casing, but since it was only my initial walkthrough I left it at the house. *I can't believe Chase built us a house.* I smiled to myself. The mansion he had built was probably one of the biggest houses I'd ever seen except for Frankie's. I pushed the thoughts of my father out of my head, not wanting to ruin the moment. First thing I had done last night? Taken a very long, hot bath in the giant tub before passing out until late morning.

And now, a few hours later, I'm here, I thought as I looked around. The area was spacious, but not outrageously so since there were essentially three mini-neighborhoods within the borders of the compound. The perimeter of the Aces' acreage was a tall chain-link fence with the traditional barbed wire wound in a curly-q on top. I spotted one or two cameras on pretty much every lamp post, but there were taller masts that held clusters of cameras as well as siren speakers. I mentally noted the precautions making sure to mark that I would need access to their video feeds to check for any blind spots as well as determine how often these were monitored. *Because if they aren't, they'll need another perimeter monitor.* I grumbled and dug my fingers into the dirt right inside the fence. *It would be way too easy to tunnel under this before someone noticed.*

I wondered if the fence was electric as I stared at it and debated if I wanted to test it, but smarts won out and I walked away. *Don't want to fry myself or stop my heart.* Turning to scan the area some more, I spotted what Brooks had brought up as miscellaneous buildings, and if my mental map was correct, *which of course it is*, it would be the southeast building. I had just gotten near the small stone structure when I heard a rumbling. Glancing around, I caught sight of a large militarized truck heading straight for the fence, two beat up pickup trucks right behind it. I sprinted the last bit of distance to the building as they smashed through, but the door was locked and before I could unlock it, rough hands grabbed my upper body.

I let loose a scream as I kicked out and caught one of the men in the stomach as he attempted to secure my legs. Turning sharply to the right, I loosened the steel grip around my torso just enough to grab my gun, but my shot went wide and into the stone building's side as a third burly man tugged on my arm. He twisted sharply, and my grip slackened at the stabbing pain and my gun thudded on the ground. Immediately, my vision was filled with the butt of a gun swinging toward my temple. I rocked backward and the hit barely grazed above my left brow. An explosion of pain radiated through my skull, while warm, sticky liquid poured down my face. *Fuckers!*

I heard shouting as the three bastards tried to wrestle me back around the building. There was a large group of fist and knife fighting, while a few gunshots rang out intermittently during the brawl. I couldn't tell who was who unless I focused on their cuts, but at this rate my only goal was not being taken wherever they were dragging me off to.

"Fuck you!" I screamed, and tight hands clamped even more around my arms and legs as the three assholes hoisted me into the open back of the humvee. Yanking and flailing my limbs, I couldn't loosen their grips. Blood soaked the left half of my face, my hair sticking to the wet pool. The cut above my brow throbbed, but adrenaline helped numb the pain. I heard Garrett's harsh voice hollering somewhere, but I couldn't turn my head to see.

"Shut the fuck up, bitch!" the guy holding my arms shouted as they finally got me into the metal contraption. A new set of hands grabbed me, and a familiar scarred face filled my vision as the truck started to move.

"Hello, Kiera." Jace's voice made me shiver, his hands like steel bands around my biceps. I kicked out, but Jace, who had always been faster than me, easily stepping out of the way of my boot's path. "Still feisty I see." He pressed his face into the crook of my neck and inhaled, his tongue darting out to lick my skin before pulling back to look at me with his one good eye.

Gross. I shuddered. The sound of the wind filled my ears as we started to pick up speed as we moved away from the compound. *I have to fucking get out of here.*

"It's been a long time since you and I have gotten some quality alone time," he murmured in my ear.

I clenched my fists tightly, the urge to punch him in the face pouring through every inch of me. I stood still, hoping if I didn't react at all he would let go or at least loosen his grip. My attention darted around the small space. The canvas top was draped over several steel bars that enclosed the back of the large metal contraption. Dark grey or black painted benches lined either side of the truck bed, and Jace and I stood between the two long rows. I held back a very sarcastic reply along with the churning in my stomach that had me nearly retching, and I focused on trying to come up with a plan, but there was nothing back here except us meaning it was up to me to get out of this shit situation.

"Cat got your tongue, pretty girl?" Jace's lip curled unevenly at his own *terrible* fucking joke. The unscarred, abnormally perfect side of his face was barely visible in my peripherals as he leaned into my neck again. "Don't worry, we have plenty of time to catch up, and soon enough you'll be begging and screaming my name."

"Fuck you, psycho," I snapped unable to keep the bland facade up as fear flooded my system. *I was not going to do anything of the sort. I would rather die, as cliche as that is to say.* His rough chuckling filtered through my growing panic, the graze of teeth making me yank away as far as his iron grip would allow.

"There's my Kiera. I was starting to worry if that step brother of yours had finally broken your fiery spirit." Pulling back, he looked down at me.

I stared straight ahead, my eyes glued to the pulse that thudded rhythmically in his neck. *I'm going to enjoy cutting open your throat.* My resolve steeled at the thought.

Doing something I knew I would throw up over later, I calmed myself enough so as not to puke as I pressed my lips on his. His scars were rough against my lips as he tried to deepen the kiss, his hands starting to shift away from my arms. *Bingo.* I took the opening, shoving him away from me and snatching my knife from my boot. His eyes flared in hunger as I squared up against him, thankful that he was dumb enough for it to only be me and him back here. The only Alloy Kings on the humvee were in the cab of the truck.

He moved, his strikes hard and fast as I attempted to counter them. Even after years of training, he was still quicker than me. When he landed a punch to my bruised ribs I couldn't hold back the cry of pain; stars burst before my eyes. His other hand grabbed a fistful of my shirt to yank me back to him, his lips pressing against mine before he bit down on my lower lip. Blood flooded my mouth and dripped down my chin as his vicious bite brought another scream of pain. Trying to push through the haze of agony that pulsed through my body, I swiped the knife, but he caught that as he smiled down at me, my blood coating his teeth and lips. His tongue darted out, lapping at the blood on his mouth as he leaned in for another kiss.

Fuck you, asshole, I snarled mentally before smashing my forehead against his nose.

He stumbled back clutching his gushing nose. I turned and, without any thought or hesitation, I launched myself out of the back of the humvee making sure to angle off to the side of the road and hoping to land in the grass. *Fuck, this is going to hurt.* I curled into myself, dropping the knife so I didn't accidentally stab any part of me, before smashing into the desert ground. I rolled in attempts to ease the pain from the impact, but I was still breathless and throbbing from the landing. Opening my watery eyes, I watched the humvee continue down the dirt road.

"Ow, fuck," I whimpered on all fours, slowly climbing to standing. Bracing against my knees as a wave of dizziness passed over me, I focused on not throwing up. *I kissed Jace*

Corden, fucking disgusting. When I was able to stand fully, I limped over to my knife that had landed blade down in the dirt before pulling it out and tucking it away. *I wish I had my gun*, I thought sullenly. If only it hadn't gotten knocked away when I was jumped by those stupid fucking bastards.

"Well, could have been worse I guess," I said to myself, tallying my injuries. Bruised and bloody face, *check*, most likely a sprained wrist, *check*, new bruising on my ribs, *check*, what I'm sure will be severe bruising on the side that landed on the ground, *check*, but at least nothing was broken. Surprisingly.

With that, I started limping back toward the compound, my leg still aching sharply from the impact on the ground. *That's* definitely *going to be a wicked fucking bruise.* I had only walked a few moments before I saw the Aces' crash SUV come barreling down the hill at an incredibly dangerous speed in pursuit of the humvee. It skidded to a stop about fifty feet from me when they realized I was standing on the side of the road. All the officers hopped from the car and sprinted the distance between us. Garrett reached me first.

"Oh, my fucking god," he muttered as he took in my still bleeding face that I'm sure looked terrible. It was covered in dirt, grass, and my own hair that I could feel sticking out at funny angles. "Are you okay?" I tried to chuckle, but cracking a smile ripped the wound on my mouth open further, causing me to whimper instead.

"Hurt," I admitted with a huff, my words sounding funny due to the puffy, wounded, and still gushing bite on my bottom lip. "I just fucking jumped out of a humvee hauling ass down a fucking dirt road. Did any of you see it? I'm sure I looked fucking badass."

Garrett shot me an exasperated look, while Stone facepalmed and Brooks rubbed his eyes with a groan at my attempt to be funny. Only Chase chuckled finding the humor in the situation like I knew he would. Nate, who I spied over the shoulders of my men standing a few feet back, gave me a thumbs up and a small smile.

"What's bleeding?" Stone gestured to my face with a bloody hand, his knuckles split. I realized then that he was wearing only his cut over his bulky muscles, the dark skin dusty with dirt and blood splatter.

"Forehead—one of the fuckers attempted to pistol whip me. Only hit a bit since I moved out of the way fast enough," I explained. I took a deep breath and tried to ready myself to reveal what had happened to my mouth. "Lip." My attempts were unsuccessful as I felt my stomach turn and the thought of kissing Jace finally settled in. Dropping to my knees, I lost my lunch in several waves of sickness. The pool was mostly blood, as the retching made the blood flow in faster waves onto the dirt ground.

"It's all right, Kittycat," Chase soothed, rubbing gentle circles on my back as I shifted to sit back on my heels.

"What happened to your lip?" Stone asked, leaning forward to inspect my face. I glanced at Garrett when I spoke.

"Jace was in the back of the humvee," I muttered softly. Rage exploded in Garrett's eyes as he started to pace. "He's still faster than me, so I did what I had to to get him distracted." Garrett stopped his stomping to glare at me, angry that I had been in Jace's general vicinity to begin with. "I kissed him." I retched again but didn't puke. "Ended up fighting but he fucking kissed me again, bit the hell out of my lip."

"He fucking bit you?" Garrett fumed. "Enough to bleed

that much?" He took Chase's spot next to me and dropped to a crouch. His rough hands grabbed my jaw lightly to angle my head the way he wanted to be able to inspect my wound. "I can't believe that little fucking... I'm going to fucking murder him, slowly and painfully," he raged, his gaze glued to my wounded lip. "After I fucking cut off his tongue and his lips, and pull his teeth out for this." I placed a dirty hand on his, and Brooks' grasped Garrett's shoulder in a comforting gesture.

"Not if I get to him first," I joked, and his eyes darted up to mine, "then I get to do all of that, and trust me I have much more planned especially since that bastard licked and bit my neck." Finally, after a few more moments of coaxing from me and Brooks, Garrett calmed enough to help me to stand.

"Why'd you throw up?" Brooks asked softly as we walked to the SUV. Nate held open the door for me in the back so I could be between Brooks and Garrett.

"Because I had to kiss that fucking bastard." I shuddered in disgust. "I almost threw up on him thinking about it; wondering now if that would have worked better." The drive back to the compound was quiet, all of us lost in our thoughts as Nate took us around the compound to the front. When we finally reached the front gate, I was feeling the pain throughout my body, the adrenaline having dissipated.

"Did anyone get injured or killed?" I realized I wasn't aware of what had happened; I only knew there was a giant fucking fight as I was driven off with a damned psycho.

"A few knife wounds, two gunshot wounds, handful of minor cuts, scrapes, and bruises from fighting but nothing fatal on our end. We have two Alloy Kings secured; one has a concussion while the other is just bloody from getting his ass kicked," Stone explained from behind me as he held onto the jump handles.

I felt my brows rise. It was the most he'd spoken in one go without sounding all judgy or like his usual jerk-off self. *Hey, maybe he was starting to like me.* I tried to smile to myself, but hissed at the tearing in my lip.

"Fuck me." The swelling was getting worse and my eyes started to well up with the growing agony throughout my body. "Please tell me we have some damned good medicine around here," I whined as we pulled up to the clubhouse, "because I'm really starting to feel that whole 'jumping out of the back of a humvee like a badass thing.'" They chuckled lightly as we exited the car.

"Yeah we do, the doctor should be here already looking at everyone," Brooks explained as Chase acted as my crutch so I wouldn't topple over. The bar was crowded with members, most just holding ice packs to their faces or knuckles with a few bandaged cuts and injuries. Only three were being assisted by an elderly man with bright white hair, his knobby fingers stitching the gunshot wound in Rider's leg with ease and precision.

"Doc." Brooks approached him as he finished tying off the stitches. "Got one more for you." He hitched a thumb over at me, and Rider's eyes flicked up to me as he grimaced with sympathy. The doctor's eyes were a dark blue behind a set of wired frame glasses that were perched on his crooked nose, his tanned skin full of wrinkles as he looked over me.

"What happened to you? Get into the guys' fight?" he questioned moving toward an open seat. I bristled at the thought that because I was a woman I couldn't fight along with them. Stone understood the question and answered for me, his words stunning me into silence.

"She's just as much one of us as the rest of the guys, Doc." Stone's dark eyes sought out mine, a miniscule smile curled his lip. "She's quite the brat though, so fair warning."

I flipped him off, but inside I melted at his acceptance. *These assholes are just turning me into an ooey-gooey mess of emotions*, I mentally chuckled. I sank onto the seat the doctor patted.

"Well, then, welcome to the Aces..." he trailed off since he didn't know my name.

"Kiera." I tilted my head down in a polite nod. His hands stopped moving as he looked at me, his face moving close to mine.

"I knew you looked familiar." The corner of his eyes crinkled in amusement as he fought a smile. "Nice to see you again, Miss Casterelli." Silence reigned around us, and I realized no one other than my men had known who I was. "Winter Gala of 2006, I believe." I scoured my memory and when I realized who was sitting in front of me, I burst out laughing despite the pain in my face and bruised to hell body.

"Anyone want to tell us what's so funny?" Brooks raised a brow and glanced between the two of us. I finally quieted enough to lean back and let the Doc rinse the blood from my face with a squirty-type bottle.

"I was nine," I started, once the dried blood had been washed away. The feeling of the wounds continuing to bleed barely registered in my mind. "Frankie loves his stupid fucking parties, and I loved to cause trouble."

"Who would have guessed." Stone rolled his eyes, but his tone was warm. I chuckled before biting back a long string of obscenities as Doc washed my forehead and lip with antiseptic.

"I went around pickpocketing all the guests and collecting all the goods before putting it in the Head Chef's office. He was a huge dick to me, so I didn't want him around anymore," I explained seeing the scene in my head as if it were yesterday. *An older gentlemen dressed in a hand-me-down suit watched me curiously as I exited the office, his dark blue eyes sparkling.*

"I asked her if she knew what she was doing," Doc took over for me, "and she gave me this little self-assured smile before waving me behind one of the double doors to a large pantry. We watched the chaos that reigned after they realized their precious jewelry and goods had been stolen, peering through the crack of the door. After a few minutes, the chef had been kicked from the grounds. It was a huge scandal for months afterwards."

"You didn't tell anyone it was her?" Garrett questioned softly, and Doc shook his head looking at me with the same sparkle in his deep irises.

"Everyone who goes to those things deserves far worse than having their shit missing for an hour, but I asked her why. Know what her response was? 'Some people deserve to be knocked down a little, and karma takes too long.' After that, how could I turn such a cute, clever little girl in?" He smiled at me and I rolled my eyes. That dress I had worn that day had been itchy, uncomfortable, and most of all, ugly as fuck. My men watched me all lost in thought as Doc worked through patching me up.

"You're full of surprises," Brooks finally spoke, a small smile on his handsome face. Chase chuckled, his eyes sparkling at the little slice of the past that wasn't all darkness and demons, while Garrett did the same. Stone just shook his head at me making me chuckle as I sat up from the chair.

"So what's the plan, Boss?" I asked eagerly as Doc moved onto another Ace who needed patching. The officers' eyes lit up, the patch holders around us all watching with nosy expressions.

"You want to help take down the Alloy Kings?" Brooks questioned. Chase's excitement was palpable, his jacket swaying as he bounced on his toes. I smirked as well as I could with my bandages.

"Fuck, yeah. Let's show those bastards who the real kings are." A round of shouted cheers went up through the members, and a sense of purpose filled me as I eyed my men.

Oh, yeah, we're fucking doing this...

MAY 8TH
WEDNESDAY MORNING
KIERA

Everything hurt. I thought I might have fucking died and gone to Hell, but then I realized I wouldn't hurt like I had jumped out the back of a humvee if I was in Hell. *Hopefully.* A drawn out groan escaped me, and I peeled my eyelids open. The large California king was empty except for me and a large tangle of blankets. My black and blue bruised skin was dark against the white swaths of satiny sheets, my comforter having long since fallen to the floor in my night of restless tossing and turning.

"Ow, fuck me," I whimpered as I shuffled as gently as I could off the bed. Even the pressure of standing hurt, my leg and side throbbing when I stood. "Fuck, shit, fuck." Cursing worse than a sailor wouldn't help the pain, but it certainly helped me feel better since I couldn't beat the shit out of my punching bag in the basement. The delicious smells of breakfast wafted up the wide staircase,

Chase's soft singing accompanying the sound of a whisk and sizzling bacon. He was wearing his usual lounge attire of grey sweats and form fitting black shirt, his lean muscles deliciously on display as he whisked the bowl of batter.

"Morning, my little assassin," I murmured when I made my way into the kitchen, heading straight for the refrigerator. Chase immediately jumped in front of me causing me to nearly stumble at the sharp movement.

"Good morning, Kittycat." He very gently directed me to the bar stool. "You sit and I'll get your morning lifeline from the fridge."

I rolled my eyes, thinking, *I'm injured, I'm not dead*, but I obliged him anyway because I knew he'd be upset if I didn't.

"Thank you," I muttered against his lips as the cold can bit into my hand. I shook the last of the sleep from my battered body. He refused to lean any closer, my bandage and cut up lip making him cautious in kissing me. Biting down on the irritation at him not wanting to kiss me, I rerouted the conversation. "What's for breakfast?"

"Pancakes, eggs, toast, fruit," he rattled off some items cheerfully, pointing at each item as he talked. My brows furrowed; I couldn't understand why he would make so much.

"God, how are you so fucking jolly this early in the damned morning?" Stone's soft question had me whipping around to face the hallway momentarily forgetting I was injured. The twisting of my torso made me whimper as shooting pains radiated from my ribs. "Good one, brat, that's a good way to injure yourself more." I flipped him off, unable to snark back as I pushed the pain down.

"I'm always jolly." Chase perked up after a thought. "I'm

like Santa!"

Stone scoffed and slipped around the island to pull out a coffee cup, filling it to the brim with the already made brew. "Except you bring death instead of presents," he argued.

After playfully waving his arms in front of him, Chase went back to cooking without further exchange. Stone stood stoically sipping his coffee, his jean covered hip resting against the smooth counter. I watched the suspicious enforcer out of the corner of my eye, observing the way his muscles twitched and bulged as he shifted ever so slightly, as if he was readying for a fight despite the fact he was drinking coffee in a house we're supposed to share. I couldn't help but appreciate the way his body moved though; it made me want to rip his shirt off and revel in what laid beneath. *Don't turn those judgy eyes on me, I'm in pain, not blind.*

"Morning, baby." Brooks' typically smooth voice was rough with sleep, his golden blond tresses messy and flopping into his face. The change had me squeezing my thighs together; the 'just fucked' look only seemed to heighten his sex appeal. I hummed a quick good morning as he pressed a kiss against my unbruised temple. Brooks shuffled over to the coffee maker following Stone's lead in filling a mug up until it seemed like he would spill it. Carefully, he brought the steady cup to his lip and sipped until it didn't look about ready to splash everywhere and make a mess of my kitchen.

Well, I guess our *kitchen now.*

That's going to take getting used to.

"So," I dragged the word out, my eyes narrowing on the two officers, "did you guys just get here? I didn't hear your bikes." Brooks had the balls to chuckle at my question, while Stone shook his head.

"They stayed last night, Kittycat." Chase cocked a brow at me, a smug smile curling his lips. I wasn't sure if it was the drugs from Doc that was making me slow to understand this morning or the fact my energy drink still hadn't kicked in.

"You were out before we even left the compound," Brooks added, his observational skills apparently telling him I was still confused. "Chase drove you home, and we followed. Several hours later, here we are." He gave a small flourish of his hand at the end of his statement.

"Thanks, Sherlock." I rolled my eyes, but I was unable to keep my smile to myself. *He might be a prick, but he's my prick.* I was startled by my own sappy thoughts, so I did what any normal person would do.

I stuffed them way in the back of my mind where I couldn't acknowledge them.

Garrett was the last to join, nearly stomping into the kitchen a few minutes later. He growled when his green eyes landed on me seated safely on the stool. Knowing him, he had probably been worried I was out doing something risky.

"I went to go make sure you were okay, and I found you missing," he ground out, "thought you had gone running off to go steal some rare piece of art or go take out a bunch of rivals."

Knew it, I mentally scoffed, *naggy asshole.*

"No, Gar," I huffed in irritation, my energy drink still working its way through waking me up, making me extra irritable. "I decided to come down to the kitchen in *my own house,*" I emphasized, "because I couldn't sleep any longer." He grumbled under his breath, but I was too tired to argue about it as he lined up next to his president against the counter, coffee clutched tightly in his hand. Chase was lost in his own little world singing and dancing as he finished up breakfast. He plopped a very full plate down in front of me.

"You three better be happy." Chase waved the spatula in the direction of the MC officers. "I even made bacon. For you guys." I rolled my eyes at his dramatics, but secretly my heart warmed at his thoughtful gesture because that was a big thing for him. Chase normally refused to handle meat unless it was absolutely required. I hid my smile behind a glass of juice he set down, and the rest of the guys piled up their own plates before joining me at the bar. The only one who continued to stand was Stone, and that was mainly because he was practically glued to the coffee machine, his cup refilled at least three times already.

"So," I started when it looked like most of us were getting full. "What's the plan, now?" I immediately focused my full attention on what we were going to do against those fucking bastards in the Alloy Kings.

My injuries pulsed at the thought of our rivals, my stomach rolling as the memory of Jace's violation attempted to invade my mind. I shoved it down before I threw up the delicious breakfast my little assassin made for us. *You can't stop now*, my mind whispered, *if you stop working now, you'll be left with the memories what happened running on repeat*. With that nauseating reminder, determination steeled through me. I was silently glad none of them recognized the turbulent thoughts that raged through my mind as Brooks answered my question. It was unsurprising that he took the lead since he was *the Boss* of their little leather-wearing boy band. His grey-blue eyes centered on my face as he spoke.

"If you're up for it, we need a list of security precautions for the compound." I nodded my agreement, happy to have a job to do so I wouldn't be sitting here lost in thought. "Stone and I will be surveying everything around the compound to see if there were any other issues after the attack, but we'll be mainly focused on ground zero." Brooks turned to look at Garrett on his other side. "You'll be working with Nate on moving out the families or anyone who wants a safe haven off the compound. We don't know how bad this is going to get, and I don't want anyone caught in the crossfire if they don't have to be."

"What about me?" Chase bounced on his stool, his messily combed bedhead shifting with his playful banter. I chuckled, cutting Brooks off from talking since his question wasn't directed at him. *He'll hopefully learn that soon enough*, I thought.

"Go through Harbold's files, pull anything and everything to do with the Alloy Kings and see if you can get in touch with some of your old contacts about anything we can use." I groaned as I stood, waving away the guys who all attempted to take my plate and glass to the sink. "I can do it," I snapped, glaring at all of them. *I didn't need any of them to pamper me or take care of me.* I'd broken myself of the need to depend on anyone long before today, and despite their good intentions, the coddling wasn't wanted.

The thunk of the steel lock clicked behind me and my bodyguard; a sense of dread flowed over me as a mix of rage and sadness bubbled in my chest. The decadent silk sheet covered mattress in the far corner taunted me, the rest of the room blurring behind a watery wall of unshed tears. Don't cry, *I commanded,* you know what happens when you show weakness. *Steeling my spine, I mentally prepared myself for what I was going to have to do.* One day, *the*

promise whispered through my mind as I stepped forward,
I'm going to kill them all.

Damsel in distress?

Not anymore.

EPILOGUE

MAY 10TH
FRIDAY NIGHT
JACE

The thumping music rattled the signs on the walls as I weaved my way through the collection of bikers. I kept my arms pulled in; their dirty bar had me eyeing the place with disdain. We normally didn't have to meet at their compound, opting to gather in a neutral location, but the plans had changed after the botched attempted on the Aces. I stepped into their back room; the empty space held a few chairs and a table pressed up against one wall while a mirror hung on another.

Looking at my reflection, I took in my appearance. My black suit jacket was buttoned, the deep red dress shirt underneath pressed and starched. The iron lines perfectly straight on my dark grey slacks. My shined dress shoes were bright against the dingy tiled flooring. I shuddered at what was touching my expensive shoes. I had a meeting with my boss after this, and he was like me in the taste department: expensive, lavish, and perfect.

Lastly, my gaze landed on my scarred, and now bruised, face that stared back at me, a taunting reminder that my Kiera had gotten away. Again. I thought of my Kiera, how close I had been to having her and how her lips felt against mine as she kissed me. I growled deep in my throat as my body thrummed with need. But now, because of these incompetent assholes who dared call themselves a motorcycle gang, my need would have to wait. The gun tucked in its holster called to me, the urge to shoot one of these fuck-ups following the desire that flooded me.

Leaning back against the table, I pulled out my blade and cleaned my nails while I waited. The bite of the sharp point against my thumb sent a shiver down my spine. When the blood welled up enough, I sucked the coppery tang off. *I would rather have it be the blood of the president, but this will have to do. Lucky for me though*, I thought cruelly, *the president and his VP would be joining me shortly.* As if I had spoken the magic words, the door opened immediately after my bloodthirsty thought, and the two people I wanted to hurt stepped into the small office.

"Let's get started," I commanded sharply. My fingers twitched in my violent urge to break each of their fingers for losing Kiera. I took that urge and focused on running the blade lightly against my palm, not enough to cut skin, but enough to keep the sadistic tendencies dancing through my mind at bay. My cock stirred in my slacks at the hint of pain. "We have lots to cover before I meet with my boss."

"We going to start by talking about how I'm now down two more members?" Bryce Hill copped an attitude, clearly forgetting who the fuck he was speaking to. I sneered a ruthless smile and brushed my open hand down my jacket in an attempt to hold off on hurting him... for now.

"Are we going to discuss how your little pitiful gang here lost me Kiera? The one object of importance to me *or my boss?*" I emphasised Frankie in the question despite that the pursuing of Kiera was solely for my own compulsion. Ron scoffed, his eyes rolling as he spoke.

"Maybe it would be best if the Alloy Kings reconsidered their alliance with the Solace mob if its only focus is one little girl," he hummed, shrugging his meaty shoulders indifferently.

Red flooded me at the disrespect, and I snapped. I gripped his burly, bushy jaw tightly within my grasp, the knife point only a milimeter away from his pulse that throbbed in neck. I glared at down him, and he visibly paled. *My reputation precedes me*, I noted as another sadistic impulse to maim him washed over me.

"I suggest you remember who you're speaking to," I ordered. "You're on Frankie's payroll, and I'm sure I don't have to remind you what would happen if you upset him."

"What about that Kiera bitch?"

My cock throbbed at the mention of Kiera's name, but my temper grew at the bitch comment. *No one calls my Kiera a bitch*, I roared. I released Ron and stalked to the president, my height easily allowing me to tower over him.

"Nothing, you little fucking imp of a man," I muttered, rubbing my blade gently against his cheek as I watched him cower before me. "You don't do a fucking thing, but if by some stroke of dumb luck you happen to find her, you hold her for me. But if I find that so much as one hair on her head was damaged by any of you, I will not be pleased. Be thankful I didn't castrate the man who pistol whipped her, and you personally should be on your knees kissing my feet that I don't skin you for referring to her in such a vile manner." He paled in fear, eyes widening as he nodded his head shakily.

"Understood," he whispered in a cowering tremble.

I nodded sharply and stepped back, reeling in the urge to fulfil my threat. *My boss might not be pleased if I do so, but I'm too valuable to him to punish.*

"Good. Work on your plan for your next move." With that, I tucked my knife away and strode out of the room. I made my way out of the wretched bar and into the Alloy Kings' main compound parking lot where I sank into the smooth leather backseat of my waiting car. As the driver started toward the exit, I rolled up the partition between the front and the back. When I had my privacy, I dug out a familiar worn white card that I had had tucked in my wallet for the last seven years. Pulling my knife from its home once again, I ran the blade discreetly along my inner thigh. The sharp edge didn't cut my pants, but it solidified my cock behind the tight fabric into an aching erection. I brought Kiera's signature calling card to my nose and inhaled as if her berry and grease scent lingered on the matte cardstock. It had long since faded, but since I had gotten so close, it was as if it was really there. My eyes rolled back as a moan worked its way up my throat at the delicious scent I so desperately craved.

Soon enough, I thought in my lustful haze, *Kiera will be mine, and the rest of those little boys will be taken out of the equation.*

Very soon...

Adversary

BOOK 2 OF THE ACES SERIES

AVAILABLE NOW

ACKNOWLEDGEMENTS:

Jake, my amazing husband, who supported me and cheered me on even when I doubted myself!

My dad for covering my expenses while I waited to get paid from Amazon so this book could actually be edited professionally!

My beta readers-Michelle, Jessica, and Cassie-you guys are awesome and made this entire process so much more enjoyable!

Finally, for all of my readers, this wouldn't be possible without you.

ALSO BY A.J. MACEY:

ABOUT THE AUTHOR:

A.J. Macey has a B.S. in Criminology and Criminal Justice, and previous coursework in Forensic Science, Behavioral Psychology, and Cybersecurity. Before becoming an author, A.J. worked as a Correctional Officer in a jail where she met her husband. She has a daughter and two cats named Thor and Loki, an addiction to coffee and swearing. Sucks at adulting and talking to people, so she'll frequently be lost in a book or running away with her imagination.

STAY CONNECTED:

Follow A.J. on Facebook:
https://www.facebook.com/author.ajmacey/

Join the Reader's Group for exclusive content, teasers and sneaks, giveaways, and more:
https://www.facebook.com/groups/authorajmacey/